Praise for LESLEY

RECIPE FOR A GOOD LIFE

Globe and Mail bestseller, Indigo's Top 100 Books of 2023

"Reading *Recipe For a Good Life* was like being on the receiving end of an enormous hug just when you need it most. Bursting at the seams with heart and humour, this book is a most glorious love letter to the amazing women of rural Cape Breton. I now want to get a time machine and move to South Head Road!"

–BIANCA MARAIS, *The Witches of Moonshyne Manor*

"Maybe even her best novel yet.... Lesley Crewe hits the nail on the head with her descriptions of life in rural communities. As with all of her novels, the cast of characters in this story are well-developed, with very unique personalities that you can't help but fall in love with."

–THE MIRAMICHI READER

"Notting Hill meets Cape Breton—if Julia Roberts was a bestselling author and Hugh Grant a clandestine baker instead of a bookseller. With Crewe's signature wit and a cast of cheeky characters, lolloping dogs and heaps of food, this is a warm hug of a book."

–NICOLA DAVISON, *In the Wake*

"Fans of the delightful Lesley Crewe know that she can skillfully make you weep or laugh at the drop of a noun. In her latest novel, *Recipe for a Good Life*, she weaves loneliness like silk into the soul of a person with a stitch of humour. This clever author knows that the heart can teach you more than you will ever teach it."

–BEATRICE MACNEIL, *Where White Horses Gallop*

LESLEY CREWE

Death
& OTHER
INCONVENIENCES

Vagrant
PRESS

Vagrant Press is an imprint of
Nimbus Publishing Limited
3660 Strawberry Hill St, Halifax, NS, B3K 5A9
(902) 455-4286 nimbus.ca

Printed and bound in Canada

Nimbus Publishing is based in Kjipuktuk, Mi'kma'ki, the traditional territory of the Mi'kmaq People.

Editor: Penelope Jackson
Editor for the press: Whitney Moran
Cover design: Heather Bryan; cover cross-stitch created by Mary Tinney
Typesetting: Rudi Tusek
NB1740

Library and Archives Canada Cataloguing in Publication

Title: Death & other inconveniences / Lesley Crewe.
Other titles: Death and other inconveniences
Names: Crewe, Lesley, 1955- author.
Identifiers: Canadiana (print) 20230591884 | Canadiana (ebook) 20230591892 | ISBN 9781774712795 (softcover) | ISBN 9781774712818 (EPUB)
Subjects: LCGFT: Novels.
Classification: LCC PS8605.R48 D43 2024 | DDC C813/.6—dc23

Canada Council Conseil des arts
for the Arts du Canada

Nimbus Publishing acknowledges the financial support for its publishing activities from the Government of Canada, the Canada Council for the Arts, and from the Province of Nova Scotia. We are pleased to work in partnership with the Province of Nova Scotia to develop and promote our creative industries for the benefit of all Nova Scotians.

To my girl Susie,
through thick and thin for fifty years

Chapter One

OBITUARY

Richard (Dickie Bird) Ambrose Sterling
Fredericton, New Brunswick
1960–2023

The family is horrified to announce Dick's sudden and totally expected passing thanks to a chunk of ham sandwich while he sat in his living room recliner watching the Stanley Cup Playoff finals between the Vegas Golden Knights and the Florida Panthers. He would want me to mention that his favourite team won. Go Vegas.

He was born in Bathurst, New Brunswick, to parents Jerry and Doris, I think. They're dead. Survived by stunned and furious wife Margo (Donovan), a vegetarian hockey hater, his daughter Velma and her latest partner Joanne something, and his long-suffering (in her own mind) first wife Carole. He never saw his siblings so no need to mention them, other than he called them Larry, Curly, and Moe, along with their spouses April, May, and June.
Can you believe that?

Dick was a butcher. He loved barbequing, watching hockey, gambling and drinking beer. Look where that got him.

Arrangements will be announced.

Honest to God.

How many times had Margo told Dick to stop wolfing his food? But he never bloody listened. In truth, for a few years now he had hardly registered she was around. He was totally preoccupied with something and she was totally preoccupied with her grandchildren, so when he'd pat her head and tell her not to worry, she didn't.

But then that's how Margo coped with everything in her life. She tried not to ponder too far ahead. Thinking was upsetting and totally unnecessary. Unless the situation had her by the balls, as it were, it was better forgotten.

Her ex-husband, Monty, had a problem with that, which is why he ran off with his chiropractor, Byron. She drove her over-achieving daughter, Julia, up the wall, but Margo knew all mothers and daughters had their moments. Thankfully her son, Michael, never mentioned it. Come to think of it, Mike didn't mention much.

Even though Dick was getting on her nerves after ten years together, and her daughter called him Tony Soprano behind his back, she still cared about him. She loved their sex life. After almost thirty years of mediocre and infrequent intercourse with Monty, she was almost relieved when he ran off with a man. It kind of explained everything, and Dick promptly clarified what should have been happening all along.

She was going to miss Dick the prick.

She hadn't expected to miss him so soon. He was only sixty-two. Her age, even though everyone thought she was in her early fifties. Margo was a wizard with beauty products and makeup. She'd been manager of the Shoppers Drug Mart cosmetic counter forever. Makeup was not only her job but also her hobby. How many times had Julia lost her mind when Margo applied another coat of lipstick staring into the sun visor mirror at a red light in downtown Fredericton? But Margo chucked her job in when her first darling granddaughter, Posy, was born five years before. Life was too short. And when Hazel came along two years later, Margo's life was complete. The girls called her Gogo. It didn't matter that Gogo looked like a *Zoomer* cover girl with her mid-length sassy blond haircut, petite figure, and manicured nails. She was Grandma Walton underneath the façade.

Margo was searching for the bottle of nail polish she'd left in the den when she walked in front of their blaring sixty-five-inch television and discovered Dick slumped in his chair, his face a horrible shade of dead.

She screamed, as if some hapless victim in an HBO murder special. Then she ran to the kitchen to call 911 and couldn't understand why the phone wasn't on the wall anymore. It took a full five seconds to remember that Dick had thought they should cut back on expenses and get rid of the landline. So where was her cellphone? Still shrieking, she went from room to room trying to find it. When she finally did on the back of the toilet, it had no power.

"Is everything dead!?"

She hightailed it across the lawn to her neighbour Harman's house and banged her fist on the door. Harman looked alarmed when she opened it. "Margo, what's wrong?!"

"Dead. Meat."

After that Margo had no idea what happened.

Until now, when all the large strangers and policemen and coroner finished their investigation of the scene and carted Dick's body off to the morgue. His death was ruled an accident, but it was no accident. Dick was responsible for his own piggish ways. He could suck back an entire roast chicken in three minutes, with not enough meat left on the bones to make soup. That's why Margo told him she was a vegetarian for the most part. She couldn't stand to watch him act like a caveman. Dick never noticed that she'd stopped eating with him. He'd take his platter and hunker down in front of the television, happy to be left alone with his side of ribs and TSN.

Harman told her she couldn't believe it when she moved in. "I always told Dick he was Fred Flintstone with those ribs of his, and there you were, a Doulton figurine."

And now here it was, late at night and her daughter was in her kitchen, looking like she just got out of bed, which she had. Harman had called her and she stayed with Margo until Julia showed up. Margo was still shaking with the shock, despite the hot tea spiked with sherry and warm blanket wrapped around her.

Julia held the obituary, hastily scribbled on the back of an envelope.

"Mother! Seriously?"

Margo grabbed several tissues out of a box on the kitchen table and blew her nose, as Julia dropped into the nearest chair. "Mom, you can't use this obituary."

"I can't? Why not? It's the truth. Isn't that what you're supposed to write? The truth."

"There are levels of truth. First of all, don't put 'Dickie Bird.' It's gross. And speaking of that, don't say he 'choked on a late-night snack.' Let them assume it was something dignified, like a heart attack or stroke."

Margo kept dabbing her eyes.

"Also, the language you use is important. You don't say his parents are dead—"

"They are dead."

"You say 'He was pre-deceased by his parents, blah blah. You can't say 'expected death,' it's supposed to be *unexpected*, and 'furious wife' makes you sound like a harpy."

"But I am furious! All of this was totally preventable."

Julia sighed. "Take out 'vegetarian,' because you're not. 'Hockey hater'...no one cares. And for God's sake find out Joanne's last name. Also put in his brothers' real names. Don't mention Carole at all if you can't say something other than 'long-suffering.' You don't want to be sued for defamation."

Margo was exhausted. "You sound like a teacher going over my homework. I'm reeling, Julia. I'm distressed. I just found my cold, dead husband in a chair, so stop giving me grief."

Julia put her hand on her mother's shoulder. "You're right, I'm sorry. This is awful, but please don't feel you have to do this right now. Or would you like me to do it?"

"You do it. I can't believe I'm a widow. I look terrible in black."

"You'll be fine, Mom. Think Jackie Kennedy."

"That's true." Her mother wandered out of the kitchen with the blanket trailing behind her. Julia sent her husband, Andre, a text because he'd asked her to. *Kill me now*

He replied, *Do not take over!*

Then she texted her brother Mike. He was a night owl. *Dick died*

Three little dots started moving on the screen. *WHAT? The dickster? What happened?*

He choked on a ham sandwich

Totally not surprised but shit...poor dude. Should I call mom?

No. Tomorrow...she's lying down.

Julia knew she had to call her aunt and uncle even though it was really late, because if she didn't, Aunt Eunie would give her an earful about how they were always the last to know anything.

Aunt Eunie and Uncle Hazen had never married and lived in their childhood home together on the outskirts of Miramichi, about two hours away. They were ten and fifteen years older than her mom, and so she never felt like she had a lot in common with them. Her mother confessed that she was a little leery of Hazen because he'd tell her off. Uncle Hazen was a straight shooter.

The phone rang three times and then there was a fumbling sound, followed by coughing. "Hellooo?" Aunt Eunie sounded befuddled.

"Hi, Aunt Eunie! I'm so sorry to wake you. It's Julia."

"Julia? Are you all right, dear? What's wrong?"

"Don't worry, Mom is fine, but her husband, Dick, died tonight. I thought you should know."

"Oh no!! The poor soul. Was he ill? She never told me, which isn't a surprise—"

"He wasn't sick. He choked on a ham sandwich, unfortunately."

"Oh, dear heavens. That's terrible, just terrible! Oh, just a second...It's Julia, Hazen. Dick died tonight...choked on a ham sandwich..."

More rustling noises. Uncle Hazen must have grabbed the phone. "Julia? When was this? Tonight?"

"Yes, I just found out myself. Mom's neighbour Harman called me. Mom ran over to her house."

"Of course she did. Never thought to call an ambulance first, I imagine. Probably couldn't find her phone—well, it's true, Eunie... the girl has no sense."

The fact that Uncle Hazen still called her mother a girl was a riot.

"I hate to say it but it's not a surprise. That Dick fella ate like a golden retriever. Was he starved as a child?"

"I wouldn't know, Uncle Hazen."

"When you comin' to the house? I've got two donkeys now. Bet your little ones would like them."

"I'm sure they would. I'll be in touch. Right now, I'm dealing with this situation."

"Don't be a stranger." And he hung up. She wanted to say goodbye to Aunt Eunie, but no doubt they'd be talking before too long. That was one thing about having a death in the family. You suddenly had a kin convention.

Now to call Dick's daughter, Velma. The police suggested it was better coming from a family member, but her mother naturally fell to pieces at the thought and said she didn't have her number anyway; it was on Dick's phone. Julia found it beside the uneaten half of his sandwich on the coffee table. She felt terrible. Firstly, she always got stuck with her mother's problems. Secondly, it was now two in the morning. Thirdly, she was about to give Velma a message that would change her life forever; and fourthly, she knew that Velma hated Margo and anyone associated with her.

Hardly surprising, since her mother was Dick's bit on the side before he divorced Velma's mother, Carole.

Ring. Ring. Ring.

Another sleepy "Hello? If you're a goddamn telemarketer I'll rip your face off! Do you know what time it is??"

"Velma? This is Julia Donovan Paris—"

"Who?!"

Julia took a breath. "Margo's daughter."

Now Velma took a breath. "Margo the man-eater?"

"Yes."

"What's wrong? Where's my father? Why are you calling me?"

"I'm so sorry, Velma. So very, very sorry. Your father died tonight."

There was a howling over the line and Julia burst into tears at the sound of it. For the first time, the enormity of what had happened hit her. Dick was someone's dad, not just her mother's second husband. She didn't know what to do. "Hello? Hello?"

A woman's voice came on the line. "What's going on? Who is this?"

"I'm so sorry. This is Margo's daughter, Julia. Velma's father died tonight and the police wanted me to call her. It's terrible news and I'm sorry to have to tell her over the phone."

"What happened? Did he have a car accident?"

"No. Nothing like that. He...he died eating a ham sandwich."

"A ham sandwich? What the hell difference does it make what he was eating? Why not say he choked to death?"

"I'm sorry! I don't know what to say. I've never done this before. Please give Velma my sincere sympathy."

"So where is he? What are we supposed to do?"

"I really have no idea. Call the coroner's office, I suppose. Or the police. I don't have any more information other than what I've told you. Everyone's left. I'm here by myself with my mother. Again, I'm very sorry."

She ended the call. This was going to be bad. Julia wiped her eyes and knew she had to go to her man-eating mom. But she needed help, so she called her dad. His was the voice of reason. He always reminded her of a British general, mainly because he was British and he loved rules.

He picked up first thing. "Have you been drinking and need a ride home? You're a little old for that now, darling."

"Dad, Dick died tonight."

She heard an intake of breath. "Bollocks. You know what this means."

"Yes. I'm going to lose it."

"I forbid it! You are not your mother's keeper."

"Then you better help me with this! She won't cope and I'll be left with the mess. You know how she is."

"Julia. Stop hyperventilating. That's your mother's first reaction to absolutely everything, and you are not your mother. You take after your old man. Ice in your veins. Remember that. We'll get through this."

"I'm not so sure."

⁃↝⊝

Velma was, of course, distraught. Her partner, Joanne, ran around in a dither while Velma sat in the middle of their bed in the lotus position, focusing her upset on the one person who had caused her father's death.

Her sobbing stopped long enough for her to shout, "I know that bitch made his ham sandwich! Probably cut chunks big enough to choke a horse. She's to blame. I'm going to strangle that woman when I see her. Let her find out what it's like not to breathe."

Then she went back to wailing. Joanne had to calm things down, or at least share this misery. "Why don't you call your mom? I think you need her."

That set Velma off again. "This will kill her!"

"Haven't they been divorced for a decade?"

Velma held her shaved head in her hands. "Don't you understand anything? He's her baby daddy!"

Joanne made a face. Not exactly.

They'd been an item now for going on a year and Joanne was realizing that Velma had a lot of issues and could be quite emotional, especially when it came to her mom, Carole. Carole had recently started to use a cane to get around because after two bouts of Covid, she wasn't as energetic as she used to be.

Apparently, this was Margo's fault too.

"Don't you understand anything?" Velma cried. "Stress causes symptoms to worsen. Margo has caused my mother more stress than anyone on earth. It's her fault she's got that stupid cane. Not just her bad back."

The realization that Velma and Carole would spiral into a vortex of despair because of Dick's passing sent a shiver down Joanne's spine. And being told she didn't understand anything several times a week was annoying.

Eventually, Velma calmed down enough to call her mother's number. She put it on speaker. It rang several times.

"She sleeps like the dead."

A voice finally shouted into the phone, "What's wrong?!"

"Daddy died!" Velma cried. "That miserable bitch killed him!'

Joanne grabbed the phone out of Velma's hand as she collapsed in a heap. "Carole? This is Joanne."

"What's going on? What's she talking about? Something about her father and a bitch? Was he mauled by a dog?"

"I'm so sorry. Dick died tonight while eating a ham sandwich...I mean, he choked to death."

"What?! What?! Someone killed him?"

"No, no one killed him. It was an accident."

"Oh my god! Richard's dead? The father of my child is dead? That means I'm a single parent!"

This catastrophizing seemed to run in the family.

It didn't bode well.

Chapter Two

Julia was an accountant who ran to her car and drove to the office daily. Her husband, Andre, worked as a graphic designer for a marketing firm. He didn't run anywhere except after his kids, ever since his firm downsized their office space after Covid. He worked from home.

Which freed Julia from worrying about her girls, since Daddy was there when Posy got on and off the school bus, and he walked Hazel back and forth to a private daycare just up the street.

She took the day off work to take her mother to McNally's Funeral Home. Mike did offer, but Julia was certain he would let their mother buy a bronze casket. She never really listened and agreed with people without thinking of the consequences.

Julia was on guard. And numbers were her life.

She drove the ten minutes to her mom's place. She and Andre had bought a house in the neighbourhood of Hanwell after her mother moved in with Dick. Julia was pregnant with Posy at the time, and Julia realized she could use her mother as a handy babysitter after her maternity leave was up. She knew her mom would sit outside on their doorstep anyway as soon as the baby arrived.

Her mom wasn't waiting for her now, but if Julia had had the girls with her, Margo would've have been pacing in the driveway. She parked behind her mother's red Mazda 5 and Dick's enormous new Silverado. God only knew what that had cost.

She ran up the stairs to the back door, knocked, and turned the door handle, not expecting it to give way. "Mom! I told you to keep this door locked!"

Her mother didn't answer. That wasn't a good sign. Neither was the fact that there were dirty casserole dishes around, no doubt belonging to Harman next door. Her mother was an extremely neat person. To see the kitchen so untidy brought the situation home. Her life had been upended with no warning.

Julia found her mother sitting on the edge of the tub, a tube of mascara in her hand, staring at nothing.

"Are you okay?"

Margo looked up, black mascara circling her eyes. "I can't stop crying. This is supposed to be waterproof."

"Don't worry. We'll clean you up."

Her mother stood up and took four sheets of makeup remover and held them to her face.

"What are you doing?"

Margo looked confused. "You said I had to clean up, didn't you?"

"I meant your face, not...everything! Here, let me." She took a corner of one makeup sheet and wiped gently around her mother's eyes. "There. Just put a little concealer back on and it's fine." She left the other three sheets to dry up by the sink. What a waste.

"I have to change my false eyelashes. If you cry too much, they start to look like soggy spider legs."

"We don't have time, and you look great."

A normal person wouldn't be wearing false eyelashes to a funeral home, but Julia's mother wore them to take out the garbage.

When they arrived, Margo wouldn't get out of the SUV. She was like a five-year-old on the first day of school. Julia felt sorry for her. She held the door open and extended her hand inside. "It's okay. I'm with you."

The funeral director was extremely efficient and knowledgeable. He handed them a folder containing everything they needed to know in the days ahead, and that took up the first half hour. When they got to the large array of options available, Julia's heart sank.

Her mom couldn't order from a Wendy's menu, let alone decide how Dick was going to meet his maker.

"I want the best for him," Margo said shakily.

That option was put on the table. Julia kicked her mother's shin.

"Perhaps something a little less extravagant," Julia said. "Right, Mom?"

Margo looked down at her hands. "Right."

The last option was a pine box. They both agreed that was taking it a little too far.

The gentleman was very patient with them. Julia didn't know how he could stand it. Her skin was crawling, it was taking so long.

"What about cremation, Mom? Have you considered that? Did Dick ever mention it?"

Margo was getting desperate with the indecision of it all. How could she know what he wanted. They'd never talked about it. "Dick was so big. I can't imagine him in something the size of a box of Premium crackers."

Julia squirmed in her seat while the funeral director waited placidly. Then she had a thought. She grabbed her mom's arm. "What was Dick's favourite thing in the world?"

"Meat?" Her mom looked at her hopefully.

"He loved to barbeque! I don't think he'd mind being cremated one bit, do you?"

Her mom sagged in her chair and said quietly, "Yes. You're right. That's what we'll do."

They decided on a date, time, and place for the wake and funeral, and this part of the ordeal was over with. Two hours later they were back in the car, both of them wiped out. Margo took Julia's hand. "Thank you, sweetheart."

Julia gave it a squeeze. "You did a good job, Mom. I'm desperate for a cup of coffee. You?"

Margo nodded.

It was waiting in the drive-through at Starbucks when Julia realized her mistake. "What would you like, Mom?"

"What would I like?"

Her mother always answered a question with a question. It was irritating. Andre told her it was because it gave Margo time to think. Julia replied her mother didn't think.

"I'm only going to give you three choices. A medium roast, an Americano, or a latte."

"Umm…"

Julia was pulling up to the speaker. She needed to get home before supper. "We'll have two venti Americanos, cream and two sweeteners."

"What's a venti?" her mother asked.

"Doesn't matter."

ᏋᎦᎧᎩ

OBITUARY

**Richard Ambrose Sterling
Fredericton New Brunswick
1960–2023**

We are deeply saddened to announce the sudden passing of our loved one, Richard Ambrose Sterling. Dick died peacefully at home on June 3 in Fredericton at the age of sixty-two.

He was born in Newcastle, New Brunswick, and was predeceased by his parents, Jerry Sterling and Doris (Page) Sterling. He is survived by wife, Margo, daughter, Velma (Joanne Talbot), first wife, Carole (Zapt) Sterling, brothers, Larry (April), Carl (May), and Mortimer (June), and nieces and nephews.

Dick was a butcher. He enjoyed hunting and fishing and loved the game of hockey.

Visitation for Dick will be held June 8, 2023, from noon to 3:00 p.m. at McNally's Funeral Home, 1200 York Street, Fredericton. The committal will take place after the visitation at Forest Hill Cemetery. Memories and condolences may be shared with the family by visiting www.mcnallys-funerals.com

Family flowers only. Donations to a charity of one's choice.

"Hi, Eunie."

"How are you, Margo, dear? Any better?"

"Any better? Not really. It's only been a few days. I'm calling to tell you that Dick's obituary is in the paper this morning. It's not long, but he really wasn't that interesting, was he?"

Eunie couldn't say. "When's the funeral?"

"Wednesday. Are you and Hazen coming?"

"Of course, dear."

"Oh good. I think I need some support. I only have the kids and my neighbour Harman, and a few friends I worked with at Shoppers. I need more on my side."

"Your side?"

"I'm walking into a lion's den, Eunie. Carole will be there with her pitbull daughter, Velma, and her partner, not to mention Larry, Curly, and Moe and their families. And I didn't know Dick's friends from work."

"The Three Stooges? Aren't they dead?"

"Dick's brothers. That's what he always called them. I don't think they were that close, but apparently Carole is still on good terms with her ex-sisters-in-law. So, they'll be gunning for me too. What did I ever do to that family?"

"Ahh..."

Margo's voice got higher. "You know darn well that Dick told me he was separated when we met. I'd never go out with a married man on purpose. You of all people know me, Eunie!"

Eunie did know her. Margo was the most naïve person on the planet, and she did believe her sister when she said she had been unaware of Dick's marital status. She was unaware of most things. That's why Eunie never liked Dick. She believed he used that to his advantage.

Margo continued. "I mean, that was a decade ago, and he divorced her. Monty and I have managed to stay friendly. It took a couple of years, but still. Just because a marriage ends doesn't mean you have to hate someone forever. Actually, I wonder if Monty and Byron can come to the funeral. That would bulk up my troops."

Dick's funeral was shaping up to be a battlefield. Eunie wondered if it was too late to get out of it.

When they hung up, Eunie heard the back door open. Hazen coming in from giving Fred and Ginger their breakfast. She ladled some porridge into a bowl from the pot on the wood stove and brought it over to him. Hazen reached for the bowl of brown sugar and shaker of cinnamon on the table before pouring on the cream.

"Dick's obituary is in the paper."

Hazen grunted, picked it up, and opened it to the right page. He perched his reading glasses on the end of his nose. "Oh look! Wilfred Jackson died. Well, well."

"Who's Wilfred Jackson?"

"Someone I worked with at the sawmill. Look here, says he had twelve kids."

"Obviously he couldn't keep it in his pants."

Hazen looked at her over his glasses. "You're a hard woman, Eunice."

"I'm a smart woman. Unlike poor Mrs. Jackson."

He shook the page. "Oh, here it is." He read it out loud and snorted when he came to the part about what he did for a living. "A butcher being done it by a piece of ham! Wilbur and his ilk have had the last laugh. I love it."

"For pity's sake, the poor man died. We're going to his funeral on Wednesday."

Her brother took off his glasses. "We are? Do we have to? We only met him half a dozen times."

"Margo needs us there. She's worried that his first wife and daughter are going to make things very difficult for her. She'll need her big brother to stick up for her."

He closed the *Daily Gleaner*. "She should've thought of that before she hopped into bed with a married man."

"She didn't know he was married—"

"You can tell yourself that all day, and if you want to believe it, fine, but that girl keeps her head in the clouds on purpose. It's her way of abdicating responsibility. She's got it all figured out. She played Mom and Dad like a fiddle and you're jumpin' to her tune too. But she doesn't fool me."

Eunie knocked back the rest of her tea. "Well, maybe you're right, but she's our flesh and blood and her husband just died and it must have been a terrible shock. You can afford to be charitable. It's what families do."

"If you say so."

Monty and Byron were in the sunroom at the back of their house overlooking the rose bushes when Monty spied the obituary. "Oh dear. It's in the paper." He read it out loud.

Byron was already on his second espresso. "Well, that was short and sweet. Remind me not to let Julia write my obit."

Monty cut into his eggs Benedict. "Listen, the poor child was terrified of saying something she shouldn't. She even added Carole to placate the daughter and took out the names of her own family in case that was upsetting. If it was left to her mother the poor man would have no obituary, just a big empty space with the words *Hold on a minute...I can't think of anything.*

"You are a cruel man, Monty."

"Am I wrong?"

"No."

A notification buzzed on Monty's phone. "It's Mike. I wish these kids would just ring." He opened the message. *Hey dad... mom wants to know if u & B can come to the funeral on wed. She's looking for backup*

"Oh, blast. Mike says his mother wants us to go to the funeral."

"Really?" Byron took a bite of buttery toast. "I'd rather stick needles in my eyes."

Monty typed back. *I don't think so, Mike.* He waited for a response, but after getting no answer for a full minute, he typed, *We'll be there.*

Three little dots danced. *I knew you'd see it my way*

Monty put down his cell. "That boy loves his mother."

"Shit, we're going?"

ᦉ

Velma's mother called her. "Did you see your dad's obituary?"

"No! Let me get my phone." Velma started to hunt in the messed-up duvet and found it at the bottom of the bed under Joanne's nightshirt.

"She made him sound as interesting as a facecloth."

"Just a sec. Let me read it." She couldn't believe she was looking at her father's name in the paper. "Why did she pick that picture? I hate that picture. He looks like Barney Gumble on *The Simpsons.*"

"Who?"

"Your name is in here. I didn't expect that."

"He liked to hunt and fish? When was the last time he went hunting? Or fishing? He had other hobbies."

"He did?"

Her mother sounded huffy. "Sure he did. He loved to barbeque. He always put up a brand new Canadian flag every July 1. He collected ball caps. He recycled. The list is endless."

"We should have been consulted on the obituary. I should have written it. I've known my father for forty years. Margo's only known him for ten."

Her mother scoffed. "They were *married* for ten years. Who knows how long the affair was going on before that?"

"I'll kill that woman." Velma sniffed. "Why is she alive?"

"The good die young."

〜

Julia honked the horn outside her brother's townhouse. He was never on time. So laid back she called him a speed bump. Mike was a thirty-five-year-old computer genius who only bought the place after Julia nagged him about it. It never occurred to him that owning was an investment. He had the money to do more with it, but buying it was as far as his efforts went. After a year it was still filled with packing boxes. His desk, chair, chunky recliner, and elaborate computers were the only furnishings in the living room. He'd been sleeping on the floor since he broke his Ikea bed frame.

He had an on-and-off girlfriend, Olenka, who he'd been with since high school, but neither of them seemed in a hurry to do anything about their relationship. They loved video games and ate at A&W three times a week, but she still lived with her mom. She was a biologist, whatever that entailed.

Julia drummed her fingers on the steering wheel. His lawn needed mowing, the green cart was knocked over with the grungy lid open, the siding was desperate for a pressure wash. Honestly.

Her brother finally appeared with bedhead wearing his uniform: an oversized T-shirt, nylon shorts to the knees, hairy legs, black socks, and Crocs. And the minute he did, the girls whooped and hollered out their back windows.

"BOOBOO!!!!"

He pretended to fall down the steps and they squealed with delight. Julia grinned. Her girls loved their uncle Booboo. No one could remember why Posy called him that to begin with, but Hazel continued the tradition, and half the time that's what Julia called him. It got confusing at times when Booboo and Gogo were in the same room.

He got in the front seat and his knees hit the dash. Mike was a big guy. He turned around to look at his nieces. "How are my blueberry muffins today?"

"I'm not a blueberry muffin!" Posy yelled. "I'm a pancake!"

"Oh no! And what are you today, Miss Hazel?"

"A egg!"

He reached into his pocket and took out two packages of gummy worms. "Even pancakes and eggs need a treat now and again." He passed them back.

"Thank you, Booboo!!" They set about ripping them open.

Julia backed the SUV out of the driveway. "A box of raisins wouldn't go amiss."

"Not a chance."

"Thanks for coming. Andre had some work to catch up on."

"Oh, I love going to Costco. I live for these occasions."

"I'm stocking up for Mom. She's not cooking. Harman is bringing over delicious meals, but that can't last forever."

While Mike pushed a cart with the girls in it, Julia reached for the things her mom might need. Definitely Kleenex. When she tried to put a twenty-four pack of toilet paper into her cart, Mike made a face. "There's only one bum in that house now. This will last her until next Christmas."

"Exactly. One less trip for me."

While the girls were occupied looking at the new *Frozen* figurines Booboo had thrown in the cart for them, he said, "Jules, Mom knows how to drive. Just because she's lost her husband doesn't mean she's going to stop living."

Julia turned away and her eyes filled with tears. "Yes, it does! That's exactly what will happen, and it scares me to death."

He tsked. "You are not responsible for her. She's a grown woman and you treat her like a child."

Julia wiped her eyes. "It's so simple for you, Mr. Easy Come, Easy Go. Some of us aren't built that way."

"I don't judge Mom like you and Dad do. She is who she is. She doesn't always know her own mind and people get mad at her. She's like me, and you're being super unfair to us sloths."

She laughed and hit him on the shoulder. "You big dope!"

"Mommy! You called Booboo a dope. That's a bad word."

Mike put his hands on his hips. "Yeah! That's a bad word. Let's get her!"

Chapter Three

When Mike and Olenka, wearing a somewhat wrinkled Athleta hoodie dress, walked into the funeral home for the wake, the first thing they did was sign the guestbook and put a sympathy card in the slotted wire circle. Mike didn't think they needed one, but Olenka insisted.

"My mom wrote your mother a message in the card. She knows what it's like to lose a husband."

"Oh, that's kind."

"Do you know our mothers have never met in person, except at graduation? That just occurred to me yesterday. They've talked on the phone, but how long have we known each other?"

"Fifty years at least."

She elbowed him. "Feels like a century."

They walked into the adjoining rooms. Mike blinked. "Oh no. Pistols at dawn."

Dick's urn was at the end of the room on a table surrounded by family flowers and a big picture of him wearing a Vegas Golden Knights hockey jersey and holding a beer in one hand and a rack of ribs stabbed with a barbeque fork in the other.

Now, most wakes have a line of family members snaking along one side of the room so people can pay their respects before they wander off to the next room and mingle with people they don't know well, all of them looking pained. Although there are always those individuals who forget where they are for a moment and see someone they haven't run into for a long time and start a delighted, animated conversation until their mates give them an elbow and they revert to reverent tones.

In this case it transpired that two lines were formed. Obviously, Velma was not going to stand with Mike's mother, so she was on the opposite corner of the table, glaring at everyone, with Carole sobbing in a chair beside her and a super long line of people after that who had to belong to the Dickster. His three brothers looked exactly like him, big guys with thick black eyebrows and five o'clock shadows.

Mike's heart gave a little tug as he watched his mother, looking so small and poised in a beautiful black suit with a white silk blouse, wearing high heels, with her makeup and demeanour just flawless. He was always so proud of her. How was it possible that she and Jackie Gleason were married? Olenka always said that biology worked in mysterious ways.

He saw his mom notice him for the first time and her face softened. He patted his ill-fitting suit and she gave him a thumbs up. Julia stood beside her, almost a carbon copy of their mom. She seemed very relieved to see him, Andre next to her, holding her hand. He was a great guy. He gave Mike a nod. Andre and Mike were as different as chalk and cheese, but they clicked.

His debonair dad and bearded sidekick, Byron, stood next to Uncle Hazen and Aunt Eunie, both short like his mom but heavyset. They reminded Mike of two dumplings.

Aunt Eunie kissed him and tweaked Olenka's cheek. "You never come to visit!"

"We will, I promise."

"I've got donkeys now," Uncle Hazen said. "Can't wait for the family ass to meet mine!"

Mike loved the old guy. Even when he said a little too loudly, "So who's the widow here? I say it's the one blubbering over there in the chair. God almighty, what a racket."

It was a long three hours. Every time a couple showed up in the doorway, they had a panicked look on their faces. It was like a contest after a while. Which line would they go to first? He and Olenka started counting on their fingers to keep score. It wasn't looking good for their side.

At a lull in the mourners coming through the door, Mike saw his mother, looking pale, lean on his sister, and Julia took her by the arm and left the room. He looked to Olenka. "Don't worry," she said. "She probably needs some air, or the washroom."

As they disappeared, Carole, the grim weeper, took her cane and struggled off her perch to follow his mom—but she seemed to be in slow motion. Velma practically marched on the spot behind her. Uncle Hazen slapped his knee. "Gunfight at the O.K. Corral."

This wasn't funny. Mike sidled off, with Olenka on his tail. Everyone else pretended nothing was happening.

He heard shouts from inside the washroom and went to shove the door open. Olenka pushed him aside. "Mike! Don't! You'll make it worse. Just let me handle this."

Leave his girlfriend to handle what was essentially *Call of Duty*. This should be good.

Olenka opened the door and found them facing off by the sink. Females fighting over a male. Behaviour as old as time.

Carole was wielding her cane like a weapon. "You man-eating bitch!"

Velma whirled towards Margo. "You made that ham sandwich, didn't you? You killed him!"

Julia had her arms around her mother, protecting her. "Don't you dare suggest such a thing. If your father ate like a normal person instead of gobbling everything in sight without chewing, this wouldn't have happened."

Velma nostrils flared. "Sure, blame him now that's he's dead. My father was a saint! And by the way, that obituary was a snore-fest. Why didn't you ask us? You kept us out of everything, even the plans for his funeral. Who do you think you are?"

"She's his wife," Julia shot back.

Velma took a step towards her. "And I'm his only child!"

Carole teetered and put her cane back on the floor. "And I'm a single parent," she wailed. "Thanks a lot, you hussy."

Julia's mouth dropped open. "A single parent to a forty-year-old gym teacher? Are you serious?"

"Enough!" Olenka shouted. They all looked at her, surprised to see her in the washroom. "This is ridiculous. You're behaving no better than a couple of honey badgers, who face their enemy, produce a rattle-roar, stand with their hair on end, emit stink bombs, and then charge. Basically what you're doing now, in this public washroom, during a civilized wake for the man you supposedly loved. Now get out there and conduct yourselves appropriately. This is a solemn occasion. Stop with the spectacle."

Both Julia and Margo looked grateful for the intervention and left quickly. Velma and Carole were confused. "Who are you?"

"Animal control."

They both gave her dirty looks, but they left.

Olenka took a quick minute to pee while she had the chance and joined Mike, who stood there looking perplexed. "What just happened?"

"It all comes down to biology, Michael. I told them they were acting like honey badgers in the wild and they couldn't calm down fast enough."

Michael blinked and stared at his best friend with her cat's eye glasses and very short bangs who even with her dress on had a pocket protector and a few pens. "I love you."

"Get over it."

At the cemetery, the farce continued. Dick's brothers manoeuvred Carole as close to the small dug grave as humanly possible, while Margo stayed tucked under Michael's arm. They didn't know the officiant. Margo hadn't been to church in years, which her sister, Eunie, lamented over. Carole sobbed, "WHY?" every thirty seconds, punctuated with an occasional: "DICK, DON'T LEAVE ME!"

Julia looked around. Both her dad and Byron were holding their fists to their mouths trying not to laugh. Uncle Hazen was wide-eyed and Aunt Eunie looked scandalized. Mike was stoic, trying to be a comfort to their mom. Andre held one of her arms and Olenka held the other. Good thing, or she would have punched Carole in the face.

And then the strangest thing happened. Her mother extricated herself from Mike's embrace, picked up Dick's urn, and put it in Carole's hands.

"You want him, you can have him." And she walked away.

&ppppp;

Back at the house, while Olenka made tea and passed around sweets from Harman and a few other friends, the guys grabbed a beer from Dick's stash. Margo hadn't said a word in the car and she was now in her bedroom.

Her family looked at each other.

Michael took a swig of beer. "Wow. Just wow."

"She took the wind out of that banshee's sails, didn't she?" Uncle Hazen grinned.

"That woman turned a religious ceremony and dignified affair into a comical farce," Aunt Eunie scowled.

"I'm gobsmacked," Monty admitted, leaning forward holding his beer bottle between his knees. "Margo shut her down brilliantly."

Julia leaned back on the couch and rubbed her aching forehead. "Don't make it sound like she planned it, Dad. Mom didn't want to show Carole up, just shut her up."

"Well, she succeeded. Did you see that harpy's face?" Uncle Hazen slapped his thigh. "Glad I came, but we need to head back. It's been a long day and we have a two-hour drive home."

"I need to say goodbye to her." Aunt Eunie swallowed her last bite of date square and chased it down with the dregs of her tea. Then she got up and went to Margo's bedroom door and knocked softly. "Only me, dear."

She opened it and there was Margo sitting at her dressing table holding the brush of their mother's ornate, silver-plated dresser set.

Eunie sat on the edge of the bed and looked at her baby sister in the mirror. "You've had a terrible day, lovey. We have to go, but you better come and stay with us for a while."

"You and Hazen? I'll think about it."

"I know what that means. Margo, your brother and I aren't getting any younger."

Margo turned around and grabbed her sister's hand. "Don't. Not today."

"You're right. Take care of yourself and call me if you need anything. Why don't you come out and be with your family?"

Margo followed her and said goodbye to Hazen. "Didn't know ya had it in ya!" He squeezed her shoulder and shut the door behind him.

She flopped on the couch in the living room. Julia brought her tea and Olenka had a plate of funeral sandwiches. She waved them off.

"Eat something, Mom. You need to keep up your strength."

"Do I?" Margo grabbed an egg sandwich triangle, took a nibble, and put it back on the plate. But she did drink the tea.

Byron was anxious to go and gave Monty their signal. It wasn't subtle. An index finger to his temple.

Monty stood up. "Well, my dear, I'll leave you with the kids. I'm sorry it was such a godawful day. Are you going to leave Dick with his ex? I'm assuming you paid for that plot."

"He can moulder away on her mantel for all I care. You can throw me in the one I just bought and Byron can have mine next to yours. That way they're all used. Okay?"

Monty quickly kissed her cheek and they bolted.

Julia looked at her watch. They needed to get back to the kids.

Margo saw it. "Please, you guys go home to the girls. I'm fine." She stood up to make it clear she meant it. Andre was the first to give her a hug. Then Julia held her tight. "I'm so proud of you."

Then there were three. Margo always relaxed with Mike and Olenka. They were so easy and never had expectations. Life unfolded for them. They weren't frantically trying to control it.

"Thank you for today, Olenka. I'd still be stuck in that bathroom if it wasn't for you."

"Sneaking off to confront you in a washroom was cowardly. And Carole was deliberately trying to take the focus off of you at the funeral. You calling her bluff was masterful."

"I wanted her to stop, that's all. I didn't think about it."

Mike put his beer bottle on the coffee table. "What if you regret it?"

Margo sat back on the sofa and sighed. "Me? Change my mind?"

The kids smiled.

She looked at them seriously. "Things weren't good between us and I ignored it because I didn't know how to handle it."

Mike looked concerned. "You should have said something, Mom."

"What could you do? The horrible part is that when I found him dead, I wanted to kill him again. And I know I'm crying, but not for him. For myself. I'm so angry. I'm furious that I never stood up to him and now I'll never get the chance. So no, I don't want him back. Carole is welcome to dust him forever. In my current mood I'd use his ashes to fertilize my perennials."

After the kids left, Margo had to remember to lock the door. Dick had always done that. The house was so quiet. The television wasn't blasting *Hockey Night in Canada*. She couldn't hear him stomping around in his slippers, clearing his throat. His glass and plate weren't in the kitchen sink, his clothes weren't on the floor by the hamper, the toothpaste tube wasn't open by the bathroom sink, and when she crawled into bed, she had to remember again that his warm body wasn't going to be there to hang on to. She always put her cold feet on his shins. She was so incredibly weary, but sleep wouldn't come, so she had a bath instead.

That's when she bawled her eyes out. For him.

⁊∾⊖

The Sterling side of the family congregated at Carole's condo off University Avenue. It was a tight squeeze. It didn't help that it was so cluttered. She bought it when she and Dick divorced and he paid her for her share of the marital home. She moved on to a smaller place, knowing she'd never live with a man again. Even male cats and dogs were out of the question.

June, May, and April had brought over casseroles, a baked ham, potato salad, and rolls. Anyone would think that the widow lived here, what with Dick's urn on the coffee table.

They sat around and stared at it while they ate. Eventually the brothers and their families trickled away.

Velma and Joanne sat in chairs opposite the couch. Carole was sprawled on it with a heating pad on her back, and an ice pack on her ankle. She'd tripped in the hole as she was leaving. Luckily, she didn't spill Dick.

"So, what did we think of Saint Margo?" Carole took a big gulp of wine. "Miss Butter Won't Melt. Trying to show me up with her designer outfit and high heels. I have to wear orthopedic shoes because of my back. She wanted me to look like a frump."

Velma held up her glass and twirled it with her fingers. "She reminded me of a mannequin with all that goop on her face. Don't you think?" She looked over at Joanne.

Joanne took a sip of coffee. "I thought she looked overwhelmed."

Velma rolled her eyes. "Never mind, Mom, she's being neutral and professional. God forbid she have an opinion."

Joanne wanted to get the hell out of this space. When she'd woken up this morning, she hadn't realized it was going to be the longest day in the history of the world.

Carole downed another glass of wine. That was her fourth. Thankfully Velma noticed, even though she was half in the bag herself. "Don't take more painkillers for your ankle, Mom. You might overdose and then I'll be an orphan."

"Perhaps we should let your mother rest, Velma. It's getting late."

Carole flung her arm towards the urn. "If you go, take him with you."

Joanne couldn't help herself. "You didn't want him to leave you and now you're kicking him out?"

Carole's eyes narrowed. "What's that, Josephine?"

"It's Joanne."

"Keep it up, Joanne." Then she looked at her daughter. "You take him. You're his only child. I can't have my ex following my every move."

"Dad on my bureau gathering dust?"

"Why not?"

Joanne jumped up. "I have to go, ladies." And out the door she went.

Velma couldn't believe it. "You think someone would support you on the worst day of your life."

Her mom groaned as she moved her leg. "Exactly. Why do you go out with her? She's very unpleasant."

In a matter of minutes, Carole and Velma both nodded off and began to snore. For the first time in over a decade, the nuclear Sterling family spent the evening together.

Chapter Four

Mike poured Honey Nut Cheerios into a mixing bowl because all his cereal bowls were dirty. Olenka was not the sort to wash his dishes to help him out. She'd let mould grow on them just to make a point.

She'd spent the night because Mike came home with two whole pizzas out of the twenty given away at end of the computer conference he'd attended the day before. He was annoyed he'd grabbed one with ham and pineapple on it, but Olenka didn't care.

"They were free. Quit bitching." She raced down the stairs with half her clothes in her hand and papers hanging out of her knapsack. "I'm late." She threw her UNB hoodie over her head and struggled into it. "A bunch of third graders are coming to the lab at the university, because my boss forgot she was in charge of the end-of-year field trip at her son's school. You watch, I'll be babysitting the little brats all day."

Mike grabbed a wooden spoon to eat his cereal after pouring in about a quart of milk. "You have such a motherly way about you. Remind me never to leave my nieces alone in your company."

There was a quick knock on the front door and Julia burst in. "Hi! Just me, and I have to be at the office, but since you refuse to answer my texts, I had to come see you face-to-face the way humans did back in seventies. Oh, hey, Olenka. My god, this place is pathetic."

Olenka grabbed a half-eaten piece of pizza out of the box and put her knapsack over her shoulder. "Sorry, can't chat. I'm about to make a bunch of eight-year-olds scrub out an old octopus's tank. I'll see ya in two days, Mike. Have to help Mom with a Lithuanian Festival she's involved with. God knows what I'll be doing."

"If it involves potato pancakes, bring me a bunch," he shouted.

"Yeah, yeah." She ate her pizza on the way out.

Julia couldn't help herself. She started clearing up Mike's dishes. He didn't say a word, afraid she wasn't aware of what she was doing and that she'd stop if he pointed it out. "You have to do me a favour. Mom needs to find a bunch of documents and go to the bank. Can you take her? I'm afraid if I go, I'll have a brain aneurism."

Mike kept shovelling in his cereal and between bites said, "I had to go over to show her how the remote worked, the thermostat, and do her recyclables. Will you be doing anything, or is having two kids and a full-time job going to be your excuse?"

His sister had her blazer off by this time and was rinsing the dishes before putting them in the dishwasher. "You have no idea how often she calls me. Yesterday she wanted me to walk her through how to turn on the heat pump. And you're going to have to mow her lawn before too long. She has no strength in those skinny arms of hers and besides, she'll worry about breaking a nail. God only knows what she's going to do this winter. She'll be snowed in for months."

"Andre and I can take turns shovelling. He can bring the girls over. That will make her happy."

Julia nodded. "Speaking of happy, I wanted to kiss Olenka for her performance in that funeral home bathroom. She's a feisty little honey badger herself. Why don't you put on a ring on that and give my girls some cousins?"

"It's always about you."

Julia looked down at her hands. "What am I doing? Clean up your own mess." She put her blazer back on. "Call me when you get back from the bank, and wash that bowl."

He reached over and turned her around. "You can go now. You'll be late for work and I have a Zoom call in three minutes. I'll text you later."

She made her way to the front door. "Are we going to survive this?"

He sat down in front of his computer. "You're going to drop dead and I'm going to walk over your cold body. See ya."

☙❧

As it turned out, Michael was going to drop dead. Thank the lord Julia had been wise enough to give him this mission. Mike knew his sister would have strangled their mom by now. Margo couldn't find anything. Their files and documents were a complete mess. She could lay her hands on her birth certificate—the one thing they didn't need. And she had Dick's death certificate, but only because it was still in her purse after the funeral director had given it to her.

"Mom, think carefully. Where are the wills?"

"What wills? The only will I had was with your father."

"So you never changed it after you got remarried?"

She shook her head. "Was I supposed to? Don't wills last your whole life?"

"No. Think about it. Would you still want Dad to get everything when you die?"

"But you kids were listed too."

Mike rubbed his eyes. "We'll get you a new will. Things change. Posy and Hazel are here now."

Her mother clapped her hands. "Of course! I'll leave everything to them."

"Don't be hasty." He kept rummaging through the file folder. "But we're not worried about your will right now. Where's Dick's will?"

"I don't even know if he has one."

"That's just great. He better have one so you can be his beneficiary. Are you sure you kept everything in here?"

"I guess so. Where else would it be? Dick handled all this. Unless he's got a hiding place I can't find, and I've looked everywhere."

Mike sat back. "Why did you let Dick deal with your finances?"

Margo looked alarmed. "He didn't. I have a chequing and savings account in my name. Your dad helped me set that up. But I let Dick manage our joint account because your father always did and it was easier. I'm no good with numbers, or anything else for that matter." Her eyes filled with tears and Mike put his hand on her shoulder.

"Stop it. That's not true. What is true is that Dad is straight as an arrow and trustworthy. Was Dick?"

"I guess so. Although he did gamble."

The hairs on the back of Mike's neck stood up. "What?"

"It was just a hobby."

Mike tried not to panic and went back to the file. "Okay, where's your marriage certificate? Did the bank say we needed that?"

"I don't think so. Just the death certificate so I can close his accounts."

"What about an insurance policy?"

His mother looked uncertain. "I think he has one. It must be in there."

Mike eventually found some paperwork indicating that four years ago Dick had cashed it in. Mike felt sick to his stomach. He didn't tell his mother. There was nothing she could do about it now.

They finally gathered what they needed and were about to head out the door to the bank when Margo suddenly decided she better go and powder her already-powdered face. Mike had no choice but to wait.

She finally returned. "All set."

Mike looked sternly at her. "Where's your purse?"

Back she went for her purse, and then they went out the door and shut it. Halfway to the car Mike turned around. "Did you lock the door?"

"Yes." She looked for her keys. They weren't in her purse. "No." She went back up the stairs and disappeared.

"God help us," Michael said before she emerged holding the keys over her head in victory and walked away without locking the door. "Did you forget to do something?" She locked the door.

They were ten minutes late for their appointment. Mom passed the banker Dick's death certificate. "I'm here to close out Dick's accounts."

By the look on the guy's face, Mike knew he was about to get an ulcer. The man put his arms on the desk and clasped his hands. "I'm afraid I have bad news."

"What do you mean?" Mike's mother grabbed his hand. He held on tight.

"Your husband has no money in his accounts. All of them are overdrawn and he owes an astonishing amount thanks to his maxed-out credit cards."

His mother went white. Mike leaned over the desk. "Is my mother's name on any of them?"

The banker looked down at the sheets of paper in front of him. "They had one joint account they set up ten years ago..."

"When we got married." Margo looked at Mike desperately. "Don't all married couples have a joint account?"

"I think so, Mom."

The banker nodded. "Most of them do."

"So that wasn't wrong?"

"No." The banker continued. "And her name is on a large loan they took out last year."

Mike looked at her. "Mom? What was it for?"

Margo pulled a wad of tissue out of her purse before answering. "It was for that ridiculous souped-up new truck and fancy barbeque. He was so down in the mouth about everything and I thought if he got what he wanted it might make things easier for me at home. I'm such a fool." And she began to weep.

So did Julia, when Mike took her and Andre into their backyard to break the news while the girls watched *Bluey* downstairs with a bowl of cut-up veggies and hummus their father made for them.

Julia paced back and forth with her hands on her head. "This is unbelievable! Why didn't she come and ask me if she should be taking out a huge loan at this stage of her life?! I'm an accountant."

Mike was just as upset. "Because you would have bitten her head off!"

Andre held out his hands. "Okay, guys, calm down. So, what does this mean?"

"She's screwed!" Julia shouted. "It means whether he has a will with her named as beneficiary or not, she won't get a cent, because the estate has to pay the bank first, and since he gambled away all his goddamn money, they will take his assets, and the only asset he has besides that goddamn truck is his house, and they will foreclose on the goddamn house and Mom will be homeless, and if that doesn't cover everything, including the credit card debt, they'll take the rest of her money since she was a co-signer on the loan and the goddamn joint chequing account!"

Andre had to sit down on the girls' swing. "Oh my god."

"What are we going to do?" Mike bit his lip. "Of all people. A woman who doesn't know how her cellphone works."

"I knew Tony Soprano was a gangster. There was always something unsavoury about him. I should have listened to my gut and told Mom not to go near him. She's so naïve and foolish. How could she so stupid?"

Mike shook his head. "No. Leave her alone! She's gullible and trusting, that's all. And she's done more for you than all of us put together, taking care of your daughters whenever you need her, so don't you dare call her stupid."

Julia started crying again, as she walked up to her baby brother and hugged him. He hugged her back.

Hazel poked her head out of the sliding door. "Mommy? Why are you sad?"

⌒⌒⊖

Everyone in the rest of the family was sad too, but first they were incredulous.

"What did she ever see in that tosser anyway?!" Monty boomed. "Why didn't she come to me?"

Aunt Eunie was bereft. "Oh, that dear girl. What's going to happen to her? I never liked that fella. Anyone who eats as if the cops are on his tail is bad news."

Uncle Hazen nodded knowingly. "I always told you that one had her head in the clouds. Tiptoeing through the daisies isn't going to help her now. Not when life has just jumped up and bitten her in the ass."

Olenka shook her head. "Poor M. Just like a chimpanzee. They are significantly more likely to voluntarily place resources at the disposal of a partner. A risky but potentially high-payoff option. But this case it didn't work."

Margo needed to hide away from everyone. She was horribly ashamed and didn't want to see the kids. They must have told Harman, of all people, because more casseroles showed up on her doorstep after Margo refused to answer the door.

She was a charity case. She'd worked her whole life and now she would have next to nothing for her retirement. The only way to cope was to not think about the future. And she was so livid with Dick that she didn't want to stay in his crappy house anyway. She was glad the bank would foreclose on it and cart off his idiotic truck that had so many extras in it a person could set up house. And she hoped they'd take his prized television too. And the poor deer head with antlers on the wall that she'd always hated, along with his stinking lounge chair.

She didn't want to live here. But where was she going to go? It was all so horribly unfair, not to mention massively inconvenient. Moving from one husband's house to another's had been enough for her to know she hated packing. And now she had to do it again, because Dick was...a dick.

She took a chair, stood on it, and struggled mightily to get the deer head off the wall. It was incredibly heavy and she marked up the Gyproc when it fell. She didn't care. Then she dragged it out of the house, down the steps, and along the path to the garage door, pointed the fob, opened the cab of the truck, and heaved it behind the steering wheel. She slammed the door. The deer looked like he was going to drive away.

"You get the last laugh, Bambi."

She looked down and realized she'd broken a nail. That's when she began to kick the truck tires. Harman ran out her back door, hurried across the lawn, and put her arm around her to take Margo back to her house for supper. She'd made tandoori chicken.

❧

Harman phoned Julia that evening to tell her that her mom wasn't starving to death, and that Margo said she didn't want to see the kids. "She wants you to stop calling. She thinks you all hate her and she doesn't want to deal with it."

"I hope you know that's ridiculous, Harman." She was in front of her washing machine sorting darks and whites, her cell cradled between her chin and shoulder until she remembered she could put her on speaker. "And hiding away isn't going to solve anything for her. We're here to help."

Harman sighed. "Your mother is very insecure. You know, she put on lip liner at the dinner table tonight. She took a compact mirror out of her pocket and applied it before dessert."

"I know! It's ridiculous. Why is she like that? She's such a beautiful woman, you'd think she'd be supremely confident."

"Looks have nothing to do with it. Makeup is her protection. A mask she hides behind."

Julia bent over to pick up more clothes but stopped. "I never thought of that before. How did you get so smart?"

"I'm a psychologist, remember? I suggest you and your family come up with a plan for her, since she isn't in the position to make any kind of decision—"

"She never is."

"And that is why she's hiding, Julia. Remarks like that."

Julia was immediately awash with shame. "I'm sorry."

"Her life is out of control right now, so take it out of her hands for the time being. You and your brother talk to your dad. I'll make sure she's fed in the meantime, because she doesn't want you around."

"It's so sad. I can't believe she doesn't want to see the girls. They're such a source of comfort to her."

"She doesn't feel she deserves comfort."

A few minutes after Julia hung up the phone, Andre found her weeping into a dirty towel. He knew better than to ask what was wrong. He pulled her and the towel close and wrapped her in his arms. "It'll be okay."

"This is all my fault," she wailed. "If I wasn't always so impatient with Mom about her dithering, maybe she would've confided in me and I could have advised her on what to do in a calm, professional manner, like I do with my clients." She wiped her runny nose on the towel. "Instead, I act like a sulky teenager around her and look what's happened. That bastard has left her with nothing. And I helped him do it."

Andre stepped away but held onto her arms. He gave her a little shake. "Stop that right now. You've always been there for your mother, and I hate to say it because I love her too, but she can be very exasperating. Every time I ask her a question, she cocks her head and says 'Sorry?' like she didn't hear me. She doesn't concentrate on anything. The only time I see her focus is when she's in charge of the girls. Then she's hyper-aware. That means she *is* capable of focusing, she just doesn't bother. So don't put all the blame on your shoulders. She owns some of it too."

Julia grabbed him and held him tight. "Do you have a will?"

"You know we do."

"Do you secretly gamble?"

"I forget the rules to Go Fish."

"Please don't ever eat too fast."

"I'm a vegetarian. I'll never choke on a baked pig."

Chapter Five

The next night Posy and Hazel were thrilled to be having a sleepover at their Grammie and Daddad's house. Andre's parents had eight grandchildren, so they weren't as available as Julia's mom, but they were always happy to help when something came up. Andre called them and said Julia's family had to have a meeting and their place had been selected because Mike didn't have enough chairs.

The girls ran to their grandparents as they came through the door. Bernice and Clarence had offered to pick them up, and that was a big help. Andre went out with his dad to install their car seats. Bernice helped the girls on with their sweaters while Julia went through their bags to make sure they had everything.

Her mother-in-law laughed. "Honey, they'll be home tomorrow. Don't fuss."

Posy had her unicorn, Rosette, in her arms. "Grammie, can I have lunch before bed like last time? Alphabets?"

"I want Sugar Pops!" said Hazel as she jumped around with Burt, her lion.

Bernice gave Julia a look. "Don't tell Daddy."

"Never. Mom, could you put the girls' hair in braids? I try and try and still can't get it right. I'm too impatient."

"My pleasure. That's when Sugar Pops and Alphabets come in handy. It keeps them still. That and *The Little Mermaid*."

Daddy came back in and they hugged their parents goodbye. He kissed his mom. "Now remember, no junk or sugar cereal."

"Yes, dear."

Thirty minutes later, Mike, Olenka, her dad, and Byron showed up and sat at their dining room table. Andre passed around sparkling green tea and spinach artichoke dip with rice crackers and Julia handed out notepads and pens.

Mike took his glass. "Got any beer and Doritos? I'm going to need some. Julia wants us to do homework."

"Stop talking, Mike," Julia said as she sat at the head of the table.

"You asked us here to talk," Olenka reminded her.

"Not about beer and Doritos. Honey, could you set up the laptop, please?" Andre placed it at the at the other end of the table, put up the cover, and turned it on.

"What's that for?" her dad asked.

"We're having a Zoom call with Aunt Eunie and Uncle Hazen. Their boarder, Holly, is setting it up for them. They are part of this family and should be included."

"Am I considered part of the family now?" Byron looked pleased.

"Only because you refuse to go away," Michael said.

His father gave him a look.

"Dad. I'm joking."

Julia took a sip from her glass and put her reading glasses on the top of her head. "Now I'm going to tell you about my conversation with Harman before the Zoom call starts. I don't need Uncle Hazen weighing in with his thoughts on psychologists."

She gave them the lowdown.

Mike drank his green tea in one gulp and set it back on the table with a bang. "You see? This is what you and Dad have been doing to Mom for years. Always getting annoyed at her because she's not as driven or as focused or as highly efficient as you two. I know what that's like because you've both insinuated that about me all my life." He looked at Olenka and she put her hand over his clenched fist on the table.

"I can vouch for that." She nodded. "You often make Mike feel like a nurse shark. The couch potato of the sea."

Julia and her dad looked at each other in dismay.

Mike continued. "The other day you walked in, Julia, and the first thing out of your mouth was how my place was pathetic. You don't even realize you're doing it. No wonder Mom wants to hide away. She knows exactly what you'll say."

Mike didn't know he would be so upset. He shoved this chair back and stood up. "The brilliant architect and amazing accountant being fast tracked to be a partner at her firm. Mom is talented too, you know. She does makeup, and she does it better than anyone. And yet you make fun of her for it. I've heard you."

Julia's face crumpled. Andre went to the fridge, opened a beer, and gave it to his brother-in-law. "Sit down, Mike. I want you to know that Julia had a bad day yesterday when she realized, without your help, that she'd been unfair to her mother, and that's why she's facilitated this meeting. I don't want a shouting match in my home. We all make mistakes and we're here to try and help Mom with hers."

When Mike sat down, Olenka turned to Andre. "This is why I love you, dude. A peacemaker. There are many peacemakers in the animal world who will frequently intervene to break up a fight among their neighbours. Take the Tonkean—"

Monty raised his hand in the air. "Sorry, Olenka, we need to keep this on track. I, for one, apologize to you, Mike, if I've ever made you feel less than. It was never my intention. I'm proud of you, except for your Croc-wearing habit. I'll be aware of it from now on."

"Sorry, Michael," Julia chirped. "I always think of you as my stinky little brother. It's a bad habit."

"Even with an apology you both managed to insert an insult." Mike laughed.

Then their dad drummed his pen on the table. "Guys. Focus. I want to tell you that your mother called me and I made sure she knew that my lawyer is at her disposal. Apparently, she's been told that the bank is going to foreclose and take Dick's assets, but as far as she knows that should cover the debt, so it looks like her money won't be touched."

They all flopped back in their chairs, mightily relieved.

"Now, here's the problem," he continued.

Julia interrupted him. "Why is she calling you if she doesn't want to speak to us?"

"Your mother always calls me."

"That's for sure. Constantly." Byron looked fed up.

Monty gave him a side-eye. "She's the mother of my children, Byron. May I continue?"

Byron folded his arms. "Don't mind me."

"She's allowed to stay in the house until the foreclosure process is compete. A few months to a year. The trouble is, your mother doesn't want to be there. She's sick at heart over all this and she's so angry at Dick she's developed hives and isn't sleeping. The sooner we get her out of there, the better. Any suggestions?"

"She can stay with me," Michael said.

"Sorry, Mike," said Julia immediately, "I don't want to be disparaging a minute after my apology, but the fact is you have two chairs and sleep on a mattress. Now, obviously she can't stay with Dad and Byron..."

"Obviously," Byron chimed in.

"So that leaves us. I'll turn the kids' playroom into a bedroom."

"That's the room next to our bedroom," Andre reminded her.

Julia shrugged. "What are you gonna do? Move your office upstairs and she can stay down there?"

Now Olenka held up her hand. "Won't she be taking her furniture? The stuff that's hers, anyway. She can move that into Mike's."

Mike looked alarmed. "All that flowery stuff?" He dunked three crackers into the dip and shoved it all into his mouth.

Andre looked at his watch. "Time another country was heard from." The Zoom call connected and Aunt Eunie's face popped up inches from the screen, looking down at them like a confused vulture. "Ya there? Hello?"

"Hi, Aunt Eunie!" Julia waved.

"Where are ya, dear? I can see a bowl."

Andre adjusted the screen.

"Oh! There you are. Hazen! They're on! Just a second, he'll be right back. Had to give Fred an extra pear. Can you believe that, giving my expensive fruit to a donkey. If he keeps it up, he won't know what hit him."

The screen went wonky and suddenly Uncle Hazen loomed over them. "Now ain't this somethin'. No, Eunie, I'm not hogging the screen. So what's goin' on?"

"We're having a family discussion," Julia said. "And we wanted to include you."

"I should think so. I am the head of the family. Why, even Hazel's named after me."

Until that second, the connection had never occurred to either Andre or Julia, but it made perfect sense that Hazen would think so. "That's right, Uncle Hazen. And we were wondering if Mom could come and stay with you and Aunt Eunie for a while."

The others looked relieved and everyone gave her a thumbs up for her quick thinking.

"How long?" Uncle Hazen asked.

The screen moved again and Hazen was gone. Aunt Eunie was back looking annoyed. "Of course she can come. For as long as necessary. Yes! That's what I said, Hazen. You stay out of it."

The family meeting was over.

⤙⤚

It was a perfect early summer day. The Wildsmiths' old house looked inviting, with the flowers and hedges starting to bloom in the gardens, along with the fruit trees and berry bushes dotting the property. The oak trees out front were bright green with new leaves and hid the house, painted white and needing some work, with a covered front porch that looked out over the highway. Eunie and Hazen couldn't see their neighbours, but they weren't far along on either side. The paddock was between the house and the barn, a fenced green space where Hazen's donkeys, Fred and Ginger, spent their days lounging under the trees, but when they got the chance, they'd follow Hazen around like dogs. But he was watchful. The highway was close by and the house was on a straight stretch, and more often than not, cars went by too fast. Whenever Hazen went up to the mailbox at the end of the driveway, Eunie would see him shaking his fist at a passing car. She said one day some yahoo was going to get out of his truck and pound him.

Hazen would pull up his trousers and spit, "I'd like to see him try!"

At that moment, Holly pulled off the highway and drove into the yard with her old rattletrap of a car, creating a cloud of dust. She bounced out of it and shouted over to Eunie, who was hanging up tea towels on the line. "Heya! I took home some cinnamon rolls they were going to throw out. If you and Hazen don't want them, Fred and Ginger will. I'm sick of the sight of them."

Eunie smiled at her. It was such a change having a young person around. Holly was all arms and legs, her brown hair always in a knot at the top of her head. She ran up the stairs and disappeared inside. Oh, to be young and have your body move like that.

The year before, Eunie had been driving into town and saw Holly hitchhiking. She stopped when she realized the young woman was crying. Eunie told her to get in. When she noticed the girl's bruises, she nearly died. Holly said her parents had kicked her out and she had nowhere to go. Eunie said, "Oh, yes you do. You're coming home with me."

Now Holly had a job waitressing at Cora's in town, she'd bought an old used car, and she insisted on giving Eunie and Hazen money for room and board. Eunie didn't want to take it, but Holly said it made her feel like a real person. Eunie squirrelled it away for her. She and Hazen had managed to keep the place going all their lives. They didn't need Holly's hard-earned money.

Eunie followed Holly back into the house. "Did you have a nice time with your friends last night?"

"It was a blast. Drinking, toking, fornicating. The usual."

Holly put down the cinnamon buns and opened the fridge. Taking out a large yogurt container, she brought it to the table, proceeded to take the lid off, and ate out of it with a soup spoon.

Eunie sat opposite her. "Would you like a bowl?"

"No, thank you. There's not much left." Holly looked down at the elderly dachshund curled up in the basket by the wood stove. "That critter was there when I left yesterday. Are you sure he's not dead?"

"Wilf! Are ya dead yet?" Eunie asked. He looked up sleepily, then closed his eyes again. "Nope. He's fine."

"Anything happen while I was gone?"

"I did the crossword puzzle and Hazen farted all night, thanks to my baked beans. It was a good evening for you to be out." Eunie picked at the placemat and plucked up her courage. "Holly, should I be worried about you? I know you're nineteen and your life is your own. I have no business telling you what to do, so I'm unsure if I'm stepping over the line here."

Holly scraped the side of the container with her spoon. Eunie wished she had more experience talking to young people.

"I've never had anyone worry about me before." After taking the last few mouthfuls, Holly put the container on the table and looked up. "I've been around drugs my whole life. I've seen what they do to people. I have the occasional toke with my girlfriends. I'd rather have a cooler, to be honest. I don't intend to ever become my parents. So no, Eunie. I don't think you have to worry about me. At least on that score. You have my permission to worry about me for everything else though. It feels nice."

Eunie quickly grabbed a tissue and pretended she had to blow her nose. Holly grinned and got up to rinse out the container in the sink. "Any more of those English muffins?"

"Yep. In the breadbox."

As Holly set about making her breakfast, Eunie poured herself another cup of tea and sat back down. "We're having company on Friday."

"Do you want me to get lost? I can stay with Amber, we're on the same shift." Holly came back to the table with her plate.

"No, child, that's not necessary. It's my sister, Margo. The one I told you about who lost her husband recently."

"Oh yeah. How's she doing?'

"It's been hellish. She's losing the house because of her husband's debts."

"No shit? That's awful."

"She didn't want to drive, so her ex-husband, Monty, and his partner, Byron, are bringing her down. They'll stay for the weekend and go back. She'll be here longer."

Holly's English muffin didn't make it to her mouth. "Fuck right off! She's still on speaking terms with her ex and the new guy? Amazing."

Eunie always flinched at Holly's language, but she heard the f-word constantly now. The way the world was at the moment, it might as well be its motto.

"How old was this husband?"

"Sixty-two."

"Old, then."

"Maybe to you, but trust me. I'd love to be sixty-two again."

Holly nodded. "Well, this situation I've got to see. And maybe I can help your sister."

"Why do you say that?"

"I'm an expert on unhappiness."

Eunie tsked. "Oh, you dear child. When you say things like that, my heart breaks."

"I'm not unhappy anymore, so you don't need to worry."

"You just told me to worry." Eunie sipped her tea.

Holly licked jam off her fingers. "Oh yeah. Keep worrying."

Chapter Six

Monty and Byron took a shared overnight bag and went to pick up Margo. She was on the back porch surrounded by luggage, obviously anxious to go. The truck was gone and Margo's car was in Harman's driveway. As they pulled out onto the street Monty said, "Shouldn't you keep the car in your driveway so it looks like someone's home?"

Harman waved them goodbye from her back step and Margo waved back before she answered, "It's not my driveway. And I hope they rob the place blind."

"Margo—"

"Monty, I'm grateful for the drive, but I don't want to talk about it."

"I was about to ask if you would like to see Julia and Mike before you go. They're so anxious to see you."

"I can't. Look, it's hard enough not seeing the girls, but I'm not ready."

"Fair enough."

Once they were out of the city, it was a little over two hours to get to the homestead, a pleasant drive with endless trees, fields, lots of bridges, and small rural properties dotted along Route 8. As they passed the familiar communities of Doaktown, Renous, and Newcastle, it became more overcast.

They decided to stop for a coffee. Margo had touched up her lipstick in the washroom. Back on the road, Byron passed back her coffee and an oatmeal raisin cookie. She broke it and gave him the other half. "I hope it doesn't rain all weekend."

"Are you planning on hiking?" Monty glanced into the rear-view mirror.

"No. Eunie will grumble about Hazen's wet boots and cover the kitchen floor with newspaper."

Byron talked over his shoulder. "I'm intrigued. Why did your siblings never marry, why did they stay in the family home?"

Margo took a sip of her coffee. "Why? Well, Eunie's young man died in a motorcycle accident on his way home from giving her an engagement ring. It was so tragic. She never got over it. And Hazen? He's been an old goat since he was a kid."

Byron grinned. "Did Eunie ever work?"

"Yes, at a local gift and jewellery shop. She's always been attracted to shiny objects and sentimental gifts, and she's a sucker for commemorative plates. She's still got her Princess Diana memorial plate on the mantel, if you can believe that." She took another sip. "And then one night she spun out in the car and landed in a ditch on icy roads coming home from work. She was stuck until a neighbour drove by and found her. She was chilled to the bone by then, bruised and bloodied but nothing broken. Eunie told me that she'd never seen Hazen so angry, and she didn't appreciate being yelled at, until realizing it was his fear and upset. She could have died that night. So she decided to call it quits workwise. She didn't want Hazen fretting about her and she never wanted to be that cold again."

"That's awful."

"Accidents happen on ordinary days, don't they?" Margo looked out the window then, and the three of them finished their coffee quietly.

Monty got them there safely, tooting the horn as they pulled into the dirt driveway. Almost instantly, Eunie opened the back door and waved, her fluffy white hair and large gold-rimmed glasses framing her smiling face.

"I told you she'd have an apron on," Margo said.

Hazen emerged from the barn wearing coveralls under a checkered flannel jacket, workboots, and an ancient ball cap.

"Does the man know it's summer?" Byron marvelled.

The donkeys ambled out behind him. "And there's the posse."

Once out of the car and after hugs all around, Margo followed Eunie into the house. Hazen wanted to show the guys the new front-end loader he bought for his lawn tractor. "It's sure come in handy." Fred and Ginger joined the men.

Eunie hustled Margo into the kitchen and made her sit in a chair, as if she was an old lady. "Have some lemonade while we wait for those three to come in for lunch." She disappeared into the pantry.

Margo sat at the table and looked around. Wilf was in a dog bed by the woodpile. "Are you sure that dog's not dead?"

Eunie reappeared with two glasses and then brought out a jug of cold lemonade from the fridge. "Wilf? You dead yet?"

Wilf picked up his head and yawned.

"No. Not yet."

"I always love coming into this kitchen. Nothing changes. You still have the same wallpaper you and Mom put up thirty-five years ago."

Eunie made herself comfortable at the table. She poured their drinks. "Mom loved this wallpaper. Tiny blue-and-white flowers are calming, don't you think?"

A skinny black-and-white cat jumped on the table and startled Margo into nearly spilling her glass. "Oh! When did you get a cat? Is he allowed on here?"

"Of course he is. Stan showed up last year, didn't you, Stan?"

Purr-meow. He walked to the windowsill and sat down, watching the action out in the yard.

"See that! Say his name and he'll answer you."

"He will? Hi, Stan. It's nice to meet you."

Stan completely ignored her. Eunie couldn't believe it. "That's never happened before! Talk to him again."

"Hi, Stan."

He remained unblinkingly focused on the window.

"He's just doin' that for dirt now," Eunie tsked. "Stubborn little monkey. Stan!"

Stan looked at her quizzically. *Meow?*

Eunie slapped the table. "If that don't beat all. What a cat!"

"Can we not talk about the cat?"

"Sorry." Eunie leaned over and patted Margo's hand. "How you holding up?"

"Not good. I'm getting sick staying in that house. All I want to do is take a sledgehammer to everything. He lied and lied and lied, Eunie. I know I'm not the brightest bulb in the family, but I feel like a complete fool."

Eunie grumbled. "Now, stop putting yourself down. Is that why you won't see the kids?"

Margo grabbed her hand and held on. "Yes! I'm so ashamed, I can't look them in the eye. Julia already thinks I'm useless. She's always so exasperated with me. I'm afraid to tell her anything."

Eunie looked concerned. "Really?"

Margo nodded. "At least Michael doesn't do that, and I'm grateful when he's around, but he's not very often because he's some kind of brilliant programmer and civilization as we know it would collapse if he wasn't at his keyboard. Olenka might as well be Jane Goodall. They are all so brainy. What else can they be thinking except I've been an idiot?"

"The only thing your kids are thinking is how much they love you."

Margo ran her fingers through her hair. "Maybe."

"I'm starting to have an inkling about kids, now that Holly's here. It's amazing how someone can get under your skin so quickly. Hazen and I suddenly feel like parents. It's lovely, all very *Anne of Green Gables*, except Hazen is no Matthew Cuthbert, and Holly isn't an orphan." She reached over and stroked Stan's back. His tail twitched. "Do you remember that family down by the river when we were growing up? The kids used to call them the river rats?"

"Yes, I remember. Multiple generations of the same clan in squalid conditions. A bunch of rundown buildings and junk in the yard."

"Holly had to get out of there. I offered her a place with us. Best thing we ever did. She's a lovely girl but she says *f-u-c-k* a lot."

Margo grunted. "So have I, lately."

The fellas came in for lunch, canned mushroom soup and chicken salad sandwiches. Eunie had made an apple pie at the crack of dawn in the regular oven. It was too hot to put on the wood stove.

No outdoor living-room set on a patio in this household, so they took their tea into the den crowded with a hodgepodge of out-of-date, mismatched sofas and chairs. Fortunately, there was a heavy-duty revolving fan in the corner. Eunie took in the bemused expression on Byron's face.

"Are you decorating in your head, Byron?" she laughed.

He crossed his legs and held up his teacup. "Just a tad."

Monty looked at Byron with great affection. "I can't take the man anywhere. We were having the car serviced and he starts telling me how they should rearrange the car showroom. What's in a showroom? Cars and a room! What can you possibly do with that?"

"A few potted plants to soften the place, an accent wall, attractive art."

Hazen slurped his tea. "I'm thinking of building a lean-to for Fred in the paddock to keep him out of the rain. He's a nosy so-and-so and doesn't like to be kept in the barn during the day even if it's spilling out. If you fellas help me, we could get it done this weekend, and you can decorate it, Byron. I think he's partial to the Impressionists myself." He slapped his own knee and cracked up.

To Eunie's surprise, Monty and Byron said they'd be happy to help Hazen build a shelter, so when he said, "No time like the present," the three of them got up and left in Hazen's truck to drive down the road to his friend's sawmill.

Margo took four trips to the car to get all the cases from the trunk, and she took her time bringing the luggage upstairs. She wouldn't let Eunie help her. "I'm not completely useless."

Then she told her sister she was going for a walk around the property to visit Mom and Dad. She always called it that. Visiting. She didn't want company, so Eunie and Stan watched her from the window. She crossed the yard and went up to the paddock. The donkeys were looking for treats; Eunie grabbed a couple of apples from the fridge and went out on the back porch. "Here! Give them these. They always expect to be fed."

Margo came back and thanked her and left again. Eunie went back inside and continued to keep an eye on her.

She was so small. Eunie was sure she'd lost weight, despite Margo telling her over the phone about Harman's lovely food offerings. Their mother had always worried about Mary-Margaret, and their parents had always let her get away with things. Who could say no to that little face? The trouble was, Margo felt things very deeply and was always afraid of making a mistake. She could never make up her mind and people would get impatient with her, but Eunie knew it was just as frustrating for Margo to feel that way.

They sat down again that night to a glorious supper of fresh poached salmon from the Miramichi River, with egg sauce, new potatoes, carrots, and string beans. A meal fit for a king, finished off with blueberry cake and brown sugar sauce.

The only fly in the ointment was when Hazen brought up the situation. "Just want to say you should've had more sense than to marry a gambler. They're madmen. It's like a virus in their blood."

"Is it? Well, I didn't know he had an addiction, and you're not my father, Hazen."

"If Dad were here, he'd be saying the same thing. Were you going to get to drive that truck or cook on that barbeque? You were getting nothing out of that loan, the selfish son of a bitch."

"You're absolutely right."

And that was enough excitement for one day. Everyone headed to their respective rooms. As they went up the stairs, Margo asked Eunie where Holly was.

"It's Friday night. She's out with pals. Most of the time she's back by midnight."

Eunie doled out towels for everyone. Monty and Byron were in Hazen's room, since he didn't like his new mattress and preferred to sleep in the lounger in front of the television. Margo was in the guest room, and Holly's room was next door to Eunie's. Eunie was smart enough to get into the bathroom ahead of Margo; she knew from experience that once Margo got in there, she'd be a half an hour at least.

"Goodnight, fellas." Eunie gave them a wave as she left the bathroom and shuffled down the hall in her bedroom slippers.

"Thanks, Eunie! That meal alone was worth the trip," Byron said.

"Want some more? I've got another whole salmon Hazen caught in the freezer."

Byron bit his knuckles, and as he did, Monty dashed by him and got in the bathroom first.

Eunie shook her finger at Byron. "Ya snooze, ya lose." She disappeared into her bedroom.

⁂

Margo sat up. She'd forgotten to take her pill. She got out of bed and turned on the bedside lamp, knocking over a bowling trophy as she did. Eunie had more stuff than a Dollar Store. But really, this home had been their grandparents' house when their parents had moved in to take care of them, and now by default it was Eunie's and Hazen's. People throw things away when they move, but otherwise possessions accumulate around them unnoticed.

She started to rummage through her bags. She knew she'd brought them. And then it hit her. She had on her light summer jacket. Maybe she left the pill container in the pocket. Eunie had hung it up in the downstairs hall closet. She needed those pills. She had a bladder infection on top of the hives. A terrible nuisance.

Margo crept down the darkened hall. Eunie had a bad habit of never leaving any lights on when she went to bed. It was a good thing Margo knew her way around. She went down the stairs and was thankful for the glare from the television set in the den. Not that Hazen was watching it, judging by his snoring.

When she opened the closet door, her heart sank. It was stuffed. How was she supposed to find her jacket? Then she

59

remembered that this closet had a light. She pulled the string hanging down and an ungodly glare lit up the entire space. It was such a surprise she was momentarily blinded.

That's when the yapping and barking started, and the sound of toenails clicking on the wooden floor got closer by the second. Her ankles were immediately surrounded by a very confused Wilf. She waved her arms around trying to get rid of him and shush him at the same time, but then the closet door slammed open fully and a shadowy figure towered over her with what looked like a mallet. She screamed and tried to protect her head. There was hollering in the background and a great thumping down the stairs. The dog continued to have a fit until someone yelled, "SHUT THE FUCK UP!"

The overhead light came on and Margo saw Eunie, Monty, and Byron on the stairs, Hazen in the den doorway, and a young woman with a broom in the hall. Margo clutched her chest. "I'm sorry! I didn't know Wilf would have a meltdown."

Eunie bent down towards the dog. "Wilf! Stop your nonsense and get back to bed." He left with his tail dragging.

"You put on a light, you silly girl!" Hazen grumped. "He thought you were a burglar."

"So did I," said the young woman.

Eunie introduced them. "Everyone, this is Holly. Holly, this is my sister, Margo, and her manservants, Monty and Byron."

They nodded hello at each other before Holly said, "I didn't mean to frighten you. When I heard the dog go berserk, I thought something was wrong."

"No harm done," Margo said. "But Eunie, why do you have a hundred-watt bulb in the closet? No one needs to read in here."

"It was a mistake, obviously. Hazen put the ladder away before I could change it again."

"That's right, blame me. Now everyone, get to bed." Hazen turned away and returned to the den. Holly took the broom back to the kitchen and the fellas disappeared up the stairs, clearly not comfortable standing around in their pyjamas with mixed company.

"What are you doing in the closet, anyway?" her sister wanted to know.

"I'm looking for my jacket. I think I left my pills in the pocket." She slid the jacket off the hanger and checked. "Oh, thank goodness. They're here."

There was no point in trying to hang it back up, so she turned out the light and shut the closet door. Holly came back from the kitchen without the broom. The three women went up the stairs. At the landing, Margo turned. "Holly, I'm glad you're looking out for these two. It makes me feel better to know that someone is here to protect them."

"Oh, no one's going to bother them. They're too boring. This is the most excitement I've had since I've been here. Eunie, I left more cinnamon rolls on the counter downstairs. Night, all." And she went in her room and shut the door behind her.

The sisters said goodnight and Margo went in the bathroom to pee yet again and take her pill. She threw her jacket on a chair, crawled back into bed, and turned off the light. After that rush of adrenaline, she knew she'd have a hard time going to sleep. Just then, there was a quick jump on her feet and a rapid catwalk over her body right up to her face. Stan stared at her in the dark.

"Hello, Stan."

He still wasn't speaking to her.

"I thought my door was closed, but okay, if you'd like to stay, I could use the company."

She closed her eyes and Stan settled himself along her chest. She put her arm around him and he was lovely and warm. An unexpected comfort. She slept through the night for the first time since Dick died.

ᡆᡢᡄ

When they convened for breakfast, Eunie was surprised to hear that Stan was with her sister all night. "I wonder why Stan slept with Margo. He never jumps up on me."

"I have loose morals."

After a breakfast of warmed cinnamon rolls, the fellas headed out to build a masterpiece. It didn't go well. Firstly, Fred was misbehaving. He would not leave them alone. It was exciting for him to have more company, and he was determined to be included. Ginger stayed politely on the sidelines.

Hazen shouted, "FRED! Stop tramping on that bag of nails!" He reached down and picked up his carpenter apron and Fred stuck his butt in Hazen's face. "Go on now! You're in the way. Get goin'." Fred moved about two feet over and figured that was enough.

They had to work around him. And then Fred decided to fart. Loudly and often. Byron was helpless with laughter. He leaned against the fence and wiped tears from his eyes. "This is the most fun I've ever had."

Not for Hazen. Monty kept questioning everything Hazen was trying to do, noting structural deficiencies as if they were building the Taj Mahal. At one point Hazen went into the house for a glass of water and found Eunie in the pantry. "Jumpin' Jesus. That one's gonna drive me nuts."

"Who? Byron?"

"NO. Monty. What is it with architects? They've all got a T-square up their arse. I can't get a thing done. Wasting time measuring and remeasuring. Fred will be dead by the time we're finished."

"Well, you opened your big mouth and asked them for help."

"Thanks for reminding me."

"They'll be out of your hair tomorrow. Just grin and bear it." He went off grumbling.

By the time they came in for supper, Monty was thrilled. "The framework is perfect."

"I'm sure Fred is delighted," Hazen said.

Monty beamed. "Gosh, thanks, Hazen. I must say that was invigorating. Byron, we must build a shed of some kind out back."

"Not unless we get a flatulent donkey."

Margo went to bed and left the door open on purpose. And sure enough, there came a soft plunk, quick paws stepping along her body, and a close stare, so close Stan touched her nose with his. "Hi, Stan." He lay down, and she put her arm over him.

Byron packed the car the next morning while Monty and Margo sat under the apple trees on a bench her father had built for her mom.

"What's going to happen to me, Monty? I can't stay here forever. I can't be away from the girls. They must be missing me."

He leaned forward on the bench and pulled a tall stalk of grass and wrapped it around his finger. "Enjoy your time here. The kids will come back and get you. And you can move in with Mike until we figure out your next move. He has the room to store your furniture, obviously."

"He does? Oh, right. Well, he can have the furniture, but I don't want to live with my kids. Can I move in with you?"

"No."

Margo waved them goodbye and wandered over to the barn. She went inside and breathed in the heavy air, the shafts of light beaming down through the cracks. Fred and Ginger placidly ate their hay and nuzzled noses over their adjoining spaces. It was calming. No wonder Hazen spent his time out here. They snorted, stomped their hooves, and swished their tails. And looked at the world with big brown eyes, not a worry in the world other than being a donkey.

From the comfort of their own home.

Chapter Seven

Carole sat on the couch glaring at Dick. He was still on the coffee table. Velma was gone when Carole had finally woken up with a massive headache the day after the funeral, leaving her alone with Dick. And he was still with her almost three weeks later. Velma always had some excuse when her mother called her up.

"Mom! I can't come over. I'm heartbroken."

"What now?"

"Joanne left me. Didn't even have the decency to say it to my face, just left me a note on top of the toaster."

"That little bitch. What did it say?"

"'Sorry for your loss. Here's another one. Don't call me.'"

Carole bit her lip. The girl was at least clever. "That's terrible, Velma. You're well rid of her."

The next time she called, Velma was ranting. "That stupid piece of shit I drive needs the engine replaced. Not a part, not a piece, but the entire engine! Have you ever heard of that? So no, mother, I can't come over and take Dad for a drive. I have no wheels."

Bad luck seemed to follow the Sterling women everywhere.

When Dick had told her he wanted a divorce, Carole was so incensed she gave it to him. A "You don't want me; I don't want you either" type of deal. And when a ward clerk at the hospital handed her a medical file and casually said, "Someone saw your ex with a very attractive blond woman. He's moved on quickly," it took everything she had not to faint. She turned on her heel and walked down the hall to the first bathroom she saw and sat in the stall for an hour. It had never occurred to her that Dick had another woman. She felt like an idiot, and never wanted Velma to know that her father ditched her for someone else. It was too humiliating.

Instead of getting any satisfaction out of her nursing career, over the years she began to resent the patients who needed help. She needed help too, but who had her back? Every day, there was yet another fat lady needing help onto a commode. On one particular occasion the woman changed her mind and tried to push Carole away. Carole ended up under her on the floor, her back frigged and her arm broken. The patient must have bounced off her butt. She was fine and in bed in no time. Carole was the one taken out of the room on a stretcher.

And she couldn't ever go back to work. All the doctors agreed it was impossible for her to continue, and she was put on disability. Now her only nursing job was to turn on a heating pad. It was just as bad as when Dick had left her for another woman. Not wanted by the man she loved and rendered useless in her profession, she was alone at an age when most couples were gearing up for retirement and maybe the best time of their lives. She was now married to feeling sorry for herself, and she had to admit she was brilliant at it.

She got drunk one night shortly after her injury, which she wasn't supposed to do while she was on painkillers, and told Velma about her father's affair. The poor kid was speechless. Carole sagged into her on the couch and slurred, "I didn't want to tell you, I really didn't, and I've kept it secret for years and years, but I have no one else. No one else."

Velma put an arm around her. "It's okay, Mom. You've still got me."

"You're the best thing that ever happened to me. You and this bottle of red."

The next morning, Velma had returned. Carole was nursing a brutal hangover while lying on the couch with a cold cloth on her head.

Velma had wanted more details.

Carole had turned the facecloth over to the colder side. "What's to know? He was cheating on me with her. End of story. And a woman who sleeps with another woman's husband is a whore. Plain and simple."

"But how long was it going on?"

"Years, probably."

"Oh my god. How could he?"

"He's a man. Most of them don't seem to have a problem with it."

"That's why I stay away from them."

"I should've been a lesbian." Carole sighed.

When the cast finally came off her arm, she had perked up slightly. Thank you, Jesus, for two hands.

That was March 23, 2020.

No one could visit. She couldn't get out. Velma left groceries for her and shouted through the door, or stood on the lawn where Carole could see her out the window, waving with her mask on.

She turned on Netflix and watched the first show that piqued her interest. Eight seasons of *American Horror Story*.

When Carole caught Covid, Velma was incredulous over the phone. "That's insane. You haven't seen a soul!"

"I went to the lobby last week to get my mail."

"Were you wearing your mask? Did you have gloves on?"

"I had a mask. I can't remember if I wore gloves. Are you supposed to?"

"Did you at least wash your hands when you got back to the apartment?"

"I think so."

"Trust you to find the one germ lurking in the elevator."

"I told you somebody up there hates me."

"You're going to be okay, Mom."

"I feel like the walking dead."

Good idea. She lay on the couch and turned on the television. *The Walking Dead*. Nine seasons, one hundred and thirty-one episodes.

She spent three years on the couch wondering why nothing had worked out for her. And now her dead ex-husband was in her apartment mocking her. Enough was enough. If Velma wasn't interested in keeping her dad close, maybe Carole should leave him at the Lady Beaverbrook hockey rink down the street. Why hadn't she let Margo bury him? Who knew she'd just give him away like a bag of old clothes?

The phone rang. She didn't recognize the number. "Hello?"

"Good morning. Carole Sterling?"

"Who wants to know?"

"I'm Gene Simmons, a lawyer representing Margo Sterling."

Carole leaned on her hand and tried to manoeuvre herself straighter on the couch. "Oh, really? Give her a message from me. Tell her to come by and pick up her husband. He'll be waiting for her outside the door."

"Mrs. Sterling, I'm making a few simple inquiries into Mr. Sterling's estate. Tying up loose ends. Do you know if Mr. Sterling had a will when he was married to you?"

"Why? If he did and my name or my daughter's name is on it, does that mean we're entitled to his money, please God?"

"Not you, Mrs. Sterling. You're divorced from the man. His daughter might be, but it's complicated."

Carole felt her face flush with anger. "Listen here. I want what's owed to my kid. She told me her dad took her for a drive in his new fancy truck and she's wandering around with no car at the moment. If she's entitled to anything, I don't want that man-eater to get it."

"No one is getting anything, Mrs. Sterling. He had too much debt."

"What? What does that mean?"

"His house is being foreclosed and the estate assets, like his truck, are being sold to pay back the bank."

"So, Velma won't get the truck?"

"No."

"That miserable creep. Wait. Does that mean Margo is homeless?"

"I'm afraid so."

"Oh gosh. My heart bleeds."

"You haven't answered my question, Mrs. Sterling. Did Richard Sterling ever have a will?"

"NO!" Carole pressed the off button on her mobile phone as hard as she could, limped into the bedroom, and took Dick's will out of the Tupperware container she kept important papers in.

She stood over the tub and set it on fire.

⌒∾⌒

Margo looked out the kitchen window at the soggy mess in the yard. It had been raining for days. Even Fred didn't want to be in his little shed and hightailed it to the barn, where Ginger was dry and content. Hazen was wandering around the property in a full-length yellow fisherman's raincoat and hat, something Margo imagined Noah had worn on the ark.

She went into the porch, took some old newspapers from a stack by the boot rack, and placed individual pages on the floor. Eunie had asked her to when Margo went up to give her breakfast. She was laid up in bed with a miserable head cold and wasn't too happy about it. Margo had to admit Eunie looked terrible, with her nose red and chapped, eyes watery, and energy gone.

"Did you take that rapid test I gave you? Just to make sure it's not Covid?"

Eunie was grumpy. "Yes, despite the fact that I know a head cold when I feel it, even if I haven't had one in twenty years. Isn't that right, Stan?"

Meow.

Margo sat on the end of the bed. "Stan wasn't here twenty years ago. How would he know?"

Eunie blew her nose. "Check to make sure Wilf isn't dead."

"I did. He's not."

Eunie fell back into her pillows, her eggs and toast finished. "I think I have a temperature."

"I just took it. You don't. It's hot and muggy out despite the pouring rain." Margo took the tray and started to leave.

"Did you feed Hazen yet?"

Margo looked over her shoulder. "Is Hazen a baby?"

"Biggest baby I know," Eunie said, coughing. "Did you make his porridge?"

"*This* is why he's a baby. No, I didn't make his porridge. I made scrambled eggs. If he doesn't like it, he can lump it." And Margo went out the door with the tray.

Eunie's voice trailed after her. "Remember whose house you're in."

"Technically, Mom and Dad left it to all of us. I'll get you more tea with honey and lemon."

Back downstairs Hazen was dripping on the paper, mopping his face with a towel. "Where's my porridge?"

Margo walked by him on the way to the sink. "Your porridge maker is upstairs feeling rotten. You'll have to make do with my scrambled eggs."

He grunted and picked up the paper.

"Feel free to make your own breakfast, Hazen. My feelings won't be hurt."

"Fine, but don't make them too wet."

Because Hazen had been up since five, his daily routine was to take a quick nap in his chair after breakfast. Margo sat at the kitchen table and looked at the paper but realized she wasn't reading it. She put her elbow on the placemat and held her chin in her hand, listening to the clock on the wall instead. Stan sat on the windowsill, but he had nothing to report.

Margo had forgotten about Holly until she showed up in an old T-shirt and shorts. Her pyjamas, presumably. Her hair was in a rat's nest at the top of her head. "Morning," she said on her way to the fridge, her fuzzy slippers scuffing along the floor.

Margo immediately, desperately missed Julia. The young Julia and the mornings she'd run down the stairs before school, telling her about some drama with her girlfriends in between bites of Shreddies or slamming cupboard doors in a foul mood before stomping back up the stairs. Where had that girl gone? Where had the years gone?

Margo didn't realize Holly was at the table, spreading peanut butter on toast. "Would you like some scrambled eggs?" she asked her.

"No, thanks." She licked the peanut butter off the knife. "You look unhappy."

Margo gave her a little smile. "Do I?"

Holly pulled her legs up and put her feet on the chair, her knees folded into her chest. Margo remembered doing that.

Taking a bite of her toast, Holly said with her mouth full, "Eunie told me about your husband. I'm sorry."

"Thank you."

"He sounds pretty inconsiderate."

Margo picked up a pen to doodle on the edge of the paper. "Yes, that's a perfect description."

"Fucking asshole is better."

Margo gave her a grin. "You took the words right out of my mouth."

Holly jumped up and poured herself a glass of milk, holding up the carton to see if Margo wanted any. Margo shook her head. Holly came back and folded herself up in the chair again. "I'm not sure if Eunie told you how I came to be here."

"Yes," Margo nodded. "A little. You were hitchhiking."

"I was alone in the world."

Margo closed her fist and put her knuckles against her mouth as she listened. Holly took another bite of toast. "I had literally nowhere to go."

Margo nodded.

"Kind of like you now," Holly continued. "And that's why you're sad."

Margo looked out the window.

"But you have literally no reason to be sad."

Margo looked back at her. "Oh?"

Holly nodded and brushed the crumbs off her hands. "The day I was kicked out of my house, I could have died in a culvert by the side of the road and no one would have been looking for me. No one would have reported me missing. No one gave a shit." Holly hugged her knees. "Now you, your manservants delivered you to this dope place and Eunie says both your kids want you to live with them. Sure, you don't have a physical house, but you have homes everywhere."

Holly drank the rest of her milk, stood up, and took the second piece of toast with her upstairs.

Ouch.

Margo was still sitting at the table when Hazen went by on his way out the door. "Rain finally stopped. You plannin' on doing anything today? You wanna shovel out the barn?"

When she didn't answer him, he grunted and went outside.

Eunie yelled, "Are you coming upstairs to bring me that blasted tea and honey?"

Margo delivered the tea and again sat on edge of her sister's bed. Eunie took a sip. "Thank you."

"Holly's quite a character. Blunt." Margo traced the pattern on Eunie's log cabin quilt.

"That girl can see through BS at a thousand paces. She told me she wants to be a police officer, like the one who showed up when she was five to arrest her father for almost killing her mother. The woman put her in the back seat of the police car and gave her a stuffed bear, a juice box, and a peanut butter cookie. Holly never forgot it."

All this was making Margo feel worse. Apparently, her own life was perfect and she was an ingrate. She got off the bed. "Hazen asked me to shovel out the barn. I think I will."

"Don't overdo it."

She didn't. Margo could hardly lift the pitchfork into the wheelbarrow, but she struggled anyway. If her seventy-seven-year-old brother could do this, then so could she. Of course, he'd worked at a sawmill all his life. The heaviest thing she dealt with on her shifts were tins of Nivea Creme.

She was making some progress. Hazen came in to take Fred out to the paddock. He was kicking up a fuss. "Fred don't like women in his space," Hazen told her. "Kind of like me."

"Shall I bring out Ginger?"

"Make sure you keep hold of her halter."

Margo went into Ginger's stall and gave her a pat. The donkey was compliant and walked with her to the barn door, but then it was as if Ginger suddenly realized Margo wasn't Hazen and violently jerked her head upward, causing Margo's hand to slip from the halter. Ginger trotted away and Margo tried to run after her. She didn't hear Hazen yell, "Stop chasing her!" and kept chasing her, because she was headed for the highway.

Before she knew it both she and Ginger were in the middle of the road playing Ring Around the Rosie. Hazen hurried as fast as a nearly eighty-year-old man can and joined them in this fun game. The minute Ginger realized Hazen was there, she slowed down and he managed to grab her just as a car came over the horizon. He pulled Ginger off the road and had to yell at Margo, who was still blindly running around in a panic.

"Get off the goddamn road! There's a car coming!"

All three of them were at the top of the driveway when the car sped by. Hazen shook his fist at the disappearing car. Then he shook his fist at Margo. "What did I tell you? I said stop chasing her!"

Margo was trying to catch her breath. "I couldn't hear you! I didn't know what to do. I didn't want her to go on the road."

Hazen was panting too. "And yet that's exactly where she ended up. Use your head, Margo."

She stomped her foot. "I know nothing about donkeys!"

"You don't know much about anything, do you?" He walked away with Ginger and Margo grabbed a handful of muddy dirt and threw it at him, hitting him in the back of the head. He turned around in disbelief, wiping away the mud. "You always were a spoiled brat, Mary-Margaret. Dad should have put you over his knee at least once in your life to knock some sense in you."

Margo wiped the dirt from her hand onto her jeans. "*I'm* a spoiled brat? Says the grown man who expects his sister to make him porridge every morning."

Hazen waved his hand, dismissing her, and walked Ginger back to the paddock, shutting the gate tight.

This was ridiculous. Margo stomped into the kitchen and sat on a chair to calm down. It took a few minutes. She looked at Wilf snuggled up in his basket. "Wilf? Ya dead yet?"

Turns out he was.

She ran out of the house. "Hazen! Hazen!"

He appeared in the barn door. "Wha?"

"The dog's dead!"

"Jesus Christ! Did you kill him too?"

Chapter Eight

When Margo finally called, Julia was so relieved. She had missed her mother and so had her girls, but she couldn't get much sense out of her at first. Something about a dog, a runaway donkey, and being a spoiled brat. The gist of it was that Mom wanted to come home; anyone's home would do.

Julia was, luckily, on vacation, and Posy and Hazel were out in their paddling pool with the little boy from next door. She called Mike rather than texting him, so she could keep her eyes on the kids.

He answered the way he always answered: "What's up?"

"Mom wants to come home."

"She finally called? Are we allowed to talk to her now?"

"She sounded pretty frazzled. We don't have enough room in our car, but if you and Olenka drive down too, she can come home in yours. Uncle Hazen wants the kids to meet his donkeys, and I'm sure Olenka would like it. How many times has Aunt Eunie asked us to visit? It would be the perfect opportunity."

"And who's she going to stay with?"

"Us, for now. Dad and I both agreed we can't take her furniture out of the house without her there, so until we ship everything to your house, she'll be okay here."

"Everything? Do I have to take that chair?"

"What chair?"

"That flowery one."

"Michael, that's a bluebird toile settee. It's gorgeous. I wish I had it, but the girls would have Play-Doh all over it in a matter of minutes."

"What about that other one I always hated? That Pinocchio chair."

"You cretin. That's a chenille velvet chaise. Another piece I want her to gift me in her will."

"Oh, brother. It will match perfectly with my ancient faux-leather recliner."

Andre appeared at the sliding doors with three small bottles of yogurt drink and cut-up watermelon chunks. She waved at him. "So, are you coming or not? How about Saturday?"

"You got it."

"Okay, great. Talk later." Julia put the phone down and the kids spied the snacks. They ran with wet feet in their bathing suits to the patio table and Andre handed out the yogurt drinks. "Thanks, Daddy," the girls said as they picked up the watermelon with their fingers.

The little boy scowled. "Ya got any pop and chips?"

⸎

Saturday morning, Mike and Olenka pulled into Julia's driveway right on time. They had to leave early since it was a couple of hours there and back, and Julia and Andre wanted to return before the kids' bedtime. Posy and Hazel's stuffed unicorns, Fantasia and Rosette, were having a knock-down, drag-out fight while their parents threw things in the car. Backpacks, a cooler, pink and purple water bottles, Elsa and Olaf ball caps, the tote bag Julia used to pack extra clothes.

"It's astonishing how human parents feel the need to bring the kitchen sink with them if they're going anywhere for a few hours," Olenka said.

"Well, humans aren't kangaroos, are they?" Mike said. "Crikey, I'm starting to sound like you."

They all agreed not to stop unless absolutely necessary, because that would delay things by twenty minutes at least. Nothing like the thought of taking kids out of their car seats to make you determined to soldier on despite a protesting bladder.

They honked their horns to announce their arrival as they pulled into the driveway at nine thirty. Uncle Hazen was out in the yard waving with both hands when they came to a stop, beside a fresh mound of dirt under the lilac tree with a sparkling beach stone on top of it. The donkeys wandered over to the fence to see what was going on. Aunt Eunie burst out of the kitchen door and came down the stairs pretty fast for a woman with a bad hip.

But not as fast as their mom.

Mike and Olenka watched the girls' faces as they bolted out of the car and tried to get to her first.

Mike smiled. "I don't think Mom loved us the way she loves them."

"Of course she did. Did you know there's new research on killer whales to suggest that postmenopausal grandmothers play a powerful role in the survival of generations that follow them?"

"Is that so?" Mike laughed.

Olenka leaned forward in her enthusiasm. "The Grandmother Hypothesis theorizes that by living long past menopause, a woman improves the survival and reproduction of her children's children and thus her own genes. Seventeenth- and eighteenth-century Catholic clergy kept church records of French settlers in Quebec and logged their births, marriages, and deaths. Researchers found that women whose mothers were still alive gave birth to more children, and the closer those women lived to their mothers, the greater the chances their kids pulled through."

He looked at her. "Do you by any chance love what you do, O?"

"Of course I do."

"You sure keep it hidden well."

Hazel jumped into her Gogo's arms and Posy hugged her around the waist and didn't let go until she spied something even more amazing by the fence.

"Donkeys!!"

"Come and meet Fred and Ginger," said Uncle Hazen. "Hold my hands. Don't spook them."

Mike and Olenka approached the railing as well, Olenka very happy to see such fine specimens. "Your uncle takes very good care of his charges. They're fortunate; not all of them are. There's something special about a donkey's face, don't you think? If a horse is the popular hockey jock in school, a donkey is the kid who gets shoved in his locker."

"You've always loved an underdog."

Uncle Hazen gave the girls a couple of apples and told them to lay their hands flat. "Now you keep your hand steady and the donkeys will take the apple from you by tickling your hand softly with their lips."

They resolutely did what they were told. When success was achieved, the sisters were very impressed with themselves.

"Now wait till you see this." Uncle Hazen went over to the barn and came back out with two big yoga balls. "This is Fred's favourite game. Watch, girls!"

As soon as he threw the balls over the fence, the donkeys went after them. Ginger nosed hers around on the ground, but Fred actually played with his. He knelt down on his front legs and picked up the ball with his teeth. Then he jumped up and ran in a circle like it was the best thing in the world.

Everyone was delighted. Especially Andre, looking at his daughters' faces. "What do you think, girls? Fred likes to play too."

"Wait for it!" Hazen shouted.

Fred instantly got up and walked on his hind legs for about twenty feet, his front legs pawing in the air, still gnashing the ball. It was so astonishing, no one could believe it. Uncle Hazen looked like a proud papa. "That Fred is quite the show-off."

Fred, with an uncanny sense of comedic timing, farted long and loud.

Mike and Olenka ended up spending most of the day with the girls, giving the adults time to chat about what lay ahead. Mike stayed out of conversations like this whenever possible. They climbed trees and clambered up rocks, picked wildflowers for Mommy, and brought their lunch outside for a picnic. Olenka told them about the animals they'd find in the woods as the girls ate the meal their father made. Hummus and carrot sticks, whole grain bagel with natural almond butter, apricots, and a square of dark chocolate.

Mike and Olenka drooled over it until Olenka ran in to make them Jiffy peanut butter sandwiches—but came out with two fresh Kaiser rolls thick with ham and cheese that Eunie had made for everyone.

It was time to go in. They'd had a lot of sun. They came around the corner of the house and a car pulled into the yard in rather a hurry. Mike and Olenka instinctively reached for the little ones, but the car stopped a good distance away. A young girl got out holding a plastic bag full of pastry. This had to be the lodger.

"Heya!" She waved. "I'm Holly. You must be Andre and Julia, Posy and Hazel."

"These are Posy and Hazel, but I'm Mike and this is my girlfriend, Olenka."

"Nice to meet you. If I have to hear your names one more time my head is going to explode. Do you realize how happy you've made Eunie and Hazen? It's a shame you can't visit more often. It can be lonely for them. Best thing Hazen ever did was buy Fred and Ginger. They keep him constantly entertained."

"They're pretty special," Olenka said.

"He fucking loves them. I hope there's sandwiches left." And she dashed across the yard and up the steps, slamming the kitchen door behind her.

Mike cleared his throat and Olenka wouldn't look at him for fear of laughing out loud. "Let's go, girls."

Their mother told them that Aunt Eunie was just getting over a head cold, and she insisted that Eunie not make one of her elaborate salmon dinners. Instead, Margo made spaghetti and meatballs for an early supper. But she had to have two pots of boiling water going, one for the whole wheat pasta and one for the white. Holly happened by and reached into the cupboard for a glass. She looked at the pots. "Why two?"

"Andre is very fussy with what his girls eat, hence the whole wheat pasta. Hazen would turn his nose up at that, as you know."

"True."

She turned to leave and Margo reached out to grab her arm. Holly pulled it away abruptly. "Don't touch me."

"I'm sorry, I didn't mean to startle you. Just to thank you for the other day. For another perspective."

Holly said, "Sure" and left. That poor child.

Just then Julia showed up and put her arm around her mother's shoulders. "Don't worry, Mom. We'll take this step by step. For now, you're going to be in the girls' playroom."

"Not in that pink fabric castle, I hope?"

"Why not? If it's good enough for a princess…"

In the middle of their meal as they chatted around the table, Posy looked up from her plate. "Where's Icky?"

All the adults froze, except Holly. "Who's Icky?"

"Gogo's friend."

Margo started to stammer. Julia glanced at Andre, but he looked like a deer in headlights.

Olenka spoke up. "Icky died, girls. Death happens to all living things. Usually for people not until they are very, very old. There are some things we can control and some things we can't, and death is one we can't control. Nobody is to blame."

Julia jumped in. "Remember, Daddy and I told you that's what happened to your pet gerbil, Stinky? Everyone and everything has a lifespan, and it's part of living. We're very sorry that Icky's gone and he didn't get to say goodbye to you, but sometimes that's what happens. We're all very sad about it."

"You are?" Posy said. "You're not crying."

"You can be sad and not cry. Sometimes we're just quiet. If you'd like to cry, that's okay. It's always a shock to find out something like this. Whatever you feel inside, in your heart or in your tummy, is exactly the way you should feel. There's no right or wrong way to miss someone."

"Did Daddy bury Icky in our yard?" Hazel asked.

"No, honey. He's with his family, just like Stinky is with us."

❧

Andre and Mike took Margo's belongings out to Mike's car. Now it was Eunie's turn to sit on Margo's bed as she packed up her cosmetics case. Margo shook her head. "Out of the mouths of babes. I can't believe we forgot to tell the girls about Dick. Not that they were around him much, but still. He was someone in their life, and to suddenly not have him around...of course they would wonder why."

"Well, you haven't seen the girls to tell them, have you? You know, you've only been here for a couple of weeks. Why don't you stay until the end of August?"

"I don't need Hazen barking at me, for one thing. And I know it will be easier for Andre and Julia if I'm around for the last few weeks before Posy starts school. I want to be useful."

"You were useful here. Making me breakfast in bed. Giving Ginger the runaround on a busy highway. Killing Wilf."

Margo zipped up her bag. "I did not kill Wilf. I just happened to discover him."

"Do you have any witnesses who can verify that?" Eunie teased. "Poor old Wilf. Of course, he was eighteen. He's been asleep for the last two years except when you turned on the closet light. But thanks for helping Hazen dig his grave. He always loved that lilac bush. His favourite place to pee."

"I'll assume you mean Wilf and not Hazen. By the way, can I take Stan with me? He's my hot water bottle."

"Not a chance. You might kill him."

They took pictures of Uncle Hazen and Aunt Eunie with the girls standing in front of them and Fred and Ginger on either side, before they fed the donkeys sugar cubes.

"I'm not sure that's healthy," Andre muttered.

Posy and Hazel wanted their grandmother to drive home in their car but were told no. Booboo suggested they could wave to her from the back seat. Julia reminded him that the kids' car seats didn't face backwards anymore. Olenka suggested they drive in front of Andre and wave to the girls themselves. Andre said that was a car accident waiting to happen. Uncle Hazen told them they were all nuts.

More hugs all around. Margo hung on to Eunie. "You'll be okay. And if your kids drive you foolish, you can always come back."

Hazen gave Margo a quick hug and kept patting her back. "Don't be stranger, now."

Off they went, honking the horns. Margo looked out the window at her childhood home and her siblings, who had always felt more like parents. They were waving with Holly, Fred, and Ginger standing beside them. "What a dear little family," she sniffed. "Thank God for that girl."

Holly shook her head as the cars turned onto the highway and disappeared. "Oh my god, they are so extra."

⌇

Andre and Julia held hands in the front seat. It had been a very relaxing day for them thanks to Booboo and O. He raised her hand and kissed the back of it.

Hazel's sleepy little voice chirped up. "No kissing I said."

Julia turned her head to the side. "Did you girls have fun today?"

"Yes!" Posy was more awake.

"What did you think of Uncle Hazen and his donkeys?"

"He fucking loves them."

Chapter Nine

Julia was on the phone when her mother came downstairs. Hazel was in her pyjamas hanging off her leg, sucking on a fruit freezie. She gestured for Margo to come and take her.

"Well, that's not acceptable," she said into her cellphone. "And I'd like it resolved as quickly as possible."

Margo walked into the messy kitchen/dining room/living room. She never could understand the fascination for open-concept living. Give her a good old wall to hide behind. Julia and Andre's house could be featured in a *Style at Home* magazine, but at the moment the place was covered in the clutter that comes with kids: tissue boxes, balled-up napkins, hair clips, stickers, drawings, crayons, balls, a play kitchen with pots, toy tin cans, and assorted groceries. This is what she used to squirrel away when people came over. Behind walls.

"Where's my sweetie pie? Is Hazel here? I can't see her. She must be hiding."

Hazel turned around, ran over, and grabbed her pants. "I'm here, Gogo. I'm sick."

Margo made a face. "I can see that. Just a minute." She reached into her bathrobe pocket and found some Kleenex. "Come, let me blow your nose."

"NOOO." Hazel turned her face away.

Margo ended up coming in behind her and smooshing the tissue into her face while Hazel wailed and tossed her head back and forth. Misson accomplished.

Hazel tried to hit her but missed. "Don't, Gogo. It's my nose."

Julia had her hand on her ear when she hung up. "Was that necessary? I was on the phone."

"You wanted me to take her."

"I wanted you to divert her attention, not make her scream her head off. I couldn't hear a thing." Julia was late for work, so she gathered up her portfolio and a soymilk and blueberry smoothie Andre had made for her. "Be a good girl, please. Mom, check her temp from time to time. There's Children's Tylenol in the cupboard. Guard it with your life. It was impossible to get last year. Daddy says her lunch today is a spinach omelette. The ingredients are in the fridge. I'll text later and see how you're doing. Andre's meeting ends at one thirty and he should be here when Posy gets off the bus. If he's not, you know where the bus stops, right? The corner by the park."

"Umm...but what about Hazel? I can't take her if she has a cold."

"Mom. It's a cold. The ten minutes she'd be outside would probably do her good."

"It would? Not if she has a fever."

Julia took a deep breath. "Okay. If Andre can't make it, I'll come home and walk a half a block up the street to get Posy and then go back to work."

Her mother looked like she was going to cry. God. Not again. She walked over to her. "Mom, it's fine. I'm sure Andre will be home. Please don't worry. I can also ask Sophie's mom if she can bring her home. It's all good."

She kissed her mother's cheek and gave Hazel a hug. "Try to get her down for a nap if you can. And no television. Bye." The door closed.

Margo and Hazel looked at each other.

"I don't want yucky spinish."

"Good. Neither do I. We'll have grilled cheese."

Hazel pushed the end of her freezie and the last bit popped up and landed on her white socks. "Oh, no. That's not good."

"It's okay, honey. Let me get a cloth." Margo walked to the sink.

"Gogo, can I watch *Paw Patrol*?"

"Your mommy said no."

"Please. I wanna watch *Paw Patrol*. Please."

"No."

Hazel blinked and blinked with her big brown eyes, her mouth gathering into a sad little pout. It was like being hypnotized. Screw the rules of only one hour total of television on a weekend. It was Friday. Close enough. "Okay."

They snuggled into the chaise longue part of the moss-green sectional for extra comfort. Hazel tucked herself under her grandmother's arm. Margo felt her forehead. "Where's the thermometer?"

"I know, Gogo." Hazel hopped back up and brought over the one from her doctor's kit.

"The real one, honey."

Turns out she knew where that one was too. Someone had put it on the edge of the stairs. "I know this goes in your ear, but what button do you press?" Hazel showed her. Her temperature was normal, thank goodness.

They settled back in and Margo picked up the remote. She pressed the power button and an unfamiliar screen came on with icons of on-demand television streaming services. She'd forgotten the kids didn't have cable.

"I'm not sure how to work this." She pointed at the screen and pressed what she thought was the right button and it sent her on a wild goose chase asking her if she wanted settings or audio hookup. "What? What's this?" It's not like she could ask Julia. Then she'd know they were watching television.

"Gogo, you have to press this."

"I do?"

Hazel pressed something with her tiny finger and the screen popped back up. "Now go here." She got off the couch and ran to the television and touched the YouTube logo. After that a bunch of children's shows came up. Obviously, a collection of shows they must have watched before. Margo didn't see *Paw Patrol*. She'd have to keep looking, and how did you do that? Fortunately, Hazel pointed to the screen. "I want this one." She ran back to the couch and snuggled in again.

"*Masha and the Bear*? Okay."

They started to watch it, once Margo figured out how the volume control worked on their slick remote. Hazel soon put her head on Margo's lap and was out like a light in a matter of minutes. The cold had taken the stuffing out of her.

The Russian cartoon was a hoot. Everything the fatherly bear did was upended by this Masha kid, and the two wolves who lived in an old run-down ambulance became Margo's favourites. Nothing went right for them.

That was familiar...but whenever Margo veered off into poor-me territory, Holly came to mind. She didn't want Hazel to wake, so she shut the television off and played with her soft dark curls.

Meanwhile Andre's meeting didn't go as planned. Their boss was in a fender bender on his way to work and had to reschedule. He and his colleagues attended to some matters, but after a couple of hours, they headed back to their home offices.

He pulled into the driveway. Margo's car took up a lot of space. She somehow managed to park it at an angle every time. He'd either have to clean out the garage, which was a scary thought, or he or Julia would have to park on the street, which would be a pain in the winter with overnight parking bans. Surely, she wouldn't still be here by then?

He found the two of them snoring away on the couch, the remote by Margo's hand. He sighed, went down to his office, and stayed there.

Hazel awakened first and patted her grandmother's chest until Margo woke with a start. She was instantly guilty about falling asleep on the job. What if Hazel has woken up, plugged in the electric carving knife, and sawn her fingers off?

Hazel started pressing a little too hard into Margo's left breast. "What, dear?"

"I'm hungry."

"Oh. That's a good sign. Let's get something to eat."

Margo lifted Hazel up onto the kitchen counter to let her butter the sourdough bread she'd found in the breadbox. It seemed a better choice than sprouted whole-grain bread. There was no margarine in this house, only real butter, so they had a devil of a time trying to spread it. Margo couldn't be bothered to soften it in the microwave, and it took Hazel an age, but she was having fun so that's all that mattered. There were no plastic cheese slices here either, so Margo cut pieces of Havarti and pieced them together.

When the sandwiches were golden brown, they put them on plates and turned around. Andre was watching them.

"Jeepers!" Margo shouted. "You scared us."

"Sorry. Home early. No spinach omelettes?"

Margo was annoyed. "Omelettes? No, she didn't want one, and when you're sick with a cold you should have what you want. What's wrong with a grilled cheese?"

"Nothing."

She didn't like the way he said "Nothing." Oh brother. It was like having a prison guard breathing down your neck.

Margo was obviously very grateful to the kids, but after six decades you get used to being a grownup. She constantly felt like a wayward child when she was with them. Of course, her three-year-old granddaughter knew how to work the television and she didn't.

Andre joined them at the dining room table with his spinach omelette. Hazel, the traitor, left her seat with only three bites taken out of her sandwich, crawled up on her dad's lap, and ate most of his lunch. "Yummy," she said.

Margo shook her fist and Andre laughed.

☙

Hazel went back to daycare after three days away. Margo held her hand and walked her up the street, Posy with them. Jenny, the minder, opened the door surrounded by three of Hazel's little pals. They looked pleased to see her, everyone shouting her name. "Say goodbye to Grandma," Jenny said. Margo was expecting a hug or a kiss, but Hazel didn't give her a backwards glance. She was dismissed. "Goodbye, Grandma," Jenny said again, as if to make up for the slight. "Bye bye. Bye bye." She shut the door firmly in Margo's face. Posy looked up at her. "She never says goodbye to Daddy either."

Margo walked Posy to the school bus stop down by the park. A gaggle of parents waited with their little ones, but Margo noticed there were a lot of grandparents like her. It made her wonder if with today's economy, families had to start living together for financial reasons.

"Don't kiss me goodbye, Gogo. I'm not a baby."

"Don't kiss you? Okay." The bus came along and Margo said, "Have a good day, sweetheart. Daddy's picking you up. I have to go to my old house today. Love you."

Posy smiled at her and waved before she climbed up the bus steps. How was it possible that her baby girl was driving away with a stranger? This bus driver better not be a drug addict or an insomniac. Margo glared at the woman and pointed two fingers at her own eyes and then at the bus driver, who looked to the heavens and rolled away. In this job, she'd seen it all.

Margo had heard from Monty's lawyer, Gene Simmons. She wondered how many people were disappointed by his plain grey suits and average-sized tongue.

He told her that the bank had confirmed she should have her belongings out of the house by mid-November. Dick had died in June. She had two months' leeway, but she wanted to get started with this. Monty was arranging for a U-Haul and Mike and Andre said they'd move the furniture, but in the meantime, Margo went over during the day with garbage bags to tidy up, wrap up dishes, and pack things in boxes. She put masking tape on the furniture she wanted to keep. Her belongings could go ASAP to Mike's. She wasn't planning to take Dick's stuff, but she'd have to ask her lawyer, Kiss, about that. She'd probably get in trouble or whatever if she left it behind, or she'd be responsible for hauling it away. It was so irritating. There were more rules and regulations to follow.

Who knew the business of dying was such an endless bog of bureaucracy? Months of continuous paperwork to be sorted out. Words like *probate court*, *executor*, *intestacy*, *chattels*, *caveats*. She started to think Dick was the lucky one. He didn't have to deal with the godawful mess he'd left behind.

There was a knock at the door, which unnerved her, but it turned out to be Harman with a steaming thermos of coffee.

"I noticed your car here," she said as Margo let her in. "I've got the morning off."

Margo cleared up the mess at the kitchen table. "Here, sit. It's so great to see you." She grabbed a couple of mugs from the cupboard. "You are the only reason I'm going to miss living here."

Harman opened the thermos, the cream and sweetener already in it. She and Margo liked their coffee the same way. "I have to admit I'm a little trepidatious about who's going to move in."

"I hope they're happier than we were."

They picked up their mugs at the same time. One had a Las Vegas Golden Knights logo on it, and Margo's read *World's Greatest Grandma*. She'd gotten it for Mother's Day.

"I didn't realize things were bad between you."

"I suppose I didn't either," Margo admitted. "I knew I wasn't particularly happy, but there are times when you aren't, in any marriage. It doesn't mean you chuck it away. Although that seems to be the way of the world now. Maybe youngsters have the right idea. Life is short. If something's not working for you, move on."

"Well," Harman said, holding her cup in both hands, "it's easier for young people. They still have most of their lives ahead of them. When you're middle-aged, it's a little harder to extricate yourself from relationships. Finances alone are more complicated, and retirement looms."

Margo shook her head. "I signed that loan without asking Julia or Monty about it first. I tried to make a decision without them. I always go hat-in-hand to them about everything, and I know it annoys them."

"No doubt that's why you didn't want to consult them. It's normal to want to avoid something unpleasant."

"If Olenka were here, she'd start telling us about how animals run away from porcupines."

"That makes sense, since humans are just mammals."

Margo kept rubbing her thumbnail along the side of her coffee cup. "That's probably why I don't want to stay here. I'm so angry with him, Harman. I can't believe he did this to me. And yet I feel guilty about feeling like this. My husband died. I did love him once. Am I a terrible person?".

Harman shook her head. "The last thing you are is a terrible person. He hurt you deeply, Margo. He was unconcerned with your welfare. He let his addiction take hold and did nothing to try and help himself. You are doing the best you can. You have to leave the home you've known for ten years; you have to move in with your adult children for the time being, and that's humiliating. It's none of my business, but will you be able to support yourself properly?"

"I'll probably have to go back to work, if they'll even take me. I'm sixty-two. Who's going to want me?"

"You need to remember that you have years' worth of experience and are a walking testament to your craft. If you were behind any cosmetic counter in any store, I'd be running over to you for advice, because it's very clear you know exactly what you're doing. Please stop selling yourself short, Margo. And the fact that you look my age is amazing. No one would think you were in your sixties, so run with that. You have more options than you think."

Margo gave her a watery smile. "I'm so glad you're my friend. Please make sure we stay in touch."

"Of course. My daughter's wedding is next summer. I'll be hiring you to do my makeup."

The minute she said it, she sat up in her chair. "My god, Margo. You could be a makeup consultant. Someone who drives around in her own car and does makeup on location, for weddings, anniversaries, special occasions, family photoshoots. If you put a notice in the paper and get a few clients, I know darn well word of mouth would have you busier than a beaver, in Olenka vernacular. And once you're really popular, they could come to you."

"Where, though?"

"Mike's for now?"

Margo shook her head. "That won't work. Mike's basically a hermit. The idea of women streaming into his place would ruffle his feathers, in Olenka vernacular."

They laughed together and Margo felt much better.

Before Harman left, Margo made her share the sandwich she'd brought with her. This time she'd used the sprouted whole-grain bread. She'd put smoked salmon, thin slices of cucumber, and mayonnaise on it, then Andre had suggested she sprinkle a little fresh mint over it. Only Andre would have fresh mint at the ready.

The minute the two of them bit into it, they decided it was the best sandwich they'd ever had.

"This son-in-law of yours should open up his own health food restaurant."

They hugged each other goodbye and Margo went back to her task, all the while thinking of Harman's idea. But the thought of driving to unfamiliar neighbourhoods and entering strangers' homes frightened her.

As usual.

And then she opened their bedroom closet. Dick might as well have been standing there. His smell was on his clothes. "You big jerk." But she smelled them anyway and immediately thought Velma might like to have her dad's hockey jerseys. He said she'd once played on a women's recreational hockey team. Margo should have offered them to her long before this...but it made sense to run from porcupines. Maybe Julia could call her. No. Margo should.

But she didn't.

Chapter Ten

Julia had flashbacks to the last time she had called Velma. She moaned about it to Andre as they brushed their teeth over the his-and-her sinks in their ensuite bathroom. "Not only am I going to have to call this woman, but Mom wants me to be there when she comes over to collect the stuff. I'd rather get a healthy dose of hemorrhoids."

Andre rinsed his toothbrush under the tap and knocked it against the sink before putting it back in its stand. "Some of your colleagues are afraid of you. Put on that Julia demeanour and she'll probably back down. Your mother is not the ogre they pretend she is. She went out with him for about three weeks when he assured her he was separated, and she gave him the boot when she found out he wasn't. She only resumed the relationship once he was divorced. Camilla Parker Bowles, she's not."

"Too bad. That one landed on her feet, didn't she? Can you do it instead?"

Andre kissed her on the nose. "Nope. I'm doing enough for your mother at the moment, like having very quiet sex so you don't freak out about her hearing us through the adjoining wall. Go ask your brother."

She did.

"Oh goody," he said.

"Listen, you. You're her child too, so you get to be involved."

"I'm not sitting on my ass, Jules. I'm the one physically moving her furniture."

"Big whoop, so's Andre. Listen, this Velma person is pretty hefty. If she goes off on a rampage, Mom and I could use a burly guy there."

"What a sexist thing to say. I'm a manatee. A very large creature who is nonetheless gentle and slow-moving. Ask Olenka."

Julia always parked her car ten blocks from her downtown office. It gave her a brisk ten-minute walk in the morning and a bit of fresh air before she drove home in the evening. She also walked on her lunch hour over the Bill Thorpe Walking Bridge. Fredericton was such a beautiful city, with its heritage buildings, cathedrals, and churches. Her favourite place to go was the Boyce Farmers Market, only open on Saturdays. She sometimes snuck out of the house for an hour while Andre made the girls their weekend whole-wheat-and-almond-butter waffles with dollops of plain yogurt, honey, and chia-seed jam. He was a complete madman about nutrition for his children. Her girlfriends were totally jealous. She thanked her lucky stars because they'd be eating Pop-Tarts for breakfast with her at the helm.

Julia went up three flights of stairs, another nod to exercise, and greeted her compatriots before she shut the door to her office and sat behind her desk. She took several deep breaths and exhaled slowly. Velma was no match for her.

Julia called her number.

The phone rang three times. Oh good, she could leave a message—then suddenly Velma's voice was in her ear and Julia was instantly transported back to that horrible night.

"What do you want, Julia Donovan Paris? I'm about to teach a class of uninterested fifteen-year-olds how to play volleyball, which will be much more enjoyable now that I can picture your smug face as the ball."

"What I want, Velma Sterling, despite your unpleasant and thoroughly unnecessary vitriol, is to extend you an invitation to your father's house on my mother's behalf. The bank is foreclosing, and she is losing her home thanks to your father's gambling debts. But before she vacates the premises she wondered if you would like to have anything, specifically your father's clothes, hockey sweaters, or other personal effects. She would have been in touch sooner, but as you can imagine she's been overwhelmed with the change in her circumstance through no fault of her own."

There was a long silence before she said, "When?"

"This Saturday. Ten o'clock in the morning."

Velma hung up, and Julia looked at her cell. "You're welcome."

☙

Velma went straight to her mother's house after her last class. Julia's phone call had thrown her for a loop. She wanted to keep hating Margo, and she needed her mother to fan the flames.

As usual, she found her mom asleep on her living room couch, surrounded by Chinese takeout containers, crossword puzzle books, prescription bottles, empty Coke cans, and *People* magazines. Why not read about other people's lives instead of partaking in one yourself?

"Mom...MOM."

Nothing. She better not be dead, but it was more likely she didn't have her ears on, as she called her hearing aids. Her mother had been incredulous when she was told she needed them. "I'm too young to have hearing aids! You watch, it's going to be down-hill from here."

That was three days before "that fat woman," as Carole remembered her, sat on her arm.

She had no choice but to shake her awake. "MOM."

Carole lifted her head, and her hands flew in front of her face. "I have a black belt! Don't mess with me."

Exasperated, Velma cleared off the armchair on the other side of the crowded coffee table. "You're a regular Jackie Chan."

Her mother groaned and had a hard time manoeuvring into a more-or-less sitting position. "I'm parched. Get me a Coke, will ya?"

"How about a glass of water?"

Her mother dropped her chin and squinted at her over her dirty glasses. "How about a Coke?"

Once she delivered the soda, Velma sat in the chair and put her hands on her knees. "Julia called."

"Who's Julia?" Her mother took a huge gulp straight from the can.

"Man-eater Junior."

Velma belched. "Why is that stuck-up princess calling you?"

"To ask me over to Dad's house on Saturday morning to gather up his personal effects, if I want them. Stuff like his hockey jerseys."

"Do you want them? It took you nearly three weeks to come and get the man himself."

"Only because I was busy trying to get my life back on track after my car and girlfriend dumped me. I wasn't purposely rejecting him. He's on the shelf in my bathroom now."

"Excuse me?"

"How many hours did he spend in there? I figured he'd like it."

Carole downed the rest of the can. "I'll come with you. To make sure you get what you deserve."

On Saturday morning, Julia heard her mother gagging in the bathroom. Posy was outside the door. "I don't think Gogo feels good."

Julia knocked. "Mom? You okay?"

"No. Yes. No."

"Come downstairs. Andre's making you normal pancakes. He bought a small bag of white flour just for you."

"Thank him, but I can't eat."

While Julia ate her mother's pancakes, she called her dad. "Wish me luck."

"Good luck, honey. Byron says to break a leg."

"That's what I'm worried about."

Margo came downstairs looking like she might be going to the Oscars, but Julia bit her tongue. Her makeup was her protection, Harman had said, so Julia refrained from making a comment.

Hazel did. She ran over and hugged her grandmother. "You look like Barbie!"

When they picked up Mike, he was naturally running behind, so Julia had to hop out of the car and go pound on his door. Olenka answered in her bathrobe. "He'll be right down. He's on the john."

Olenka looked past Julia and waved to Margo sitting in the front seat. She gave her a thumbs up and Margo blew her a kiss.

"How is she?" Olenka asked.

"She looks like Cleopatra."

Olenka knew about Harman's theory. "Classic defense move. Some animals build a shell that they can hide their soft bodies in. Take snails, for example..."

Thank God Mike showed up just then. He gave a Olenka a peck. "Come and get me if these women beat me up."

"You've got this. You're an alpha male. A silverback. Did you know that—"

Both Mike and Julia hurried down the steps. "Later, babe."

When they arrived at the house, there was already a car in the driveway. "Okay, let's do this," Julia said. She got out and so did Mike. He opened his mother's door and she sat there. "Come on, Mom."

Margo didn't move.

Mike leaned down and whispered, "Olenka said to tell you that you are a naked mole-rat."

Margo looked at him with dismay. "I am?"

"It is not uncommon for a naked mole-rat to have a bloody skirmish when another female is challenging the queen."

"Mike, I love Olenka, but this isn't helpful."

He nodded. "I'm delivering the message, that's all."

Margo took a few deep breaths and got out of the car. Velma got out of theirs and Carole struggled to get out of her seat. Mike offered her a hand.

"I'm not an invalid."

He backed off.

Julia used her executive voice. "Good morning. Did you bring some boxes or containers or garbage bags?"

"We're not stupid," Velma answered as she opened her trunk. Mike asked if she needed help and she ignored him.

So far this was going well.

Mike gave his mom a gentle nudge and she walked to the back door and opened it, the others behind her. Julia was surprised when her mother spoke up. "I organized your dad's clothes on the bed, so you can see what's there. All his hockey jerseys are in one pile."

Velma started to cry.

"Look what you've done!" Carole yelled. "You made her cry."

"This is going to be very emotional for her, Mrs. Sterling," Julia said. "Would you like some water, Velma?"

Velma shook her head.

"We'll give you some space."

They stayed in the kitchen and sat around the table while Velma sobbed in her father's den.

"I feel sorry for her," Margo whispered. "It's very hard to say goodbye to your dad."

"I suppose even rude people have feelings," Julia said.

"You'd know," Mike said. Julia punched him in the shoulder.

Carole limped back in with her cane, brandishing it like a weapon. "Where's that deer head? He shot and ate that animal himself. It was his prized possession."

"It drove away two weeks ago."

"Excuse me?!"

"I didn't realize it was something you or Velma might want," Margo said. "It ended up on the curb and someone took it. I apologize."

"You owe us one deer head."

"We'll go hunting when we're finished here," Julia said. "What's your address?"

"You little smartass."

Mike held up his hand. "Let's be civil. This is difficult enough."

Carole glared at Julia and left the kitchen. Now Mike hit Julia in the shoulder. "Stop stooping to her level."

Julia rubbed her shoulder. "Mom, Michael's hitting me."

Velma eventually started to cart out boxes of clothes and accepted Mike's help with the heavier items, like Dick's hockey trophies and photo albums. Margo hoped Velma knew they were filled with pictures of her dad's hand holding a barbeque fork over every steak he ever ate. Carole roamed around and Julia began to follow her, convinced she'd pick up a nice item or two that belonged to her mother.

She went back in the kitchen and made her mom a cup of tea from the teabags her mother had left on the counter, along with a lone carton of milk in the fridge. Margo was looking peaky even through her foundation. "Mom, I don't trust that woman."

"I've already taken the smaller items I want out of here. What do you think I've been doing every day? There's only my furniture left. I'm not taking anything else."

Julia scowled. "But all this is yours by right. Marital property. Stuff like his television and lawn mower. And what about that miserable barbeque? And doesn't he have a snowblower?"

Margo rubbed her forehead. "I forgot about the stuff in the garage. And Velma is his next of kin too. She should have something. She can take everything. I do not want any of his things, do you hear me?"

Julia tried not to pull her hair out in front of her mother. "Fine. Fine. The woman can take every blessed thing. All his furniture, and give her the television too, but unless she mentions the other items, we'll just keep our mouths shut and take them away with your furniture. Mike needs a lawn mower, God knows, and a snowblower, and we could use that fancy barbeque. A reward for your pain and suffering."

"Then shouldn't they be mine?"

"We'll keep them for you until you get yourself settled."

Margo folded her arms across her chest. "You are just one step away from being a tyrant, Julia."

The other mother-daughter duo were having their own issues.

"I want you to take everything that belonged to your dad. Definitely that television and his recliner. And that hutch. We bought that years ago. I always loved it. I don't know why I let him have it."

"Because it was too big for your condo. And my new bachelor apartment is even smaller." Velma was rooting through his DVDs. "Oh god. *Caddyshack*. He loved that movie. *The Midnight Meat Train*? I never saw that one."

"The sofa and loveseat downstairs belonged to your grandmother."

"God no. That musty set is staying put. I've got his hockey stuff, the jerseys, his hockey card collection, and his leather jacket. That's all I care about."

"But I don't want that bitch to get everything. Why should she?"

"Oh, I don't know. She was his wife?"

Carole hit her cane on the floor. "Velma! How dare you talk to me like that?"

Velma paused. "Look, I've got a splitting headache."

Just then Margo came in the den, looking hesitant. "I'm sorry, it's getting late. I'm exhausted and I'm sure you are too."

Carole pointed at the television. "I want Velma to get that television and her father's leather recliner!"

"Fine. She's welcome to them. How about you come back next Saturday and take them? And anything else in here. It's not coming with me."

Carole couldn't believe her ears. "Okay."

All of them left the house, Mike carrying the last big box out to their car, while their mom locked up.

Velma actually thanked him for his help. "We'll be here next Saturday, then."

Julia let them leave first. "You're going to be busy tomorrow too, Mike."

He groaned and put his hand through his hair. "Why?

"I'm renting a U-Haul and we're moving Mom's stuff tomorrow. Text Dad and tell him."

"What's the rush?"

She told him as they drove home.

When Julia got a bee in her bonnet, there was no stopping her. Margo stayed home with the kids the next day, completely happy to be playing Hungry Hungry Hippos, while Julia, Andre, Mike, Olenka, Monty, and Byron took Margo's furniture and dishes out of the house, along with the frightfully expensive barbeque, the lawn mower, snowblower, power tools, and chainsaw. Even Harman helped when she realized what they were doing.

Everything but the barbeque landed at Mike's. "Why am I not keeping this barbeque? It's Mom's, and she's staying with me."

"Because unlike you, Andre will actually use it and what's more, clean it properly. If you take it, you'll leave it open to the elements and the grills will get rusty. If we have a barbeque, you can come over."

"Sounds fair."

They were so weary, they just plunked the furniture in Mike's living room and left it there. He'd have to deal with it later. Julia knew if she went over three days from now, it would still be there.

It was after six when Julia and Andre got home. They flopped on the couch. Something smelled good.

"Mom? Is that a roast chicken in the oven?"

"Yes!" she hollered from above.

Posy yelled too. "Don't come up here!"

"Don't come up here!" Hazel echoed.

"Oh no," Julia muttered. "What's she done now?"

Andre leaned his head back on the sofa. "Probably stuffed their faces with ice cream. You know, she bought salted caramel the other day and said it was just for her, but Hazel spilled the beans."

"Well, who cares? A grandmother is allowed to give her grandchild a treat now and again. My grandfather used to take me to the store and let me buy a huge bag of penny candy. We always ate it on the way home so Mom wouldn't know. It's one of my happiest memories."

"At this point, I don't care if they drink Kool-Aid."

"Ahh...remember Kool-Aid? That was pretty great too."

A notification dinged on Andre's phone, so while he checked it out, Julia headed upstairs. The girls weren't in their rooms. Her mom's door was partially open, so she went in. Posy and Hazel stood there wearing foundation, lots of eyeliner, penciled-in eyebrows, blush, and lipstick. Posy had shimmery purple eyeshadow and Hazel had daintily applied fake freckles. They looked at least twenty-five from the neck up. "Oh my god, Mom! What have you done?"

"They wanted to be Elsa and Anna."

Julia looked at her daughters' beautiful faces. "They look like Honey Boo Boo! Girls, come with me this instant."

As she marched them out of the room and into the bathroom, both of them started to cry. Margo hurried after them. "Julia! Stop scaring them. You're making them feel like it's their fault. It's okay, sweethearts. You didn't do anything wrong. Gogo made a mistake. I'm very sorry." She looked at Julia. "How could you? I was going to take it off. They wanted to pretend they were in *Frozen*, that's all. It was innocent and harmless, and now it will be a bad memory because you're always right and the rest of us are always wrong. Go make your own supper."

Julia was overtired. As she held a face cloth under the tap she snapped, "This is the thanks I get? We slaved away all weekend for you. Next time, move yourself."

"I didn't even want that damn barbeque! It reminds me of my own stupidity, okay? But you got greedy and made me take it."

Now all four of them were crying. Andre came running up the stairs. "What's going on?"

"Nothing!" Margo left the scene of the crime and disappeared behind the toy room door.

Andre looked into the bathroom and did his best to hide his dismay. No need to pour more gasoline on the fire.

"Oh wow, you girls look like Elsa and Anna. That was fun, but we'll take that off before supper, okay? Would you like to help Daddy peel carrots?"

They both nodded. Julia threw the face cloth in the sink. "Okay, Mr. Perfect. You handle it." She stalked off to their room.

Andre smiled at his daughters and wrung out the facecloth before applying it to Posy's face. "Mommy and Gogo are a little annoyed at each other. Does that sometimes happen with you girls?"

They nodded again.

"We're allowed to be grumpy sometimes. It's called being human."

ᗧᨀᗡ

Monty and Byron were at the house when Velma and Carole showed up in a borrowed truck the next Saturday.

"Where's the man-eater?" Carole wanted to know.

Monty spoke to her while still seated in his Lexus. "If you're referring to Dick's widow, she is feeling poorly. She asked us to open the house for you. We'll wait here."

"We could use some help."

"You should have thought of that."

They struggled out with the television and the recliner. It was a good thing Velma was burly like her dad. While they gave the two men the stinkeye every time they emerged from the house, Monty and Byron drank their Starbucks lattes and listened to classical music.

And then Carole came hobbling out of the back door and rapped at their closed car window with her cane. Monty took his time lowering it. "Yes?"

"Where's the barbeque? Velma said he has one, not to mention the lawn mower. Margo said we could have everything else because it wasn't coming with her."

"She tells me she said, and I quote, 'And anything else in here. It's not coming with me.' She was referring to the den. But she'd like you to know that you are more than welcome to cart away everything that's left inside the house today. Which is extremely generous, don't you think? She didn't have to."

"You son of a bitch."

"You're losing daylight arguing with me. We won't be back with the key, so you'd better step lively."

Chapter Eleven

Things were frosty between Margo and Julia after the makeup incident. They were perfectly civil to each other and carried on as normal, but there was an underlying tension that had nothing to do with makeup.

Margo was now packing up yet again to make the move to Mike's. She'd taken a few trips over already and was completely depressed that Mike still hadn't gotten around to doing anything about the furniture other than push it to one side. He said he'd wait for her to tell him where things went.

She thought it was obvious that a bed should be in a bedroom.

Margo was a vagabond with no one to talk to. Everyone was so busy with their own routines while she wandered around like a pinball, knocking into things. Anytime she asked Julia about what she should do about something, her daughter would smile tightly and say, "I'm not sure, Mom. What do you think?"

The day she had the last of her things packed, there was no one home. Andre had to go into the office, Julia was planning world domination at her place of business, Posy was having fun at school, and Hazel and her cronies were going on a bus ride to the local library. She knew Mike would be at his computer and wouldn't come up for air all day and Olenka was probably cavorting with silverfish.

Margo got in her car and went to Mike's. She pulled up in the driveway but didn't turn off the engine. If he looked out the window, she'd go in. But he didn't, so she backed up and drove out of the city.

She wanted to go home.

It was early October. If she'd waited another couple of weeks the trees would have been glorious along the wooded route, but they were muted at this stage. Not enough cold nights. Still, it was always refreshing to get out and see how big and beautiful this province was. So many waterways and curved, meandering roads cutting through the plush green trees, thick like a velvet rug. Sometimes it felt like the whole place was a cozy hamlet that had shattered into tens of thousands of pieces and landed wherever the wind took it.

But it didn't exactly make up for her weary view of the world this morning.

When she pulled into the yard, she couldn't believe it. It looked like there was no one around. The donkeys weren't out, the car and truck were gone. She had a moment of panic. What if she couldn't get in? Did she even have a key anymore? Did they still keep it under the old flowerpot? What the hell was she doing? Should she drive back to Fredericton or wait? Then it occurred to her that no one knew where she was. She fumbled around in her purse and pulled out her cell. Dead. She'd forgotten to charge it.

Margo stared out over the paddock and watched the trees' branches by the fence sway in the wind. She had to face facts. She was a dreary specimen with no phone, no home, no husband, no job, and zero prospects. No wonder the kids were fed up with her. And now she was showing up to inflict herself on Eunie and Hazen and even they'd run away because somehow, they'd known she was coming.

That's when she glanced at the gas gauge. Almost empty. Naturally. She turned off the car to save what little fuel she had and got out, walked up to the back door, and tried it. It was locked. Yep. They had run away. The two of them had saddled up Fred and Ginger and ridden off into the sunset, never to be seen again.

The only glimmer of hope was that Stan was in his favourite spot on the windowsill. Eunie had told her he wouldn't go outside anymore. Whatever had happened to him in the big bad world, he did not want it repeated. This place was a refuge for felines and young women. And, she was hoping, old women, but not at the moment. She tapped on the glass. Stan glanced her way but he still wasn't speaking to her.

"Okay. I have no friends, either."

It was chilly. She had a jacket on but it wasn't a fleecy fall jacket, and she didn't have gloves. She was wearing sneakers, not her casual boots. She had only meant to drive ten minutes to Mike's. This was how people ended up dead on the side of the road, frozen to the steering wheel because they weren't prepared for a New Brunswick winter. The fact that it wasn't winter didn't enter Margo's fevered thoughts. She was determined to find disaster everywhere today.

She really had no idea what to do. Did she have enough gas to get back to Miramichi and fill up? Probably, but should she chance it? At least having the car in the yard would alert her relatives she was around. Since the car wasn't going to provide any warmth, she headed for the barn.

She had never been so glad to see two donkeys in her whole life. They were contentedly crunching away and only seemed mildly surprised to see her.

"Where's your dad? Do you know when he'll be back? At least he will be, he'd never leave you two alone for long. Do you mind if I wait with you?"

Fred nodded his head up and down. It seems he did mind, but too bad. Margo sat on some hay bales and ended up taking one of the donkeys' blankets and covering herself, despite the delightful aroma and donkey hair.

She remembered hiding in this barn as a kid whenever anyone was cross with her. They often were, or so it seemed at the time. Imagine. Fifty years later, here she was, back at it. It was absolutely pathetic. She could hear Monty's voice in her head. How many times had he told her to grow up? To behave like an adult instead of a timid child.

Julia really was so much like Monty, and Michael was her mini-me in some ways. She was irritated that he hadn't put her furniture away, but maybe his tendency to be laid back was really just indecision—and that was completely familiar. If it bothered her so much in him, why did she inflict her own indecision on her kids constantly?

There was only one solution.

But she wasn't sure what it was.

She dozed off and dreamt that Dick came through the doors looking for her. He was as she first knew him, and when he saw her, his desire was thick and overpowering. He reached down and grabbed her hand, pulling her over his shoulder to carry her like an animal carcass up the ladder to the hayloft, where he made wild love to her in the manner of every Harlequin Romance heroine who dallies in a barn. This was what she missed about him. The early Richard who had lusted after her, whereas Monty had only ever loved her. She shook with the memory of it, and opened her eyes to find Holly jiggling her shoulder. "What are you doing in here?'

Margo blinked and tried to compose herself before throwing the blanket aside. "I can't tell you."

Holly tossed her head towards the door. "Take the key. I have to put these critters out first."

"Thanks." Margo was a little stiff as she tried to get up in a dignified manner. Holly wasn't fooled. She held out her hand and Margo took it gratefully.

While Holly organized Fred and Ginger for their morning playtime in the sun, Margo unpacked the car. Eunie would let her stay. Hazen might grumble, but he even he wouldn't be mean enough to tell her to get lost. Hopefully.

She was just taking the last carry-all into the kitchen when Holly appeared behind her. "Would you like some tea?" she asked.

"Got anything stronger? A rum and coke and a cigarette?"

Holly gave her a considered look. "Want an edible?"

"Isn't that..."

"Yeah, a gummy bear with cannabis in it. I have a couple, ten milligrams, which aren't very strong, but I'd only give you half."

"I won't die, hopefully?"

"Not unless you choke."

Margo's eyes widened and Holly's hand flew to her mouth. "Oh fuck, sorry. I didn't mean it that way."

"I know. You go get my vitamin and I'll put the tea on."

They sat at the kitchen table, Margo waiting for some kind of feeling other than horny despair. "I don't think it's working."

Holly tsked. "It's only been five minutes. You're not going to be swinging from the rafters, anyway."

"Oh, that's okay. I just was. Had a hell of a time until you showed up."

"Maybe it *is* working," Holly said.

"I just might sleep in the barn tonight. Do you think Fred would mind?"

"Probably. He's becoming more and more like Hazen."

Margo took a sip of tea. "Any snacks around? I have the munchies."

Holly went to the pantry and came back with a tin full of chocolate chip cookies. She placed it in front of Margo and sat back down. "You don't have the munchies. It's noon."

Margo took a big bite of heaven. "Yum. Where are my brother and sister, anyway? For some reason I only ever imagine them here in the house or in the yard."

"Hazen had to go for his annual checkup, which he was freakin' crabby about, and Eunie went to town to help with the church bazaar. I said I'd come back on my lunch hour and put the donkeys out."

"You're a good kid, Holly. Mind if I call you Holly?"

"That's my name."

Margo ate more of her cookie. "Do you remember when we first met? You called my dead husband a fucking asshole."

"Did I? Sorry about that."

Margo wiped the crumbs from her mouth. "Oh, don't be. He was an asshole. And he was very good at fucking."

Holly gave her a worried glance. "Umm...are you sensitive to medication?"

"Am I? I'm not sure. Should I be? I never know."

Taking a cookie herself, Holly bit into it before remarking, "You sure aren't like your siblings."

Margo screwed up her face. "I'm not? How do you mean? Wait a minute. Do you give Eunie and Hazen edibles? I'm not sure that's wise. Hazen might become nice and no one would recognize him." And with that, she burst out laughing.

Holly cleared her throat and looked at Stan. "I think Margo's feeling better. What do you think, Stan?"

Stan turned to look at her. *Meow. Meow.*

Holly shook her head. "You know, this cat talks, but he's kind of full of himself."

Margo grinned. "What did he say?"

"He doesn't care that you're feeling better. He wants you to get him something to eat. Listen, Stan, it's not all about you."

Margo got a fit of the giggles. "This cat is a smooth operator."

At that moment, Hazen's truck pulled in the yard. Holly grabbed three more cookies and pushed away from the table. "Sorry, I've got to get back to work. Go have a nap. See ya later."

And she was gone before Margo had a chance to say goodbye. Out the window she saw Hazen point at her car and Holly jerk her thumb towards the house.

She decided two things in that instant: 1) Holly was her new best friend, and 2) she was going to buy a shitload of edibles.

Hazen arrived in the kitchen after greeting his donkeys but still looked crabby. "Look who the cat dragged in."

"Hear that, Stan? He's blaming you."

Stan ignored her.

Hazen sat at the table with a sigh, reached in the tin, and took a cookie. "Damn doctor wants me to lose ten pounds. Says my blood pressure is a little high. Of course it is! I've lived too long to have some kid with a stethoscope tell me what to do. You get to be my age, you can decide for yourself how you want to die. And I'll die happy eating Eunie's cookies."

"I can write your obituary. 'Hazen Wildsmith, a.k.a. Cookie Monster. Me want cookie! Om nom nom nom.'"

Hazen squinted his eyes. "You okay?"

"I think so."

Hazen kept munching. "Listen, gotta ask you something. As you know, this is your house too. Mom and Dad left it to all of us and at the moment you don't have one. Not that me and Eunie are planning on going anywhere in a hurry, and you are welcome to stay here as long as you need to, but when the time comes, would you give it to Holly, so she can stay here and look after Fred and Ginger, once she becomes a police officer?"

"This house? To Holly?"

"Yes."

"How long do donkeys live?"

"Up to forty years. Fred and Ginger are only two."

Margo smacked her hand on the plastic tablecloth. "You bought two donkeys that might still be around in 2060? Are you mad?!"

He shrugged and grabbed another cookie.

Margo was sure the edible was making her hallucinate. "How do you know that Holly will even stay here? She's only a young girl."

"If we give her the house, I'm assuming it'll be a no-brainer. She needs a place to live. Who turns their nose up at a free house? And the donkeys are here, so she has to be too. You worry too much."

"But the property, the fruit trees, Mom's gardens. How would she manage all that and a job too?"

Hazen leaned over and held her gaze. He looked just like their father. "I don't give a rat's ass what this place looks like after I die and neither should you. I keep it neat and tidy because I enjoy it. Holly is a responsible girl despite her abysmal upbringing. I have no doubt she'll maintain it as best she can, but after we're gone, she can do what she likes."

Margo felt her blip of relaxation start to fade. She tried to understand what her brother was saying. It came as a bit of a shock. Her mind did its usual whirligig when presented with an overwhelming amount of information and imminent decisions.

And then he cut through it all. "Margo, you are more than welcome to have this house. It's yours. But I'd like you to look after Fred and Ginger as a favour to me. The only reason we thought of Holly is that both Eunie and I assumed you'd want to be in Fredericton with your family. That's where your life is. We didn't want to burden you with having to maintain this place. I plan on selling the two hundred acres out back past the orchard because none of us need that headache, and we can divide the money three ways. A little extra income for all of us."

Margo's mind instantly stopped being a spinning top and her shoulders relaxed. Damn. Her next big adventure was to become a dope fiend.

"I agree, Hazen. Holly is more than welcome to have this house when the time comes. My kids won't want it, but they would love to be able to have the occasional picnic with Fred and Ginger. Have you told her yet?"

"No, no. We had to talk to you first, obviously." He nodded. "Thanks. You've made me a happy man, unlike that damn angel of death at the doctor's office."

Eunie was surprised and happy to see Margo's car in the yard when she arrived home from church. Hazen came out to greet her.

"Margo's here?"

"Yep. She rolled in around lunchtime. She's been snoring on my lounge chair ever since."

"She's had a hard time lately. All that moving and upset. Still, she's made progress. She drove herself here, which is more than she did a couple of months ago. I wonder if she's still at Julia's or at Michael's now, poor kid. What an awful thing, when you think about it. Can you imagine starting over? Leaving this place?"

He followed Eunie back up the steps. "Speaking of leaving this place..."

When Margo groggily opened her eyes after the best nap of her life, she looked across the room at the blurry figure in the rocking chair. "Mom?"

"It's me, dear. Eunie." She pulled more wool up from the skein in the bag at her feet.

"Oh. What are you knitting?"

"I'm knitting you a medal. Thank you for agreeing to our plan. Hazen is mostly delighted because he doesn't have to worry about his donkeys, and I'm delighted because I didn't want to leave Holly homeless."

Margo stretched her arms over her head. "I imagine I'll get an earful from Julia and Monty about how I'm leaving equity on the table. That if you two were hit by a bus, I could sell this place and the donkeys, say ta-ta to Holly, and go my merry way with money in the bank."

"And they'd be right."

"I'm sick of them always being right, and I don't care if this is the wrong decision. It feels like the best one for you three."

Eunie counted the stitches on her needle before looking up. "You're sure now?"

"Am I sure? No. Should I do this anyway? I think so, don't you?"

Eunie pursed her lips. "Say yes, Margo. Just say yes."

"Yes?"

By the time Holly got home from work, Eunie had made sweet-and-sour meatballs with rice for supper. The three of them sat and stared at her while she ate. Holly finally dropped her fork.

"Okay, you guys are freaking me out. Have I got something stuck in my teeth?"

Hazen told her their idea.

Her face went white. "No. No fucking way!"

Margo took that to mean she was overwhelmed by the generosity of the offer.

Turns out she wasn't. "I can't. I won't."

Hazen was now really crabby. "We're offering you a home so you can stay here to look after Fred and Ginger. You said you would. And now you don't want to?"

"Not if it means you giving me the house. I'll stay here, Hazen, but I don't want to own it. I'll keep paying rent, if you don't mind. I prefer it that way. If my family finds out that I own this place, they'll come in here and destroy everything. At least if Margo still owns it, as I'm assuming she'll be the last Wildsmith standing, they won't dare, because she could call the police. My kin are geniuses at manipulating social workers and the like. They'd insinuate that I invited them to stay here since we're family. I know them. So thank you, but let's just carry on as is. And by the time any of us have to worry about anything, I'll be a cop myself with a big piece on my right hip. Boy oh boy. I can't wait."

They nodded.

"Okay." Eunie looked around the table. "Who wants pie?"

"I'll have two pieces," Hazen said. "One for me and one for Dr. Kildare."

It had been a very eventful day, and Margo didn't even think about her family or the fact that she hadn't been in touch with them. She crawled into bed and forgot to charge her phone. Stan showed up and snuggled against her chest, his second favourite spot. She put her arm around him.

"Stan, I feel like we're having an illicit affair. You completely ignore me around other people all day and then jump into my bed at night. Is that all I am to you? A hot body?'

He closed his eyes.

"Okay then."

Chapter Twelve

Once the kids were in bed, Julia poured a glass of wine and put her feet up. Andre was just going out the door to help one of his brothers install a new water heater. "What time did Mom leave today for Mike's?"

"I wasn't here when she left, remember? I had to go into the office."

"Oh, right. I wonder how she's getting along? All must be good. Haven't heard a peep."

"Must be. Back soon."

"Right. Don't let him rope you into anything else."

Andre shut the front door and Julia took another big gulp from her glass. Maybe she'd have a bath...but she picked up her phone and started to scroll through Instagram instead.

She'd had a tiring day, non-stop clients, a board meeting and quick birthday celebration in the lunch room for an office clerk she didn't know well. She signed her name on the card and gave the mail guy twenty bucks to contribute to the gift certificate for Isaac's Way Restaurant.

The little bit of wine left in the bottle called to her, so she went back to the fridge and poured it into her glass. She stood at the sliding doors and surveyed the back deck. Time to start putting away the outdoor furniture. Why did everything she look at translate into a chore that had to be done? She realized she was sighing, because it was so quiet. Normally she loved this time of day, but it felt a bit lonely, what with Andre not around, nor her mother.

She'd wished she and her mom had cleared the air before she left, but they'd both avoided it. Julia knew she'd overreacted to the makeup episode, but everything had built up and exploded after a very tiring weekend. Once more her valuable free time had been taken over by her mother's wants and needs. And that behaviour never seemed to stop. Andre had been annoyed with her that night when they went to bed, telling her she had no business arguing with her mother in front of the girls. She turned away from him to get him to stop talking.

He laughed. "You do realize, when you do that, it's because you know I'm right. You give yourself away every time."

She turned around and stuck her tongue out at him.

Well, since Mike hadn't bothered to let her know how things had gone, she gave her mother a call. She couldn't get through. No doubt she'd let her cell die yet again. How hard was it to keep a phone charged? This was just the kind of thing that drove her bananas.

She was too tired to text. She called Mike instead.

"What's up?" he answered.

She plunked down on the sofa again. "Oh, I don't know. You tell me. How did your day go?"

"Fine. A couple of pull requests on GitHub."

"Huh?"

"Proposals to merge changes essential for facilitating code reviews."

"Spare me your programmer lingo. You know what I mean. Did Olenka come over to help you? Did you guys manage to get some stuff straightened out?"

"What stuff?"

"It's been a long day; I'm not playing this game. Mom's stuff, obviously."

"I keep telling you. I'm going to do that when she gets here. Stop being so anal. It'll get done."

He sounded annoyed and that made her cross. "If you're not going to tell me, then put Mom on the phone."

"What are you talking about? She's not here."

"Oh, she ran out for a jog, did she? Hand her the phone right now. I'm in no mood."

"Call me back on a video chat so you can read my lips. Mom is not here. She never was here today. Isn't she still with you?"

Julia sat up straight. "NO! I thought she was with you. Wasn't she moving in today?"

"I don't think so. Did anyone tell me? Was I supposed to be on the lookout for her?"

Now she stood up. "Do you mean to tell me we've lost Mom? Where can she be?"

"I have no idea. Dad's? Eunie's?"

"She wouldn't drive all the way to Eunie's by herself." Julia started to pace.

"Why not? It's not on the other side of the globe. She's an adult and she can drive."

Julia started to bite her thumbnail. "But she didn't tell us she was going and her phone is dead. What if she's in a ditch?"

Mike sounded fed up with her, and Julia always hated that. He was the calm one. She didn't want him to be out of sorts.

"You're in a panic because of the way you've treated her. She told Olenka all about you freaking out over her putting makeup on the girls when all they wanted to do was play dress-up."

Julia was shocked. "She told Olenka?"

"Believe it or not, she loves talking to Olenka. She actually enjoys being with us. She says it's relaxing after spending time with you and your high standards."

"You're so mean!"

"Fine. You call Dad and I'll call Eunie." And Mike hung up.

Julia couldn't believe it. Mom talked to Olenka about her behind her back? Were mothers allowed to do that with their daughters-in-law? That's what Olenka was, even if she didn't live full-time with Mike. Wouldn't a mother be loyal to her own flesh and blood?

She realized this bombshell was making her jealous. Mom belonged to her. And suddenly she missed her very much, and poor Mom was probably in a bog somewhere, crying out for her. Or maybe for Olenka. What a slap in the face.

She called her father and he picked up after four rings. "Hi kitten, we're in the middle of a cutthroat game of crib. Can I call you back?"

"Is Mom with you?"

"No. Did she say she would be? Byron, was Margo coming over and you didn't tell me? No, Byron says he hasn't heard from her. Why? Is she missing?"

"She left the house this morning and hasn't been seen since."

"WHAT? Call the police!"

"What happened to the steel in your veins? Stop hyperventilating. Mike's calling Aunt Eunie now."

"I assumed you already had. Gather your information first before you blurt out 'hasn't been seen since.' That makes it sound like she's been missing for weeks. Why did she leave without telling you?"

"I have no idea."

There was a long pause. "Oh, the makeup incident."

"Oh, for frig's sake! Did she tell you about that too?!" Julia was now striding around her kitchen island with a paring knife in her hand. Where did that come from?

"Your mother and I talk regularly. What? You know that, Byron, so stop being so insecure. And excuse me, those are my pegs."

"Dad, are you talking to me or Byron? You have a horrible habit of maintaining conversations with everyone around you when you're on the phone."

"Well, I'll hang up. Call me when you find your mother. And you'd better hope you do, young lady."

Julia stabbed the paring knife into the wooden cutting board by the sink. Two minutes ago, she'd been enjoying a glass of wine, and now her father was blaming her for her mother's disappearance. She dialled Aunt Eunie's number, but the line was busy. Mike better call her back. She went looking for more wine.

❧

Aunt Eunie laughed. "That's okay, Michael, dear. No worries. I'd only just gone to bed. We had an exciting day here today, so we tucked up early. I was so happy to see your mother. She's dead to the world right now, with that traitor Stan snoring beside her. I don't want to wake her. I'll get her to call you in the morning. What's that? Oh, I'll tell her to charge her cellphone. Yes, I will. I might just do it myself to make sure. She's a bit of a scatterbrain, but no wonder, the poor girl. She's had quite a time of it. I never liked that Dick character. Always reminded me of Telly Savalas without the lollipop. Okay, dear. You call Julia and let her know your mom is safe and sound. Nighty-night."

Mike called his sister. He didn't get a chance to say anything before she yelled "Well?" in his ear.

"She's asleep at Aunt Eunie's. They had a nice day."

"Oh, fine for her! All of us worried sick."

Mike looked at his cell and put it back to his ear. "Jules, are you losing the plot? You only found out Mom was missing five minutes ago."

She collapsed on one of the kitchen island stools. "I think I am. What is wrong with me?"

"Perimenopause?"

Now she sat up again. "I'm only forty, Michael. And why would you even bring that up?"

"Something Olenka said the other day when we were talking about your makeup meltdown."

Julia was starting to hate Olenka. "Is that so?"

"Yeah, she said you might have depression or anxiety or mood swings. Do you have hair loss or brittle nails?"

"Do you hear yourself?"

"Ya know, Olenka told me that only three known species go through menopause: killer whales, short-finned pilot whales, and humans."

"I wasn't aware that whales had hair or nails, brittle or otherwise. I'm going to bed, Michael."

"Oh, that's another symptom. Insomnia."

She hung up on him.

⟨⟨⟩⟩

Margo slept in until ten. She loved being in this bed, and one of the reasons was that Eunie still used thick white cotton sheets. It was like being at the Savoy hotel in London. Not that Margo had ever been there, but she imagined luxury hotels had sheets like these.

And Eunie continued to iron them faithfully with their mom's iron, a weighty workhorse from the sixties. All of them thought it was bewitched, and Eunie often said that when the iron died, that would be her cue to leave this world. She wanted it buried with her.

The sisters decided to take their second cups of coffee into the den. Holly was at work and Hazen was outside mowing with his ride-on to mulch the fallen leaves into the grass, or as Eunie put it, play with his dinky.

Eunie held up her mug and blew on the coffee it before taking a sip. "It's so good to see you, dear. But why are you here?"

Now Eunie became privy to the makeup disaster moment and the fact that Margo's belongings were shoved into a corner at Mike's. "I feel unwanted. And I know if Holly was here, she'd tell me to eff off, but I need to acknowledge my feelings. I've spent my whole life running away from them."

Eunie nodded. "I think most women of our generation do. That's how we were brought up."

"You don't."

Eunie put her mug down on the armchair. "I want you to listen to me, missy. When my Ian died on that damned motorcycle, what did I do with my life? Nothing. I hid behind Mom's apron. I took the easy way out and I only forgave myself for that when I turned sixty and realized I couldn't spend my entire life beating myself up."

Margo was taken aback. "I had no idea."

"I've always been jealous of the fact that you got married, had babies who grew up to be decent, hardworking people, kept a lovely home, and worked full-time while looking like a million bucks. Does that sound like a hopeless case to you?"

"I guess maybe not?"

125

"Say no, Margo. Just say no."

⌒⌒⌒

Margo's phone was now charged, but she forgot to turn on the volume, so she missed Julia's twenty phone calls, one from Mike, one from Monty, one about bank fraud from Visa, a threatening call from the Canada Revenue Agency, a lottery scam, and a fake charity appeal.

She called Julia first, but had to leave a message. "Hi, dear. I'm fine. I didn't mean to give you a fright—"

She heard a phone call trying to come through and pressed a button and swiped but ended up disconnecting. She remembered how in love she'd been with her princess phone. Too bad they didn't still make them.

The cell rang again. It was Julia. "Sorry...I had to run out of a meeting. Are you okay?"

"Yes, honey. I'm fine. I'm sorry I didn't let you know where I was. I didn't even known where I was going until I got here, and then they weren't home at first and my phone was dead and I forgot to let you know."

"When are you coming back? The girls miss you."

"I only left yesterday, Julia. I'm going to stay for a while and help Eunie with her relish, pickles, and chow. They've still got produce from the garden in the cold cellar and I remember doing it with Mom. Holly wants to learn too. She's a lovely girl. I think I need to decompress. Spend more time lying on ironed sheets, holding Stan the man, and rocking by the wood stove. It's been a rough go."

Julia sounded choked up. "I apologize, Mom. About make-up-gate, and always being so snarky with you. I've been a beast. Mike thinks it's perimenopause."

"Mike? What does he know about it?"

"Olenka told him. Does that girl have an opinion on everything? She's a walking Wikipedia page. Oh blast, I've got to go. My boss just stuck her head out the door and is waving me back in. That woman can't do a thing without me. She's so annoying."

"Sweetheart, why don't you schedule an appointment with the Well Women's Clinic? Mike might be right."

She'd already hung up.

Margo made herself comfortable on the bed and called Mike.

"What's up, mother dear?"

"Hi, honey. How are you?"

"I'm fine, now that we've peeled Julia off the ceiling. Don't ever run away from home again without telling us first."

"Okay. I'm going to stay with Eunie for a bit."

"Cool."

"Maybe you'll have time to sort out my furniture."

"Mom, I'm not touching it until you get here. I'm not rifling through your underwear drawers."

"My delicates are neatly locked in a carry-all. The drawers are empty. At least put my bed, bedtables, bureau, and tallboy dresser in whatever room you're sticking me in. Right now, it looks like I'm sleeping by your computer, and that's not exactly welcoming."

"Okay, okay."

"And Mike?"

"Yep?"

"Could we get a cat?"

Chapter Thirteen

Olenka was trying to concentrate on a report about the infestation of the Japanese beetle in the Maritime provinces and their movement from these areas to Quebec and Ontario and what was required to prevent further spread.

But her mother, Gerda, had the stereo on full blast.

Olenka opened the door to her bedroom, which over the years had turned into a lab. Her mom refused to go in it anymore. Always afraid of what she might find after the incident with the pregnant wolf spider.

"MOM!"

Olenka lost her dad to leukemia when she was thirteen. She was an only child and felt it was her duty to stay by her mother's side. Gerda was an elementary school teacher and they lived in a shabby but comfortable upstairs apartment in an old house in Hanwell, which is why Mike bought the townhouse five minutes away. The outside of the house was old aluminum siding the colour of faded mushy peas, but that didn't faze them. The neighbours were familiar and friendly, and Olenka and Gerda never bothered the landlord because they weren't annoyed by drips, torn window screens, and stained linoleum. He loved them in return.

"Mrs. Ivanova, don't you ever leave me," he said the one time he had to come because their front door lock finally rusted out and even they couldn't ignore that.

All summer her mother had been "stepping out," as she called it, with a gentleman, also Lithuanian, who her cousin had set her up with. He seemed nice, but Olenka didn't pay much attention. There had been too much going on this summer with work and Michael's family drama.

"MOM!"

The woman was going deaf. No wonder, with that awful swing music she insisted on playing. She and this guy were taking a dance class. Olenka was glad her mom had recreational activities, but then she had always had lots of friends, unlike Olenka.

Olenka stopped yelling and went into the living room. Her mom was dancing with a broom. "Hello? I am trying to work. Could you lower the volume?"

Her mother was the epitome of pleasingly plump. She was a pretty woman with a round face and red cheeks. Always pleasant. It was a wonder she hadn't been snatched up by someone years ago, but until this character showed up, she wasn't interested.

"Sorry." She went over to the hi-fi, as she still called it, and took the arm off the record. "I think I'm getting the hang of it now."

"I sure hope so. If this continues, I'm going to live with Michael full-time."

Her mom looked at her. "I wish you would."

Olenka turned to go. "You don't mean that."

"I do, Olenka."

She turned around and for some reason was instantly furious. "You're kicking me out?"

"Of course not, you foolish child, except you're not a child. But you and Michael act like you are."

Olenka put her hands together. "What does that even mean? What Michael and I do is no one's business."

Her mom leaned the broom against the dining room table. "You've made it my business. You've got one foot there but insist on keeping one foot here, and it's becoming an inconvenience."

"I'm an *inconvenience*?"

"It's inconvenient to try and have sex at my age in the back of a car. My knees can't take it."

Olenka could not believe those words had come out of her mother's mouth. "What?"

"You of all people must know about copulation. Every species on the planet does it, and I'd like to do it the old-fashioned way. In my own bed."

Beads of sweat began to accumulate on Olenka's upper lip. "Not that I want to discuss this any further, but why can't you go to his place?"

"He lives in his sister's basement."

"Why?"

"He had some financial setbacks."

Olenka thought she might pass out. She dropped into the sofa behind her. "Why are you hanging around with a grown man who doesn't have his own home and has admitted to money issues? Who obviously wants to get his two big dancing feet under your table? I don't want you taken advantage of, and I certainly don't want you to hand over your money to keep the wolf from his door. *He's* the wolf. He'll huff and he'll puff and he'll blow your house down with you in it."

Her mother got that look on her face that meant there would be no talking to her. She seemed to get it quite often, now that Olenka thought about it. Maybe her mother really was fed up. This scenario had never occurred to Olenka. A mother takes care of her offspring. Granted, there's usually a timeline, but female orcas stay with their mothers for the rest of their life. That's why she had an orca tattoo. Orca, Olenka. Not that she'd ever told anyone that. Not even Michael.

"I would appreciate you giving me the courtesy to make up my own mind about the people in my life. You know nothing about his situation and I do." Gerda went over to the living room window and looked out through the curtains. "I am fifty-eight years old. Until recently I'd been with one man my whole life, and that was your father. The ugly incident in the silo with the farmhand doesn't count. I've been without my husband for twenty years, just as long as you've known Michael." Her mom turned around and stepped closer to her. "Did you hear that, Olenka? You've been with Michael for twenty years and you're still technically *dating*. When I tell people that they're incredulous, and so am I, because I know you love him very much and he adores you."

"We haven't been dating the whole time. We've taken breaks."

"Yeah, once for as long as four months, but you never went anywhere. You weren't with anyone else."

Olenka got off the couch. "You have no idea what you're talking about. I've been with other men."

"A quickie in a bathroom at a bar doesn't count."

She was horrified. "I have never been with a guy in a bathroom. Have you? You're watching too much television."

"Okay, this is getting us nowhere. I'm obviously not going to kick you out and I'm not moving anyone in, despite what you think. I'd just like to have an adult relationship in my life in my own home. I've earned it." Gerda stopped to wipe off dust on the bookcase with her end of her sleeve. "I've had lots of men over the years who've wanted to be with me, but I always put them off because you were here studying and then working." She sighed. "You're my beloved daughter. But I don't want to be your roommate any more. Please think about what you want from your life.

You've always said you do exactly what you want, but do you?"

Olenka folded her arms across her chest. "What's that supposed to mean?"

"You have a comfortable nest here and you're sticking to it like glue. It sounds hokey, but you need to spread your wings and fly away to your own nest. Hopefully with Michael. But if you like your arrangement, get your own apartment and still spend half your time with him. Nothing has to change except that we'll each have breathing room. I'm getting too old for this and so are you. And in case you don't remember, I love you very much."

Gerda took the broom and went to the kitchen. Olenka was going to call out to her, but she heard her go down the stairs and out the door. With her slippers on.

Back in her bedroom with the door shut, Olenka sat at her desk. She didn't give a damn about Japanese beetles. Your mom is your mom is your mom, until suddenly she's not. She's a woman with a life of her own. How did that happen? It was uncomfortable and a bit frightening. Her mother had always been her property, no one else's. God. That sounded like she was keeping her mom a prisoner. And she was, according to her mom.

For so long Olenka had been all her mother needed and that was her role. Now it seemed her mom was growing up. She hit the open book with her hand. "Whoa. Whoa. You are *not* her mother and she is *not* your kid."

How did she get so amazingly stupid?

Her mom was pipping. A chick breaking out of the shell. Or was it Olenka? She was so confused and continued to worry about the dancing wolf. She needed to talk to Michael. She sent him a text.

I'm coming over

Yep

Her mother was still wandering around in her slippers

somewhere when Olenka got in the car. She could drive this route in her sleep, and a few times she had almost nodded off leaving Michael's late at night to get home. Why? Why the need to get back? She wasn't a pack animal. A meerkat who needed to sleep in a heap over the group matriarch, who snored soundly while buried underneath her family.

She thought back to a conversation she'd once had with Julia, who said she admired Olenka for being so unconventional. Maybe Olenka was just pathetic, never striking out on her own. She lived in her mommy's house and then tripped over to Michael's when she wanted sex. That's basically what it came down to. She didn't have any responsibilities. It gave her more time to concentrate on her research.

She really *was* pathetic. If her mom and Michael dropped off the face of the earth she'd be as helpless as an altricial marsupial. By the time she got to the townhouse she was so uncomfortable in her own skin, she was hot and itchy, scratching as she walked in the door.

She threw her bag where she always did, at the top of the stairs. Mike wasn't at his desk, which was odd. His mother's stuff was still taking up all the space in the living room.

"Where are you?" she hollered.

"In the kitchen."

She walked in and saw a stranger by the stove. She screeched.

Mike turned around in alarm. "What's wrong?"

"You don't look like you. What are you wearing?"

Mike grinned and held out his arms to show off his relaxed linen short-sleeve shirt and khaki shorts. "You like? Am I eye candy? Byron was throwing them out."

"How could you?!" she screeched again. Then burst into tears, ran to the bathroom, and locked herself in.

What was wrong with her? When she'd woken up this morning all she was interested in was the Japanese beetle, and now she was having a complete breakdown about her entire life in a bathroom that had way too much hair in the sink.

There was a knock at the door. "Are you okay? What's wrong?"

"That's what I'd like to know! And I came over here to talk to Michael, only to find some casual junior-executive type making scrambled eggs in Mike's kitchen. What have you done with him? I can't take much more."

"Fine. I'll go change. Will you come out then?"

"No."

"I'll be here when you get bored."

She ended up having a bath, but had to clean the tub first. She cried again when she realized she hadn't cleaned a bathtub in years. Her long-held belief that she was an independent, cool person was dissolving much like the Comet going down the drain. Her mother had always taken care of the housework because she enjoyed it and would push Olenka out of the way when she didn't do it to her satisfaction. Mike was a grown man who could do his dishes or not. His choice. She suddenly realized that she did spend a lot of time here, but she never offered to help him with the dishes or clean his sink. So, that started the waterworks again. What did he see in her? She was useless. A big tapeworm who lived off its hosts and contributed nothing.

Eventually hunger drove her out of her hiding place. Mike was at his desk, still in his very nice shirt and khaki shorts. He didn't turn around. "I've only got eggs in the fridge, and there's bread for toast."

She didn't answer him, but threw herself into the recliner, which had been pushed to the side to accommodate his mother's stuff. She put an elbow on the armrest, and held up her throbbing head with the palm of her hand. He turned slowly in his computer chair and looked at her with his fingers interlocked across his stomach. He tapped his thumbs together.

"Bad day?"

"Why do you like me, Michael?"

He put his head back and pondered. "You're extremely clever. And fragrant. You seem to really like me and you laugh at my jokes."

"Is that it?"

"I can be myself with you. I automatically relax when you come into the room."

She sat up a little straighter and started to rock the chair. "Did you know animals like snow leopards, jaguars, and bears have all been filmed chasing off their offspring once parental dependence is no longer necessary? That's what happened today. Mom wants me to move out."

Nothing ever fazed him. He didn't even blink. "Okay. Move in here."

"I can't."

Now he blinked. "Why not?"

"I need to establish my own territory."

He pointed upstairs. "Fine. You can sleep in the other bedroom. I'll put masking tape on the hardwood to divide this space. You can have window side, because I know you like watching birds, and I'll take this side, because this desk is too heavy to move."

She got off the chair and gestured at the pile. "Have you forgotten your mother is moving in?"

His thumb tapping became quicker. "Not forever. Just until she lands on her feet. Then she and this pile of stuff, which is really starting to piss me off, will be out of here."

"If you put it away, maybe it wouldn't bother you."

He got out of his chair and pointed at it too. "Great. Help me. We can get this done in say, twelve hours, max?"

"Get Andre to help you, or your dad. Males have only two jobs. Procreating and moving furniture. And while you're at it, get your own shit together. Stop sleeping on the floor and get a couch."

"Mom's stuff is here."

Now Olenka looked at the chaise and settee. "Are you honestly telling me we'll be eating pizza on that? And she will be leaving someday. This whole house is just one big dorm room."

Mike licked his lips. He wasn't producing any saliva for some reason. "Olenka, I'd really like you to move in. Maybe I want to be more than someone's boyfriend. Lately when I'm with Julia and Andre, I spend all my time trying not to be jealous of what they have together."

"You love your nieces. That's understandable, but I'm not interested in being a mother, so what difference does it make if I'm here or not? We have what they have, just not the kids."

"Wait...you don't want kids? For real?"

"I don't think so. Is that a problem?"

Mike frowned and wandered around with his hands in his pockets. "Why have we never had this conversation before?"

"It wasn't important."

He turned and faced her. "It is now. I've been thinking about a family more and more since our trip to Aunt Eunie's, and spending that day with the girls. I'm starting to realize how lonely I've been. Aren't you lonely?"

"I live with my mother most of the time, so no."

Mike went over to her; held her hand and he got down on one knee in Byron's khaki shorts.

She nearly died. This couldn't be happening. Not today.

"This is me being serious. Will you marry me? I want to spend the rest of my life with you, Olenka, kids or no kids. Say yes."

She wanted to hit him. "I just told you two minutes ago I need to establish my own territory. I need to stop living half my time with my mother and half my time with you. I don't want to be a parasite anymore."

He got off his knee really quick. "What the hell are you talking about? A parasite?"

She stomped her foot. "I'm not explaining it properly. I can't think. My whole life was put in a blender today. My insides feel like they're hanging out. Why did you have to ask me? We always said we'd never get married, that we didn't need a piece of paper, and now you're changing the rules. That's not fair."

Mike threw his hands in the air. "Okay, well, maybe you're not the only one who's having a crisis. Ever think of that?"

She slapped her arms against her hips. "How convenient that you decide to have a crisis too."

He nodded and then hung his head. "Fine. I'm taking my proposal off the table. Go home to Mommy. Oh sorry, she doesn't want you."

That was it. That was really it. Olenka picked up her bag and walloped him on the arm. "Don't you ever come near me again, you preppy douchebag!"

She slammed the door on her way out and slammed the car door when she got in. Then she slammed the car door when she got out, and her front door when she went in. The bedroom door slammed next, and then the bathroom door, when she ran in and threw up.

She sagged against the vanity, completely spent. Then threw up again.

Dear God. Olenka looked at the calendar on her Apple watch. She was late.

❧

After Olenka stormed away Mike collapsed into his computer chair, but only after he tore off Byron's khaki shorts and shirt and threw them in a corner. They were obviously jinxed.

He felt hollow, like he wasn't home. A shell of his former self. One of those shells you find on the ocean floor and turn over hoping to find a hermit crab inside, or even a soft snail that quickly shuts its front door to keep vagrants out, but instead you get a hole. What happened? Did he just propose and did she just tell him to get lost?

WTF.

A week later, Mike was still tied up in knots. He knew what he had to do, but knowing and doing were two completely separate continents divided by the Pacific Ocean.

He ended up making a list.

Buy shit. A new couch and bed.

Buy stain remover.

A text came through from his sister.

Spaghetti & meatballs?

I'm there

While he and Hazel had a spaghetti-twirling contest, much to Julia's distress, since they got most of the sauce on their shirts and chins, he had a thought. "What kind of mattress do you guys have? Something that came in a box in the mail, or a real mattress that comes from a mattress store?"

Andre mopped up his tofu sauce with a piece of whole-grain baguette. "A Tempur-Pedic Tempur-Cloud. Came in a box. Two thousand dollars. Developed by NASA to absorb the g-force of astronauts in space."

Mike stopped twirling. "You've got to be joking."

Andre shook his head. "You spend a third of your life in bed. Why not be comfortable?"

Julia agreed. "Think of it this way. It's cheaper than eating a Double Teen Combo at A&W every day for five months."

"You guys are nuts."

"Don't say nuts, Booboo," Posy said.

"Sorry."

"Where's Lenka?" Hazel asked. "I miss her. Is she dead like Icky?"

They reassured her that she wasn't dead. And then Hazel piped up, "I wish I was dead."

They didn't do a very good job covering up their shock at this sudden statement. Julia gasped: "Hazel!" and Hazel started to cry. Then they scrambled to tell her that they weren't cross, it didn't mean anything, she did nothing wrong.

Mike helped Julia out with the dishes. "Where did that come from?" she whispered to him. "I hate it when she spouts things like that. It's creepy and upsetting."

"I bet you said it under your breath after watching *Frozen* for the twentieth time."

"You're probably right." She rinsed the spaghetti plates under the tap. "Why did you want to know about mattresses? Please God, tell me you're going to stop sleeping on the floor."

He leaned against the counter with a dishcloth in his hand. "Olenka said I should buy a bed. She told me the place looked like a dorm room."

"You've seen her?"

"No. That was the day she hit me."

Julia poked her soapy finger into his lousy T-shirt. "Think like an animal. Go after her. Even slugs have courtship rituals."

"Well, I refuse to be a giraffe. They drink the female's pee. God, the weird facts I know from hanging around with that girl."

"Michael," she said with that big sister tone of hers, "Olenka is not a girl. You are not a boy. You are a grown man. She is a woman who wants to be wooed. You have taken her for granted your entire life. Fix up your space and then invite her in. Why should she believe anything will change if you don't change anything? Buy a vacuum cleaner and mow your lawn. Dick's lawn mower is in your garage, don't forget."

Okay. This was a start.

Then he tried to find vacuum cleaners. It was hellish. The guy showed him too many options.

"We have Dysons, robots, HEPAs, handhelds, cordless, canisters, and bagless."

"Which is the best?"

"Any of them," he said without looking up from his phone.

Mike went back to the parking lot and texted Julia, who cursed back at him. Then told him two minutes later she'd ordered him a vacuum online. It would be at his door in two days.

What kind is it

It doesn't matter

He mowed the lawn and got Julia and the girls to go with him to pick out a bed and mattress. He wanted his niece's opinions on its jumping capabilities. The sales guy didn't look too impressed but Mike solved that by reluctantly handing him his Visa card. He hated using it. He was out of practice. No wonder Julia called him Scrooge.

Julia patted his shoulder. "Welcome to adulthood."

After that was done, Mike was still sitting around by himself. Now that he had improved a few things, he noticed the screen on his cellphone looked like cracked ice, so on his way to pick up his

A&W supper, he ducked into the mall to replace it. It occurred to him as he was getting out that the inside of this car looked like an active hostage situation, but Olenka didn't care about that. She transported livestock in hers.

The guy at the phone store performed the delicate operation and his cell looked brand new. He was pleased. On his way back to his messy car he went by a Hallmark store. Maybe that should be his next move. He asked the young clerk if she had anything for being a jackass.

She grinned. "We have a Love section, a Sorry section, which is the most popular, and the Thinking of You section. Sympathy might work too, or blank cards. Then you can write your own message."

Daunting.

Mike knew he wanted an animal card. That was a given, but he had to choose the right one. Not a lion, because that was too powerful, and not a donkey, because that would seem too sentimental. She did like octopuses, but the only card he could find had one tentacle hanging out of a pot of boiling water, which was super awful. There was a really cute one of a giraffe, but he couldn't get past the pee thing. She also liked three-toed sloths, but they weren't easy to find.

He settled on an orca. She had an orca tattoo; they must be important to her. The only trouble was, this cartoon was a mother and baby orca swimming side by side, and he worried she'd take that as some kind of subtle sign that he expected her to want to be a mom. But he'd run out of choices and bought it anyway.

He wanted to call Jules and ask what he should say, but he knew she'd tell him to smarten up. He'd never talk to his mom about it, that was too pathetic. His dad? Too embarrassing.

He texted Andre, who shot back an answer instantly.

Three little words. "I love you"

Chapter Fourteen

Olenka stayed away from her mother, and her mother thought she was being overly dramatic.

"I'm sorry I asked you to move out. Don't punish me. You're treating me like I'm your evil stepmother."

"I'm not mad, Mom. I'm really busy at work and I'm trying to find an apartment, but it's not easy. It's only been a couple of weeks. I will be out as soon as I find something."

Olenka had every intention of finding a place to live by herself, but she was so sick and tired. So tired and sick. And still in a state of shock. She spent her whole time reading about gestation periods. African bush elephants were pregnant for 655 days. Almost two years. Orcas for 532 days. She really wished she was a stripe-faced dunnart; 11 days and they were done.

The scientist in her knew that fewer than one in a hundred women who took the pill became pregnant in a year. Great news for ninety-nine of them. Why did she have to be the one?

She stayed away from people, because everyone she knew would be delighted with this news. And that was scary. Olenka was up and down like a yo-yo about it. No. She had a career, and she'd never looked after herself, which was mortifying, so how would she take care of an infant? She'd forget she had a kid and leave it in a car seat while she went to work.

Her hormones were doing a number on her. She barked at her boss at work, she cried at the ice cream store when they ran out of waffle cones, she went to see an apartment and told the guy she wouldn't let a pufferfish live there, let alone a real live person. For the first time in her life, she honked her car horn for a really long time at a poor old lady who looked frightened of her. And worse, she had no one to talk to. Her best friend was playing video games in his shitty chair.

She thought she'd blown her cover when she forgot to turn the water tap on in the sink as she puked in the toilet. Her mother knocked on the bathroom door. "Are you all right?"

"Yeah. I had a tuna sandwich at work. I think the mayo was off."

"Oh dear."

As her mother's footsteps faded, Olenka sat on the floor and cradled her belly, still flat as a board. "You poor kid. Stuck with me for your parental care, which is, I'll have you know, a form of altruism. It could require me making a sacrifice that puts my own survival at risk. And honestly, I have no idea if I'm capable of that."

Olenka went into the kitchen to eat another banana. She fantasized about bananas. There was a card on the table for her. It was in Mike's handwriting. Oh great. She didn't want to pick it up. This would make everything a thousand times more difficult. Who was he to get involved in this?

Oh yeah. The sperm donor.

She took two bananas and headed back to her bedroom, making herself comfortable on the bed. She couldn't remember the last time he'd mailed her a card. She opened it and clapped her hand over her mouth. An ink drawing of a mother and baby orca. Oh my god. How did he know she was pregnant? Or was this some sort of weird dig?

He had a little note at the bottom. *I tried to find a better card but this one screamed you. Just want you to know I'm here. I love you. M xo*

She stuffed her face with a banana and sobbed at the same time. It was extremely messy.

Okay, now she was officially nuts. All this sentimental hormonal slop heaving itself around her innards. How did pregnant women not just jump off the nearest cliff and be done with the whole experience? How did generations manage to keep being born, if this was the type of nonsense mothers had to go through? Was everyone like this or was it just her?

She knew what she had to do. Call Julia. She tried but it went to voicemail. She babbled something about lunch and hung up.

⁓

It was an ordinary evening. Just another hurricane blowing its way through the Maritimes, so naturally the power was out. Julia and Andre were kicking themselves for getting the girls a big trampoline for the backyard. Andre spent more evenings than not bolting it onto the lower deck so it wouldn't land in the neighbour's pool.

Julia was snuggled in, reading bedtime stories with a flashlight, and the girls were eating cut-up grapes out of a bowl with cocktail forks. They loved those silly little forks. Andre's mom had given her the idea. She had a lot of grandmother experience. Posy and Hazel were the youngest in the Paris family.

It's not easy to get kids to sleep when the power is out. They insist it's darker than dark, and spooky, and they're right, so Julia stayed with them until she was sure they'd drifted off. Then she stubbed her toe getting into her own bed. She made hissing noises and rolled around on the mattress before shining the flashlight on her big toe. "Wonderful. I just ruined my pedicure."

With the girls settled down for the night, Julia went to check her phone. Andre reminded her they were offline. She was about to put it down and noticed she had a voicemail. She thought it must be from Mom, but it turned out to be Olenka. "Holy shit, it's O!"

She listened and then erased the message. "She wants to have lunch with me, but she sounds like she's out to lunch already."

"Don't tell Mike. Don't get his hopes up. See what she wants first."

"Oh, brother."

"Yes. Your poor brother."

Andre and Monty (Byron had begged off with a sore back) heard all about the failed marriage proposal when they went to help Mike with Margo's furniture. It didn't really take that long at all since they weren't opening boxes, just putting them in designated rooms. They had her bedroom fixed up in no time and Monty knew exactly where to put the nice chairs and her wool rug.

Mike gave them a beer, and that's when he told them, because Andre mentioned that the girls wanted Booboo and Lenka to come over for supper and play tea party.

"And you haven't seen her in two weeks?" Monty said.

"Nope."

"Didn't you send her that card?" Andre asked.

"Yep."

Monty frowned. "Do you think it's because your mother will be here for a while? Maybe that spooked her."

Andre shook his head. "Stuff like that doesn't bother O. She knows Margo is in a bad way at the moment, and she'd want to help."

"I think Olenka was upset that her mother asked her to leave. She started talking about being a parasite and needing her own territory. How are you supposed to understand women?"

"Badly," said Monty.

∽

When Olenka mentioned lunch, Julia assumed they'd meet at a coffee shop. So why was she shivering on a park bench as red leaves fell around her in the wind? Squirrels went by gathering nuts for the winter. Damn. It was time for Halloween costumes. Julia hated that. Andre did a lot, more than a lot, but he refused to make a princess gown, so she was left to think up something, and she was lousy at that. Her mom could help but she still wasn't home. Maybe she was never coming back. Julia made sure she sent pictures of Posy and Hazel every day, as a reminder of what Margo was missing. But so far, her mother wasn't falling for it.

Olenka finally appeared in the distance, carrying a thermos and a small Styrofoam cooler. She'd no doubt had petri dishes in it earlier. Clearly there'd be no pumpkin-spice lattes today. As Olenka got closer, Julia became concerned. She looked dreadful, tired and pale. What the heck was wrong with those two? They were obviously meant for each other.

Olenka sat on the bench. "Thanks for meeting me. I brought lunch." She opened the cooler and took out a peanut butter sandwich. No jam, and not cut. "Or I have sardines."

Julia grabbed the sandwich. "Thanks. What's in the thermos?"

"Water."

Julia threw the sandwich back in the cooler. "Okay, what's wrong?"

"I'm doing a research paper about pregnant mammals and I need a first-hand account of how pregnancy messes up your life."

"You're pregnant?"

She didn't get an answer, not in so many words. The poor kid cried for ten minutes. Julia took Olenka in her arms and let her sob. A few people strolled by and looked concerned, but Julia gave them a thumbs up and they went on their way. Eventually the tap stopped running, and after a hunt for tissues in her pockets, which were all used thanks to Posy's latest cold, she found some in her purse that were wrinkled but dry. Once Olenka wiped up her face and sat up a little, Julia kept her arm around her.

"When are you due?"

"I don't know. Late April? May?"

"So you haven't been to a doctor?"

Olenka frowned. "I'm too busy throwing up to do anything."

"You need to see a doctor. I'll come with you."

Olenka shook her head. "I can't go. Then it will be real."

Julia squeezed her shoulder. "Oh, this is real, honey. And the baby doesn't care how you feel about it. They will keep on growing from a grape seed to a watermelon whether you like it or not. Unless you really don't want it. It's your choice of course. I'll stand behind you whatever you decide." Which was absolutely true, but Julia had to admit it would be nice to have a cousin from the Donovan side of the family.

"I was on the pill and this little kit still insists on being here. That's determination. But I'm so frightened it will ruin everything."

"What could a baby possibly ruin, except for your tits, your belly, your bum, and your precious sleep?"

For the first time Olenka cracked a smile, but ended up sighing and looking down at her cold hands. "I'm useless, Julia. I've come to that conclusion recently and it shocked me to my core. I want to stand on my own two feet, but the thought of even buying a crib seems beyond my capabilities. I have to find a place to live, and I've never lived alone before. I've leeched off my mother and Mike. It's time to stop depending on people."

Exasperated, Julia jumped up and started to pace in front of her. "Now let me get this straight. You say you've leeched off your mother and boyfriend and now, now that your child is coming into the world, is the time you want to bulldoze ahead without anyone's assistance? Do I have that right?"

"You've always been independent."

"I sucked my mom dry and then took an apartment with a girlfriend for two months before I met Andre and mooched off him for a couple of years until I made him marry me. And if you think I would have survived without the father of my children when I was pregnant and the girls were babies, you are sadly mistaken. The only reason those two girls are as sweet as they are is because their father has the patience of Job. And you know who else does?" Julia crossed her arms and tapped her foot to be more dramatic. "My brother, Mike. Who is the world's best Booboo and who will be the world's best daddy."

Olenka scrunched up her tissues and looked at the squirrel, who was now very annoyed that they were still hanging around. "I know he will, but he's not ready for fatherhood, any more than I'm ready to be a mom."

Julia wanted to jump out of her skin. "NO ONE is ready to be a parent! I don't care if you're fourteen or fifty. It's one of those situations where you learn as you go. You make a ton of mistakes and keep going because babies keep growing. No one knows what they're doing with the first kid. You can't quite believe they let you out of the hospital with this tiny, helpless creature. You can't adopt a pet these days without multiple interviews and references, and yet we can skip out to the car and drive away with a little human and it's bye bye."

"But my job?"

"I've always had a job. My kids aren't suffering. They loved daycare. So will yours. You don't have to stop being you. You'll have a ball teaching this child of yours about every animal under the sun."

"But..."

Julia sat down again. She knew she was running out of time on this lunch hour. Her boss always kept her eye on the clock. The woman needed a drink. Badly.

"Olenka, you of all people must know how important an animal pack is. You cannot survive in the world by yourself. You need your peeps. And don't worry about buying a crib. You'll have two grandmothers fighting each other off trying to buy it for you. And then they'll want to buy the car seat and stroller, and the dressing table, and a comfy chair, and before you know it, the nursery is done and you didn't lift a finger. And even if they don't, I have everything you need. I'm not using it anymore. And once we have a baby shower, you'll have enough clothes to see you through the first year. Toys? I haven't bought one yet."

Julia sat down next to her. "And then there's the wonderful aunt and uncle and cousins who will want to look after baby so you two kids can have a romantic dinner at A&W. My god, Dad and Byron will fight over the dumpling and your mother is going to lose her mind with happiness. This baby has everything it needs. It's time to invite Daddy to the party. I know for a fact that Michael Donovan loves you, and he's had a really hard time since you hit him with your purse after he asked you to marry him."

Olenka made a face. "I did? Oh yeah, I think I did."

"And yet despite that, he still wants to marry you."

"But how does he know about the baby?"

Julia looked confused. "If you haven't told him, he doesn't know."

Olenka reached into her pocket and took out the card and showed it to Julia. "A mama orca and her calf."

Julia was so damn happy for Mike at this moment, she had a hard time breathing. She pointed across the park. "Go. Now."

Olenka nodded and left in a hurry, without the sandwich, sardines, thermos, or cooler. Julia took the sandwich and broke off little pieces for the squirrel before she gathered up lunch.

She smiled. She was going to be an auntie.

☙

Mike was incredibly lonely. This must be how his mother felt. And it sucked.

He happened to be scrolling down the local buy-and-sell website and saw a notice from someone who needed a home for their cat, as they were going into assisted living. They wanted someone to love their cat. That was something his mother would say.

He called the woman and drove over to meet this character. He was a big tabby named Mr. Magoo. His poor owner was beside herself with the thought of him leaving and asked Mike for references. He said he didn't have any but he took out his driver's license and social insurance card before showing her a picture of him and Olenka and the girls on their picnic with the donkeys in the background. She decided he looked kind and said his wife and kids were lovely.

She gave him all of Mr. Magoo's belongings—he had a lot of them—and then she had a private goodbye with him in her bedroom and brought him out in his carrier, her face bright red with emotion.

"Please," Mike said, "if this is too painful..."

"No, it has to be done. Please take care of him. I shouldn't tell you this, but he can sometimes be a crank."

"Me too," Mike said.

Mr. Magoo howled all the way to the house. Maybe Mike had made a mistake.

He brought everything in and opened the carrier but Mr. Magoo didn't move. "It's okay, buddy. Take your time. I'll put your food down and kitty litter will be over in the corner for now."

He was so busy trying to get things organized he never noticed Olenka standing at the top of the stairs. He screeched when he saw her and so did the cat.

"You scared me! And Mr. Magoo."

"Excuse me?"

"He's going to be my mom's cat. He's not coming out of his carrier though."

Olenka bent down to peer inside. "He might not for a while. This is a huge shock. When you're kicked out of your house, it's an adjustment. Ask your mom. Or me."

They looked at each other. Mike put his hands in his pockets. "So, you okay?" he asked. "Did you get my card?"

"Yes. It was perfect."

He smiled. "Oh. Good."

"I'm sorry I hit you when you asked me to marry you."

"That's okay."

She looked around. "Those two chairs look good in here. And the rug."

He was about to agree with her when she blurted, "Do you still want a kid?"

"Why? Is there a sale somewhere? Look, I don't care about kids, Olenka. I just want you."

"Well, you're out of luck. I'm stuck with this one." She touched her stomach.

Mike got dizzy and his heart started to pound. It took him a minute to get his mouth to work before he croaked, "Marry me."

"That again? No, Michael, it's not necessary."

He put his hands on the back of his head and looked around trying to make sense of it all. "But you can't live alone in your own territory with a baby to look after, can you?"

"I thought I could until your sister freaked out at me. We're moving in, Daddy. Got any bananas?"

At that exact moment, Mike's mother came through the front door. "Hi honey, I'm home!"

Mr. Magoo let out an ungodly howl.

Chapter Fifteen

Olenka changed her address, despite her mother's pleas to move back home now that a baby was on the way. Gerda was very jealous that Margo was living with them.

She shouldn't have been. Margo wanted out. She knew this very early on, but her circumstances prevented her from doing anything about it. Obviously, she was more than delighted at the thought of another grandchild, and was also very happy that Olenka and Mike had settled their differences. Not that she'd known about them, since she'd been away making pickles, but Julia had filled her in.

But Mike and Olenka's lifestyle drove her up the wall. They never had a set time for meals, and mostly it was takeout. Granted, it wasn't always A&W. A lot of it looked delicious: sushi, Greek, Thai, Indian, Korean—but some of it was food she wasn't used to. Stuff that wasn't easy on her stomach at the end of the day. They'd agreed to share the grocery bill, but Margo was paying for things she'd take two bites out of. She couldn't afford to keep doing it. She was living off her savings as it was.

No wonder they had no furniture. They spent all their money on food. She asked if they could change the arrangement, which wasn't a problem (nothing ever was), and ended up cooking herself a small chop, or a piece of fish, with carrots and a baked potato every night. Boring but familiar.

The other problem was being stuck in her bedroom all day because she didn't want to disturb Mike while he was working. The living/dining room was his office, and the few times she tried to sit on her chaise, she couldn't relax because he was prattling away on headphones using an unrecognizable vocabulary. He didn't seem to mind her there. If anything, he ignored her, but the day she came downstairs in her nightgown and he waved her away because everyone on his Zoom call could see her was mortifying. She stayed in the kitchen until it was over, without her book or her phone. She just sat there.

Olenka took over the lower floor. Not that it was big, but by the time she got all her stuff in there—her lab, as she called it—every square inch was used, with the washer and dryer in the middle of it.

But truthfully it had been lonely over at Julia's too, with Andre shut away in his office and everyone gone for most of day. The one perk was that they ate regular meals at the table, and the girls were interested in being with Margo after supper. They played their favourite game on Posy's bed. Five Hundred Dollars and a Week. It involved all their stuffed animals ordering massive amounts of junk food from a restaurant, which struck Margo as funny, seeing as how their father was such a blowhard about nutrition. The restaurant guy would ask how much food they wanted. "Five hundred dollars and a week!" None of them could remember why a week was involved, but at least it was something to do. Over at Mike's the two of them played video games at night. Soldiers with guns sneaking up and killing other people or throwing bombs. She regretted giving Velma the television. She'd actually watch a hockey game at this point.

Even Mr. Magoo didn't like her. He'd finally come out of his carrier, but he crept around and kept out of everyone's way. Olenka said that was perfectly normal behaviour. He was trying to get used to the place.

Well, so was she.

Margo bought cleaning supplies just for something to do. When was the last time Mike had cleaned the floorboards? She even bought them a cool-looking hamper from Winners because she couldn't stand to see their clothes all over the floor. But the next day the clothes were thrown on the floor around it. She decided, for her mental health, to just close their bedroom door.

She kept forgetting this wasn't her house. She didn't have one. And despite the fact that the kids never made her feel like she was intruding, and said she could stay as long as she needed to, she *was* intruding. And when the baby came along, Margo knew that she wouldn't be able to keep her mouth shut and would blow up about their disorganization and lackadaisical attitude about everything.

She mentioned that to Julia when she was desperate enough to ask her if they could meet for lunch near her office. Julia made sure they were inside, in a booth, with pumpkin-spice lattes and two BLTs.

"Oh, so the great and wonderful Olenka isn't so fabulous after all." Julia smirked.

"What?"

"Mike told me that you liked being with them more than me and my high standards."

"Nonsense. And they could use a few high standards."

Julia took another bite of her sandwich and wiped a napkin down the side of her mouth. "Look, Mom, don't worry about it. Baby will whip them into shape in two seconds flat. They're going to have a schedule whether they like it or not. They will be making food, washing everything in sight, and not have a minute to play a video game. Leave the poor fools alone. Their time is running out and they don't even know it."

"I keep forgetting how smart you are, Julia."

"I know."

Margo picked up her sandwich but didn't eat it. "I don't suppose I could move back with you guys?"

Julia grimaced. "Are you serious? We just got you settled."

"I wouldn't bring the furniture."

Margo's daughter looked at her sadly. "Mom, after a week you'd be unhappy at our place again. At least at Mike's you're in your own bed. You feel rudderless at the moment. If you're that unhappy, you can always go back to Aunt Eunie's for a while."

"I can't. I have to look for a job, so I need to be here."

Julia nodded. "Okay, you get started on that, and once you have one, I'll help you find an apartment."

"They say rent is very expensive now." Margo ate a piece of tomato that was threatening to escape from her sandwich, and managed to drop tomato pulp on her scarf.

"It is! It's insane. And they'll probably want two months' rent up front."

Margo put down her messy sandwich and wiped her scarf with a napkin she dipped in her glass of ice water. "Wonderful. What if I can't find a job? What am I going to do? I feel hopeless."

Julia grabbed her mother's hand and shook it. "Don't you dare get depressed on top of everything else! Do you hear me?"

"Gee whiz, I'll try not to. Maybe I'll just drink. Oh wait, do you know where I can buy edibles?"

Julia's head went back. "Seriously?"

"Holly gave me one and it was great."

"She did? I'm not sure I like that. How does she know you don't have a heart condition or something? That was very irresponsible."

Margo tsked. "Listen to yourself. I'm not a kid."

Julia looked away and then took another huge bite of her sandwich, obviously to refrain from pointing out the obvious.

"Okay." Margo sighed. "I'm trying not to be a kid. And I realize I sound whiny. Why do you put up with me?"

"Beats me." But Julia smiled.

When Julia walked back to work, Margo strolled along the waterway and sat on a bench. It was one of those days in November when you couldn't believe it was November. She wasn't even wearing gloves and yet it was only a month until Christmas. Six months ago, she'd had a home and a life. Maybe not a completely happy one, but at least she'd kept herself busy in her own little space. Now she had no space. She could picture herself on one of those awful talk shows where relatives scream at each other. "My mother won't leave our house! She wants us to eat meatloaf and mashed potatoes at five o'clock! What kind of monster is she?"

At sixty-two and in pretty good health, knock on wood, Margo had at least twenty-five years of living left to do, according to Google statistics. She could hardly remember when Julia was fifteen and Michael was ten. How was she going to fill the years ahead? Make pickles and knit? That actually sounded like heaven, but only if she were in her own house.

Margo picked up her phone and invited herself over to Monty's for dinner. At least they knew how to make beef bourguignon. She counted on him not being quick enough to think of an excuse to get out of it. She didn't need to go, but she wasn't ready to go back to Mike's just yet and she had no money to go shopping.

Margo arrived early. She loved their house down by the river. There was always a sense of home for her when she visited, which was only natural since Monty's sensibilities had remained constant, so their style was familiar but much more sophisticated than when she and Monty lived together. They'd been raising kids, whereas he and Byron had the place to themselves, so it was usually spotless. Byron's art collection put it over the top.

This modern dwelling with its garden of rose bushes and mock orange shrubs reflected the men perfectly. Lucky bastards.

Dick's house had reflected nothing. It was depressing and had no personality whatsoever. Why didn't that bother her? Probably because she was too busy with him in the bedroom at first to even look around. When she finally did come up for air, her belongings smoothed out the rough edges for a while. It was only after Margo quit her job that the full force of the dissatisfaction hit her. But trying to get Dick interested in paint colour, wallpaper, and fabric swatches drained her to the point of not bothering. A man who had a shelf for ball caps didn't care about the finer things.

Byron's fish chowder was warm, yummy, just what she needed after that sloppy sandwich she'd left on her plate. They had the fireplace going in the kitchen and they sat at the marked-up pine table with their cups of tea and lemon cake.

"I feel ungrateful, Monty. The kids are so kind to me."

"I wouldn't want to be living with Mike either, and you and I love the guy."

"I wonder if he got any use out of the shirt and khaki shorts I gave him," Byron asked. "I was surprised when he took them. I'll give him more if he wants."

Margo cut her cake with her fork. "Oh! Were they yours? I found them thrown on the floor in the basement. I asked him if he wanted them and he made a sign of the cross, so I washed them and put them in a bag for Goodwill."

From the look on Byron's face, she realized she should have kept her mouth shut. "Sorry. I'm sure it wasn't personal."

Byron picked up his cup. "Well, he did call me a cocksucker to my face once, so there's that."

Michael's parents looked at each other.

"Well, he's not wrong," Monty said.

They had a good laugh. Margo was still smiling when she drove...to Mike's place.

When she got there, Mike's car was gone. There was a Post-it Note stuck to his computer screen. *Gone to the show.*

An evening without murder and mayhem. What a concept. Except once again Margo couldn't figure out the remote. She turned it on all right, but kept going around in screen circles. This was ridiculous and she was furious at herself. For the first time in her life, she wanted to read a book of instructions, but she couldn't find it—not that she looked that hard. God knows what she'd find in Mike's desk drawers.

She gave up and decided to have a bath, but she scrubbed the tub thoroughly first, then filled it with steaming hot water, added two Ouai Chill Pill bath bombs, and watched them boil away. She lowered herself in gingerly, adding a little cold water as she went. She wasn't a lobster, after all. At the thought of any creature, Olenka came to mind, but then she remembered the horrible diatribe about cruelty that she'd endured when she suggested a lobster boil the first week Michael brought her home.

She leaned back, comforted by the soothing feel of the slick and bubbly water, her arms floating back and forth to bring more bubbles up to her skin. Everything seemed to hurt now at the end of the day, but the heat helped her muscles relax, and the tension in her neck started to release. This was the life. Nothing felt better than—

Mr. Magoo leapt up on the edge of the tub out of nowhere. Margo was so startled she screamed, so the cat screamed back and fell into the water in his panic to get the hell away from her. They both flailed, the cat trying desperately to climb up the slippery sides while Margo tried not to drown. By the time this completely soaked cat found a paw hold on her thigh and literally flew out the door, Margo was gasping for air, scratch marks all over her body. And worse, her hair was wet. She stood up and gazed at the carnage below her head. She stomped out of the tub and wrapped herself up in a towel, dabbing at beads of blood.

She heard Mike and Olenka come in the front door and shout, "What's wrong with Magoo?

She stood at the top of the stairs. "Your goddamn cat tried to drown me. I'm gonna kill him."

"Whoa! Calm down."

"Don't you dare tell me to calm down, young man. I've been ripped to shreds."

"You decided to have a bath together? Way too soon, Mom. You hardly know each other."

"I forgot he was here! All he does is slink around in the dark. I thought I was alone in the house and suddenly I'm Janet Leigh in *Psycho*." She pulled at her towel to make sure she was covered. "Don't you dare laugh, Michael. Keep that beast away from me." Margo went into her bedroom and slammed the door. She cleaned up her scratches, thankfully superficial—except the one on her thigh. That hurt. She put ointment on it just in case. Wasn't cat scratch fever a thing? She caught a look at herself in the mirror. Her hair was a fright. She couldn't wait to get out of this house.

Olenka knocked on her closed door. "M, I don't want to scare you, but the cat might be in your room."

Margo yanked her door open and ran out in her bathrobe.

They found Mr. Magoo in her closet, and from the sounds of it he wasn't happy. They left the room with him wrapped in a towel. "This will be a setback," said Olenka. "The fact that he approached you in the tub meant he knew someone was home and he was curious to see you."

"Forget about his setback. What about mine?"

"I think he secretly likes you. Even your names are almost exactly the same."

"Wonderful. Thanks for bringing that to my attention."

She went back to the bathroom and ended up draining the water and cleaning out the mess of cat hair and blood in the tub. Just once couldn't something go right?

She wiped up the bathroom floor too. That cat must have dragged a gallon of water with him on his fur. Oh my god. He'd been in her closet. She went in the bedroom and looked down at her shoes. They were all dripping.

Margo cradled her ruined suede pumps and howled, like the lone wolf she was.

Chapter Sixteen

The weather turned really cold almost overnight, and snow covered the landscape. Instant panic. A light switch goes off in every woman's brain that Santa Claus is coming to town in a big fat hurry. Women with children were the busiest beasts on the planet during the twelfth month of the year; Julia had kicked things up to fifth gear and she wasn't available most of the time.

Margo wasn't worried about Christmas, only that it probably wasn't the best time to be looking for a job. Or maybe it was. Stores often hired extra workers to handle the influx of customers. But she wasn't looking for a temporary job. Still, something was better than nothing and she might just get her foot in the door.

Except now she worried about busy stores. They weren't the lovely hustle and bustle they used to be. Now all she saw were germs. Germs in plaid coats, hoodies, and puffer jackets. So, she was in a bit of a state on this particular morning because she had an interview at her old store, thanks to her colleague, Honey, who still worked in the cosmetic department. Margo had called her and she said she'd talk to the new owner.

"Oh? Jerry's not there?"

"No. And this new one's a pill." Honey laughed at her own joke. "Pill...get it? Drugstore?!"

"You always were a wit."

On top of her anxiety, Margo couldn't find her good boots—or any of her boots, for that matter. She knew they weren't in the closet. After blacking out momentarily when she realized her best suede shoes were toast, thanks to that drip of a cat, she took an inventory while she mopped up the rest of them.

She hurried down to the kitchen. What a surprise. The kids were at the table eating bagels and cream cheese, and before she could say anything, Olenka started talking. "Did you know that baby blue whales can gain two-hundred-and-fifty-pounds in a single day? I'm starting to feel like that could be me."

"I'm going call you Uno from now on," Mike said. "You start every sentence with "Did you know..."

"Do either of you two know where my winter boots are?"

They shook their heads.

"Think! That day Julia was determined to bring home the barbeque and lawn mower. When all of you went over and I stayed home with the girls." Margo put her hand on her forehead. "Oh my god, I shouldn't have done that. You didn't look under the stairs, did you? I think I forgot to tell you to look under the stairs. That's where Dick stored our winter boots. How could I have been so stupid? I didn't want to crawl under and take them out and I was going to tell you but in all the confusion, I forgot about them!"

"Mom, calm down."

Margo went over to the table and picked up the uneaten half of her son's breakfast. "Do not tell me to calm down ever again or I swear you'll be wearing this bagel. Do you understand?"

He held up his hands. "I'm sorry. What I meant to say was relax, chill—"

She pushed the bagel and cream cheese into his face.

⤳∞⤲

Margo walked into her old Shoppers with cold feet. She had shoe booties on, but the minute this ordeal was over she was heading over to Regent Mall to buy a pair of boots. Not that they would be as nice as the ones she had, thanks to her new reality of pinching pennies.

She was so fired up, she forgot to be nervous. No one better mess with her today. She'd loved her Stuart Weitzman knee-high zip boots. They were incredibly comfortable and she'd only had one winter out of them. She was ready to choke someone.

Actually, this was the first time since Dick's death she'd been really, really angry. Not because Dick was stupid enough to kill himself with food and gamble away every red cent he had, and not because she'd lost the house and was left with a bad credit score thanks to that loan, and not because she was miserable living with her kids—but because she'd lost those damn boots. There were five other pairs too, but she wasn't as in love with them as she had been with those soft leather knee-highs.

Honey was behind the same counter that Margo knew like the back of her hand and she gave her a big wave as she attended to a customer before holding her finger in the air to tell Margo to wait. Margo stood on her cold feet and stewed. When the dear little old lady left, Margo went up to the register. "Let me guess. Ponds Cold Cream and scented lavender powder."

"You're still a genius and you've been gone five years. How are you doing, Margo? I couldn't believe it when you shoved Dick's urn in his ex-wife's face. I didn't dare call you."

"I'm not doing a whole lot better. I shoved cream cheese in my son's face this morning."

"Much better than a dead guy." She laughed, then saw that Margo wasn't joining in. Honey cleared her throat. "The only thing I suggest you do with this new owner Ronnie is try not to gag. He's hard to take."

"Aren't most men?"

Honey frowned. "You love men. Are you sure you're okay? Maybe you should reschedule. You look like you want to bite some-one's head off."

"I can't reschedule. This is going to be my permanent demea-nour for the foreseeable future or until I can replace my boots." She stamped her feet. "My toes are frozen. Okay, wish me luck."

"You don't need it. He'd be crazy not to take you back. I told him all about you."

Margo headed for the office and staff room at the back of the store. She could still walk it blindfolded. Even the air was familiar, and a bit comforting.

She knocked on the open office door and wished Jerry was still there. He'd told her many times he loved her. He told his wife that too. She'd come by and laugh, "Margo, you're the only employee he never has to worry about. If he could clone you, he would."

Margo instantly disliked Ronnie; as he sat there and looked up, his eyes widened. A foolish smirk appeared. Did he think she'd spent the last hour making sure her makeup and hair and clothes were impeccable just for him?

"Mrs. Sterling, I presume? I'm Ronald Wells. Ronnie." He extended both hands to grasp hers.

"I apologize. Ever since Covid I don't shake hands. I'm sure you understand."

He looked disappointed. She reminded herself she needed this job and stuck out her right arm. "I'm sure I can make an exception this once."

It was a long, slow shake. So far, he was hitting every mark on her jerk checklist.

"Please sit down." He indicated the chair in front of his desk and sat on his own chair. He looked ordinary but a little sweaty and ran his hand through his head an awful lot. Margo wasn't sure if he was nervous or that he just wanted her to notice his hair.

"Honey tells me you worked in this store for twenty-five years as the cosmetic department manager. All well and good I'm sure, but before my time I'm afraid. And you've been out of the workforce for five years? May I ask why?"

"My first granddaughter was born."

He pretended to be shocked. "You're too young to be a grandmother. A fine-looking specimen like you."

She wrinkled her nose. In disgust, but he didn't know that.

"Kids today," he said. "Expecting grandparents to look after their brats. My wife was suckered into that. It still bugs me."

Margo took a moment. "I'm sure your grandchild is very lucky to have your wife...and you."

He puffed up. "We do our best. Well, Margo, it's only because you have experience in this store that I'm willing to take you on for the holiday season. It gets pretty hectic in here."

She was genuinely thrilled. "Oh, thank you, Mr. Wells."

"Call me Ronnie, please. Maybe over a drink sometime?"

"I'm sorry, I don't drink. When should I start back at the cosmetic counter?"

He looked puzzled. "Oh, you can't work there. Honey and the other two girls have that all sewn up. I'm hiring on a few people to work in the back. Handle the inventory."

Margo tried to hide her dismay. "You want me to move boxes of stock from delivery trucks?"

"Unless that's beneath you? You came in here looking for a job, I believe."

She clenched her fists. "That's right, Ronnie. I did. When do I start?"

He slapped his knees with both hands and hooted. "You should have seen the look on your face! Oh my god, that was fun. I don't suppose anyone's told you I'm a bit of a prankster."

He kept laughing as she felt her cheeks get hot.

"As if you'd be able to manage a shipping box with those arms. A Kleenex box maybe. Oh my, that was a good one."

Margo forced a smile. "I'm on cosmetics after all?"

"No! No. I told ya, we have enough staff there. I need someone on the front cash in the evenings, four to ten. Just until January second. You're going to have to work Christmas Eve, Christmas Day, and Boxing Day, all the time the regulars want off, which is only fair."

"Fine."

"You can start tomorrow. You remember how to use the cash machines, right? Come in early and we'll get your paper-work done."

Margo nodded. She couldn't feel her feet. She couldn't really feel anything.

Ronnie held his hand out once again, but she waved instead and stumbled out of the office. She didn't even stop to see Honey, but rushed to the car and willed herself not to cry. She'd wanted a job. She'd gotten one. It never occurred to her it would be at night. She'd miss the girls' bedtimes. She went over two or three nights a week. She'd miss Christmas. She wouldn't be working with Honey or the other girls. She'd be dealing with the public, not nice little old ladies looking for Pond's Cold Cream.

Still, Margo refused to cry and fall apart at the seams. That's what Julia would expect, so she absolutely wouldn't do it. Instead, she drove to the mall, rode up the escalator as though she were actually flying, and bought really, really expensive boots. She left the store triumphantly with the bag swinging on her arm.

When she got to the escalator, she turned around and marched back to the store and said she'd made a mistake. They returned her money and she bought a cheaper generic pair that would let her stand at a cash register for hours.

Margo went back to the house and found Mike at his computer with his big headphones on. He didn't hear her come in, and he jumped when she reached down and kissed the top of his head. He pulled one side away from his ear. "Oh, so now you love me?"

"Always. Sorry."

"You better be." He put his headphone back and she kissed his head again, so he smiled.

She went up to her room and laid on the bed, coming to terms with...everything. And who appeared at the door but Magoo? He sat and watched her with his big square face.

"What do you want, Mister? You owe me three hundred dollars for those suede pumps."

Meow.

She raised her head. "What did you say?"

Meow.

"Was that an apology?"

He left.

"I didn't think so."

It was Posy's Christmas concert that night. After Olenka got home from work and they had a quick bite, they hurried to the school gym to join the throng of adoring parents, grandparents, and germs packed shoulder-to-shoulder in uncomfortable chairs, overheating, holding too many coats in their arms. Andre managed to save three seats for them in the middle of the pack. Hazel wanted to sit in Margo's lap. Margo jiggled her on her knees as she leaned over and said, "I got a job."

No one heard her, so she didn't bother repeating it.

Fortunately, Posy was in the front row with her pretty red dress and patent-leather shoes on. Margo felt sorry for the parents with kids in the back rows. All that time and effort getting them ready and you only saw their heads. But when everything started you couldn't see any of them, there were so many cellphones being held in the air. Why didn't people just watch their kids? It was times like this when Margo felt removed from this generation.

They went back to Julia's house to spend time with two cranky kids. The minute Margo walked in and saw their Christmas tree, her knees buckled. She held onto the wall.

"Mom? What is it?" Julia frowned. "Are you okay?"

Everyone looked at her.

"My Christmas ornaments. They were in a box under the stairs."

Once Mike brought Julia up to speed on the boot disaster, Andre decided to get the girls ready for bed and out of the way. Julia made her mom sit on the couch, but Margo turned on her. "You were in such a hurry to get that stuff out of the house, I didn't have time to remember everything. Now my boots are gone and your handprint reindeer and Mike's pipe cleaner Santa will never be seen again! They're probably in some landfill. And oh, my mother's little silver bells." She put her hands over her face and rocked.

The kids felt terrible. And then Margo popped up again. "And I got a job today. For only two weeks and not on the cosmetic counter but stacking boxes."

"Stacking boxes?" Julia shouted.

"I mean, working on the front cash at night for the holidays. You can eat Christmas turkey without me. It doesn't even feel like Christmas." Now she turned on Mike and Olenka. "And why don't you two have a Christmas tree? Why can't you be bothered to fix up your house with a few decorations? This dear little soul is coming and what's baby going to look at? Blank walls?"

"Technically, if the baby comes now, that's...not good news," Michael said.

Margo stood up and glared at him. "Julia, do you have any cream cheese?"

"What the hell are you talking about, Mom?" she said.

Margo walked away. "I need to go. I can't deal with this anymore. Kiss the girls for me." And she stopped in the front porch. "I have no idea when I'll see you again, Julia, what with you working all day and me working all night. In 2024, I assume. I'd like to leave now, Michael."

Mike and Olenka gave Julia horrified looks before they scurried away.

Later, on their g-force mattress, Julia sat up and stared into space, even after Andre turned out the light on his side.

Eventually he muttered into his pillow, "Get some sleep."

"You know whose fault this is."

"Yours?"

"Carole and Velma. And I'm not going to let them get away with it."

Andre got up on his elbow. "How is it their fault?"

"They wanted to clear everything out and Mom wasn't in the right headspace to protect herself, so I jumped the gun and we took off without really looking in every corner. I bet they dragged off all sorts of things. I'm not going to let them get away with it."

Her husband rolled his eyes and flopped back on his pillow. "Just what we need. You picking a fight with a lunatic."

Julia sniffed. "My grandmother's silver bells, Andre." She fell down beside him and snuggled against his chest.

He patted her shoulder. "I know, I know. You feel bad."

After a sleepless night, Julia got the kids ready for the day. They were both very excited about Christmas, and kept squirming as she helped them put on their tights.

"Can Gogo come with us on Christmas Eve to see baby Jesus?" Posy asked. "I'm a donkey, remember. Just like Ginger."

Hazel kept leaning over with her foot in the air. "I wanna be Fred. I don't wanna to be a angel."

Julia's heart lurched. Her mom wouldn't be able to attend the Christmas Eve pageant at church.

After Andre left with the girls she formulated a plan. While rooting around in the back of her side-table drawer for eye drops, she saw Dick's phone. It had been in her pocket when she got home that night in June, and she'd thrown it in there with every intention of giving it to her mother, but had forgotten.

She sat on the bed and turned it on. Thank goodness for people who didn't have passwords. The screen even popped up to the contact page under the phone icon, the one she'd looked at for Velma's number. She punched in Carole's name and there was her address.

Julia didn't want anyone to know what she was doing in case it all went horribly wrong, but after seeing her mom's despair over those silver bells, she knew she had to try.

She called her assistant in the car and said she was running late. It was another bitterly cold day, but there was no snow. Just when you wanted a blanket of the white stuff to make everyone's front yards look festive for the holiday.

She parked up the street from the older four-storey building. It suited Carole perfectly. Square, squat, and grey. Julia found her name and apartment number and was just about to press the button when someone came through the door and held it open for her. The power of a nice suit.

It was the only door on the second-floor hallway that didn't have some kind of Christmas decoration on it. She knocked on it with purpose. There was no answer, so she rapped louder.

She heard "Keep your hair on!" from the other side of the door. Julia knew Carole was probably looking through the peephole and gave her a wave.

When the door opened, Carole was there in her bathrobe and slippers. All Julia could think of was Bette Davis in the movie *What Ever Happened to Baby Jane?* Give Carole another ten years.

And didn't the woman smirk just like her. "Well, well. I thought you'd show up around now."

"I knew it. You have her Christmas ornaments. And her boots?"

"She left them behind. What was I supposed to do?"

Julia tried to control her anger. "You could have called her and told her she overlooked a few very personal things, and asked if she would like them back."

Carole put her hand on her hip. "Why on earth would I do that woman a favour?"

"Then why not leave the boxes there and let them be carted away like so much garbage?"

The door to the next condo started to open and Carole beckoned Julia inside. Everywhere you looked there was disarray. If Julia wasn't so cross at the moment, she'd feel sorry for her. Carole walked to her coffee table/restaurant counter and faced her.

"Because I'm not a stupid woman. I want that barbeque back."

"To put it where, exactly?"

Carole pointed at her balcony. "There, your holiness, not that it's any of your business."

Julia stood straighter. "I thought you wanted it for Velma."

Carole reached down, picked up a Coke can, and took a long drink. "I want the lawn mower and the snowblower too. I know you think I forgot about the snowblower, and I did until Velma reminded me."

"I believe Velma lives in an apartment too. Is she going to cart them up and down in the elevator?"

"We want our stuff."

Julia pursed her lips and rocked on her heels. "It is marital property. My *mother's* marital property. Yes, Velma is next of kin also, which is why Mom gave her free rein to take not only her dad's personal affects but also almost an entire house full of furniture. Not you, Carole. Velma. And Mom didn't have to. Now, I happen to know that the snowblower belonged to *my* dad, and he gave it to Mom when he was replacing his. And Mom bought the lawn mower with her own money. She has a receipt. And they bought the barbeque with the fifty-thousand-dollar loan Mom cosigned last year. Now, if you want to get pissy, I can bring in our lawyer and we can debate this all day. And if you don't give me my mother's Christmas ornaments and goddamn boots, he will make sure you are charged with theft of my mother's property. Do I make myself clear?"

❧

The doorbell rang, which was very unusual. Everyone usually just knocked and barged right in. Mike didn't hear it, even though he was in the living room, so Margo went down the stairs and opened the door.

"Hi, Mom."

"Julia? Wat are you doing here?"

"Could you come out with me for a second? I want to show you something."

Margo tsked. "It's cold out. Is this really necessary?"

"Get your coat and boots on."

"What boots? Oh yeah, these clunky things." Margo looked at her new unexciting purchase. "Fine."

Julia led her to the back of her car and opened the trunk. When her mother realized what she was looking at, she put her hands over her face and rocked back and forth. This time with unbridled joy.

"How did you manage that?" Andre asked Julia in bed that night.

"A lot of hogwash about the snowblower being Dad's, Mom buying the lawn mower, and me bringing in lawyers who'll charge Carole with robbery."

"Wow. Remind me never to get on your bad side."

Chapter Seventeen

The only reason Margo remembered the Tim Burton movie *The Nightmare Before Christmas* was because Julia was ten when it came out. She'd begged to see it and said all her friends were allowed to watch it. Margo worried it might be too scary, but when Julia did watch it, she didn't think it was scary enough.

A real nightmare before Christmas now had Margo in its grip. It was bad enough she had missed the girls' Sunday School nativity play, but Byron had to tell her about it when she dropped by to pick up his annual gift of a dark fruitcake. Their house looked glorious with twinkly Christmas lights in all the shrubbery, so she was in a foul mood. When he laughingly described Hazel throwing off her halo and wings and braying like a donkey in the middle of "Silent Night," it took all Margo had not to shove the fruitcake into his smiling face.

Instead of hosting a Christmas Eve party for her children, Margo listened to their plans. Julia, Andre, and the girls were off to his parents' house with his brothers and their families. Michael and Olenka went to her mother's house filled with extended family and friends. They all pretended they weren't doing anything special, as if their Christmas Eve get-togethers were going to be ho-hum.

Nice try.

She called Eunie before her shift. "Please tell me you're not doing anything special today.

"As it happens a few of Holly's older friends at work want to take Christmas pictures of their kids with Fred and Ginger. Hazen bought the donkeys jingle bells with big red bows, so we're having a party with warm cider and I'm making gingersnaps for the kids. It will be fun. What are you doing?"

"Not that."

If she had to be here in the store tonight, she wished she could at least be on the cosmetic counter. They were always run off their feet on Christmas Eve, with men roaring in to buy perfume and any gift box that looked expensive and girly. They didn't care what was in them. Imagine.

But her cash register was extremely busy too. Ronnie told all of them to be on the lookout for shoplifters. There were two security people, a man and a woman dressed as customers, roaming about the store to catch people in the act. Three girls who looked about twelve bypassed her cash and headed for the door in a hurry, but the security team waylaid them and there was a ruckus before they were hauled back in and taken to the office, presumedly to call their parents. What a gift.

The woman security guard made her rounds again, and when she passed by, Margo asked her what they were trying to steal.

"In my day it was lipstick. Now it's flavoured condoms."

Margo's astonished face caused the woman to nod. "I know, right? Just kids."

Most people shopping on Christmas Eve were in a hurry to get somewhere else, so the mother and two children who wandered around the aisles for a long time were easy to spot. Margo worried about them. *Please don't let the mother get caught shoplifting in front of her kids.* She looked desperate and put things down as she looked at the price. Who invented commercial Christmas? Why put people through this every year? When she saw the security team follow the woman, Margo beckoned a colleague over and said she had to use the washroom. She went into the back room, opened her locker, and took out her purse. She'd withdrawn a hundred dollars out of the ATM earlier that day. Looking around, she folded up the five twenty-dollar-bills and put them in the palm of her hand. She walked up to the mother and said quietly, "I believe you dropped this. Merry Christmas." She quickly put the money in the mother's hand and kept going.

Margo spent the next ten minutes watching the mom let her kids choose whatever they wanted. All the things she had put down. The kids were so excited as they scooped up candy and chocolate.

The mom didn't spend all of the money. Margo was happy to give her the change. The woman squeezed her hand when she did. Off they went, the kids skipping out the door.

It was suddenly a great Christmas Eve.

But the next day that glow had worn off. Mike and Olenka were still in bed on Christmas morning as Margo went to work. Only Magoo was kind enough to sit with her as she ate her toast and marmalade. She gave him an edge of crust and he licked the marmalade off completely before starting in on the toast itself.

"Merry Christmas, Magoo."

Meow.

"Thank you. You have better manners than Stan."

She tried not to break down as she drove to work. She couldn't even look in the direction of Julia's house. Thanks to her careless husband, Margo was being denied the pure joy of being with Posy and Hazel on Christmas morning. Did Dick ever think what might happen to her with his financial situation in such disarray? She'd obviously been an afterthought. Not even that. There'd been no thought at all.

The store wasn't as busy, though the need for cough syrup, diapers, antacids, and prescriptions didn't stop because Santa was in town. Still, most people were at home arguing about what time to put the turkey on, or worse, pontificating about mask protocol and the need for Covid shots with relatives they hadn't seen in a while.

It seemed humans had something new to bicker about every blessed year. Peace on Earth was shoved aside annually.

Margo's feet started to hurt towards the end of the day. She was getting off at seven, and Julia told her they were delaying Christmas dinner so she could join them. Olenka and Mike would be there as well so the day was ending on a high note. She had ballet slippers and tutus as gifts for the girls. Their ballet class was starting in the new year. Margo's kids insisted they didn't want anything for Christmas. She was supposed to be saving her money.

A sharply dressed woman came into the store and hurried over to her. "Could you tell me where the vibrators are?"

"Vibrators?"

She looked at Margo over her thick tortoise-shell glasses. "You have heard of them, I trust?"

"Yes, of course, but I don't think we sell them."

"Is there someone you can ask?"

Margo knew who she wasn't going to ask. "One moment." She got on the phone and called the cosmetic desk. Honey's counterpart answered. Margo turned away from the woman. "Do we sell vibrators?"

"Yeah. Near the heating pads and neck braces."

"Thanks." Margo hung up and turned back to her customer. "At the end of aisle four."

The woman scurried off and soon hurried back with a package. She took out her wallet. "This always happens. You forget everything in your rush to get to the airport." She paid for the item and looked at it again before putting it in her purse. "Beggers can't be choosers, I suppose."

Margo passed her the receipt. "I hope you have a lovely holiday."

"Slightly better chances of that now, thanks."

Who walks into a drugstore and asks for a vibrator? How many did they sell in the run of a week? How did Margo not know about this? Vibrators had only ever been accessible in sex shops. She certainly hadn't needed one for the past decade, but it might have been nice to get her hands on one this easily when she was married to dear old Monty. This must be a fairly new development since she'd retired.

Then it occurred to Margo that one might be useful in her current situation, so she went down to the end of aisle four and found one solitary vibrator left.

She was supposed to be saving her money.

The coworker in cosmetics had to ring the sale through. She smirked at Margo. "Is there something I should know about, like a shortage of sex toys in this city? Maybe I should I stock up."

Good grief. Was everyone using them?

❧

Margo was tired but oh, so happy to be sitting around the table with her loved ones, all of them wearing tissue paper hats thanks to the Christmas crackers. Andre made a scrumptious turkey dinner for them but didn't eat the turkey. He was content with his nut roast wellington, a mixture of nuts, sweet squash and umami mushrooms packed in a crisp pastry. The girls, in their tutus and ballet shoes, ended up eating most of it.

They sat around the sparkly Christmas tree adorned with her mother's silver bells after dinner, eating plum pudding and hard sauce. Monty and Byron dropped by to give the girls a handmade wooden dollhouse. They were enchanted.

It was getting late. They said their farewells and Margo drove her car behind Mike and Olenka. She was surprised to see a small lit-up reindeer on their front porch. They must have done that today. Magoo was in the window waiting for them.

The kids even had a scraggly tree in the corner of the living room covered with strings of popcorn and cranberries. Dried orange slices and cut-out white paper stars hung from the branches. Margo loved this tree the best.

They settled into their rooms for the night. Margo took her purchase out of her purse. She'd forgotten it was in there. Thank the lord Julia hadn't looked in it for some reason. She started to unwrap it when there was a quick knock at the door. She shoved it under the blankets as Mike poked his head in. "Magoo is standing here. I think he wants to come in."

"Okay," she said. "Goodnight."

"'Night, Mom."

He let Magoo in and shut the door. The cat came up on the end of bed and stared at her.

"Just what I need. An audience."

It wasn't going to happen anyway. Margo had forgotten to buy batteries. She got out of bed and put her personal Christmas present inside one of her lace-up boots. No one would find it there. But now she had to figure out how to get rid of the box. She could hardly throw it in the recycle bin in the kitchen. After ripping it into twenty pieces, she placed it back in her purse to chuck into a waste bin at least a few miles away.

Back in bed, she sighed. She needed her own place.

Magoo decided she wasn't that interesting and howled to get out of the room.

⊖∾⊖

The second day of January 2024 was Margo's last day of work. What was she going to do now? The thought of trying to find another job stuck in her throat. At least being in this particular store made her life feel familiar. So much had changed in the last six months. She resented having to pivot yet again.

Ronnie called her into the office. No doubt to sort out her paperwork. She sat down reluctantly and wished it was all over.

Her boss twirled his pen in the air. "I've been watching you, Margo. I know what you've been up to over Christmas."

Oh my god. Did he know about the vibrator? Wait. Maybe it was giving that woman the money. Surely that wasn't bad? It was her money.

"Have I done something wrong, Mr. Wells?"

"Don't be such a nervous Nellie, and call me Ronnie. No, I have to commend you on your reliable work habits. I concede that widows are a darn sight more responsible than teenagers and college students."

"Oh. Well, thanks."

He nodded his head. "And because I'm such a generous soul, I've decided to keep you on full-time."

Margo leaned forward in her chair. "Really? That's wonderful! Thank you."

Ronnie jabbed his pen towards her. "Not only that, I want you to work days. No more nights for you."

She felt like she'd won the lottery. "I can't thank you enough, Mr....Ronnie. I'm so pleased."

"As am I." He smiled. "We'll get to see a lot more of each other."

Margo's heart sank a little, but not enough to take away the relief of getting a full-time job. She would soon be on the road to getting her own place.

She was still on the front cash, and Ronnie meant it when he said they'd see more of each other. Margo was sure he had enough to do in the pharmacy, but he always found an excuse to come up to the register to get a pack of Excel gum or a Coffee Crisp. She'd see him coming up the aisle and try not to catch his eye. Why didn't he pick on the younger women there?

What was she thinking? He probably did. It wasn't like he was completely obnoxious, because there were customers around, but he always stood a bit closer than she liked. That seemed to happen a lot. Older men coming in and chatting her up as they bought denture cream and ointment for toe fungus. She lamented about it with Honey.

"I don't remember this happening when I worked here."

"That's because men wouldn't be caught dead in cosmetics. At least the ones our age. Now you're right up front and everyone has to pass you to get out. Try making yourself look frumpy, if that's possible. Otherwise, they'll be hovering around you like fruit flies. It's like they crawl out of the sewer."

It was good advice. Margo started by taking off her false eyelashes. She felt naked and thought she looked sickly, but no one else seemed to notice, until finally three days later Olenka said, "You look nice," out of the blue while making a banana split.

Then Margo put CC cream on instead of foundation and only half the usual blush. Mike came out of the shower with steam billowing out after him. He looked at her quizzically, as if he was trying to figure out why she looked different.

She stopped with the lipliner and choose a softer shade of rose for her lips. That day she went over to Julia's to babysit and Julia greeted her at the door. "Do you have the flu? What's wrong?"

"That bad?"

"No, wait. Just different. Pale? Normal?"

"Well, thanks. I'm trying to tone down my look so the creepy men at the cash stop talking to me."

"I like it, and as for the men, just sneeze in their face. That'll keep them away."

Hazel ran up and hugged Margo around the neck. Then she looked at her grandmother and put her chubby fingers on her cheeks. "Did you lose your crayons?"

Chapter Eighteen

Margo adored Mike and Olenka, but they were so ruddy boring. Happy as clams to stay in their habitat and venture out only when food became scarce. They had no natural enemies, other than her; sometimes her impatience with them would come to the surface. Mike got annoyed at her one night. She was on her chaise and Magoo was perched on the end of it, looking confused as always. She'd given up trying to keep him off it. And he was growing on her. He'd plunked his bum on her feet one night and got them toasty warm.

Olenka shuffled off to the kitchen to get more bananas when Mike paused their game and looked at her.

"I do not want you putting any pressure on Olenka. We are going to get the baby's room ready in our own time."

"And when will that be? Sometime babies come early. Right now the child would have to sleep in a bureau drawer."

"We still have two and a half months to go."

She picked her magazine. "Obviously, being a mother myself, I know nothing about it."

Olenka came back in the room, her tummy out in front. "Did you know that all baby marsupials are born prematurely? That's why they have pouches."

"Are you excited about the baby shower?" Margo asked her, eager to change the subject.

Olenka nodded, placing the small carton of Häagen-Dazs over

her bump. "Sure. Just as long as they don't have party games. And if I hear one more time that we should've found out the baby's sex before the shower I'll scream. Other animals don't know what they're having. Why is it necessary to find out beforehand? I do not want to be gagged by pink and blue smoke, covered in pink or blue confetti, or eat ten cupcakes looking for the coloured icing in the middle."

"Julia wanted to know," Margo commented.

Mike grunted. "Now there's a surprise."

Fortunately, Gerda was organizing the shower at her place. She and Margo had met several times, now that Gerda had to come over to the house to see Olenka. She was shocked at the lack of furniture and the abysmal decorating. The two grandmothers bonded over that.

The shower was being held on a Saturday afternoon, and thankfully the roads were clear of snow, because Holly was driving Eunie up in Eunie's car. Julia, Margo, and Olenka waited for them and drove ahead to show them where Gerda lived. As soon as they got to the street, Olenka said, "I knew it. She's invited everyone she's ever met."

There was no place to park. The street was completely clogged with cars. Julia dropped off Margo and Olenka and Holly let Eunie out and they ended up parking two streets over. As they walked to the house together, Holly said, "I've never been to a baby shower."

Julia paused. "It's an experience."

It was a circus. There were so many women there, some of the younger ones sat on the floor. Olenka looked like a scared rabbit. Her mother had her in an armchair festooned with a lacy umbrella overhead and streamers. There were so many gifts your eye didn't know where to look. Gerda made Olenka wear a paper plate with a ribbon around her chin and stuck the bows from each gift on it. After twenty minutes, Mommy had enough and ripped it off her head. The food was glorious, there were too many party games, and their little gang never got to talk to each other because of the commotion.

The gifts were unlike anything Eunie had ever seen. When Olenka opened an automatic formula maker that looked like an espresso machine, Eunie leaned over to Holly, who was sticking to her like glue. "I'm not sure our receiving blankets are going to measure up."

They were the last to leave because Gerda wanted Olenka to stay behind to help organize the gifts. Once the cars were parked closer to the house again, both trunks were filled to the top.

Gerda hugged her only child. "I hope you had fun, little one."

"Thank you, Mama. For everything."

Gerda insisted they take a stack of plates filled with sweets and sandwiches. "For Michael."

When Olenka got back in the car, she cried the whole five-minute drive home. "What's wrong with me?"

"You're overwhelmed, sweetheart," Margo said. "It's okay."

By the time both cars were emptied and the gifts were piled on the floor, it was a bit shocking. Mike stood there eating sandwiches off a platter. "What the hell? Where's all this stuff going?"

Julia waved her hand at it. "You're going to use all of it sometime, so don't sweat it."

"When am I ever going to use a heated formula maker? I'm breastfeeding."

"You will swear undying love to that thing in the middle of the night when your sore and cracked nipples can't take one more gummy tug," Julia told her.

Olenka went upstairs to lie down and Michael and Magoo followed her. Holly kept looking at her watch. "Hazen is expecting us for dinner. He doesn't like it when we drive on dark roads."

"Quite right, my dear." Eunie put her coat back on. "So, Holly, if you ever need a baby shower, I'll know just what to do."

"I think you know what my answer will be," she replied.

"Fudge, no?" said Eunie.

Margo hugged her big sister. "Once I get an apartment, I hope you'll come and stay with me for a weekend. And when the weather gets better, I'll come to you. We do need to see each other more often."

"You just miss rolling around in my sheets with Stan."

"I do. I wish you'd give me that cat. You can take Magoo."

"I'll leave you Stan in my will."

Margo turned to Holly and knew not to touch her. "It was great seeing you, honey."

"You too." And she surprised Margo when she reached over and gave her a brief hug.

Margo and Julia waved to Holly and Eunie from the living room window. "Have I told you how much I love that girl?" Margo said wistfully.

"Too often," Julia grumped. She picked up one of the gifts. "A white-noise machine. I could use this. Do you think O would miss it?"

When Margo took off her sweater that night, she felt something in the pocket.

Two edibles.

⌁

March came in like a lion and stayed that way. It seemed Margo battled through blowing snow going to and coming home from work. Half the time Mike was able to help her clean off the car, but the other half he had meetings online, or he insisted on driving Olenka to work and back, which was obviously more important. A woman in the late stage of pregnancy did not need to be changing a flat tire in a snowstorm.

A woman in the later stages of life didn't either, but it was just what happened on the Ides of March. At first Margo thought she was stuck in a snowdrift in the parking lot, but when she got out to check, that wasn't the case. She started off again but didn't get very far. Something felt wrong.

"Well, damn!"

She got back out and looked carefully at the wheels. Did she have a flat tire? Was that flat? How can you tell? That's when it occurred to her that she'd opted not to renew her CAA card because she was trying to keep expenses down.

She didn't want to call Mike; he was picking up Olenka. She didn't want to call Andre; he'd be making supper. She didn't need an earful from Julia about cancelling her CAA card, and calling Monty was admitting defeat.

Hazen had tried to show her how to change a tire when she was a teenager but soon gave up because she couldn't get one bolt off and she'd complained about getting her hands dirty.

"Lord flyin' dyin'," he'd exploded. "You're as useless at tits on a bull."

Margo was getting colder by the minute, so she went back in the store and ran into the stock boy, Jaxon. "Honey, do you know what a flat tire looks like?"

"Flat."

Naturally, Ronnie hurried over. "What was that? You have a flat tire?"

She looked back out the door. "I'm not sure. I can't tell with all the snow around, but when I drove forward the car felt sluggish and odd and sort of bumpy."

"Sounds like it. Let me get my coat."

If it had been anyone else, she'd be mightily relieved, but Ronnie would use this as leverage. A knight-in-shining-armour kind of deal. He almost looked excited as he hurried away. She should have just called Monty. This was going to cost her.

But two seconds later he was back with his coat and gloves on.

"I'll show you where it is," she said and started for the door.

"I know your car. You stay here and keep your tootsies warm."

He knew what car she drove? She didn't like the sound of that—or being talked to like a baby. She headed out the door ahead of him and put her collar up against the cold wind. He tried to keep up, but she didn't want him walking beside her.

"Here it is," she said. "Can you see anything?"

He looked around the tires on the passenger side. "These look okay." Then he went around to the other side. "Oh look, the front tire is definitely flat."

"How can you tell?"

He pointed. "It's flat."

"But it doesn't look flat, does it?

He straightened up. "Men just know these things."

She could have kicked herself, sounding like a helpless female, but she wanted information in case it ever happened again. That tire did not look deflated to her.

"So what am I looking for?" She touched the tire and Ronnie reached over and held her hand over the problem area. "Fine. You can let go," she said. He released her.

It did look a bit saggy. She should have recognized that. *Saggy* was her middle name at this stage of life.

"Oh dear," she said. "I think I'll call my husband."

Ronnie looked perplexed. "Isn't he dead? I thought you were a widow."

"My spare husband."

"There's no need. I don't mind doing it."

"Really, Ronnie, you're very kind, but that's not necessary. This is my problem. I'm going to go in and call him." And she headed for the store before he could argue about it.

The warmth inside felt good. Ronnie looked dejected as he walked past her. "Thanks for your help." She smiled at him as she called Monty.

Byron picked up. "Hi, Margo. What's new in the retail world? Any more shoplifting stories? I used to think that was extremely rude behaviour, but with the price of everything these days, I'm starting to change my mind."

"Sorry, Byron, I don't have time to chat, is Monty there?"

"Sure thing."

Monty got on the phone and sounded cranky right off the bat.

"Am I interrupting something?" she asked.

"Nothing, what is it?"

She explained the situation, and heard him sigh over the phone. "Look, Margo, this is terribly inconvenient. I'm soaking my feet in warm water at the moment trying to soften a callous on my big toe joint that's making my life abysmal."

Well, well. When you're not as important as someone's big toe, that says a lot.

"Fine. Is Byron available?"

Monty started to laugh. "Are you kidding? He wouldn't know a jack from a jill."

"Okay, thanks anyway."

"Wait, what about M—"

She hung up on him and hurried after Ronnie.

He replaced the flat with her spare, and when she tried to give him some money he refused. "Let's grab a coffee. I could do with some warming up."

She felt she had no choice. Unfortunately, there was a coffee shop only three doors down, so they walked up the street and entered, Ronnie holding the door open for her. At least it was warm. Margo insisted she buy the coffee and anything else he might like. He chose a Danish.

Once settled at a table, they took sips of their coffee. Margo was nervous and couldn't think of anything to say other than "Thanks again for your help."

"I like rescuing damsels in distress."

Oh, yuck. She was going to take a crash course in auto mechanics.

"Are you happy working at the front cash?" he eventually asked.

Was he playing footsie under the table? Every time she moved her boots, she seemed to bump into him again.

"I'd prefer cosmetics, obviously. It's my comfort zone, but I'm not going to take away someone's job." She took another gulp of coffee. She didn't want to linger.

He bit into his Danish and managed to get a big blob of icing on the side of his mouth. She was sure he would wipe it away but he didn't, and now she could look at nothing else. It reminded her of Dick with smeared barbeque sauce on his chin.

"I'm thinking of rearranging the staff. There might be an opening in cosmetics, if you're interested." He looked at her over his drink.

"Is that so?" She took another sip of coffee.

He nodded. "It's always a good move to shuffle people around. They get complacent after a while. It causes a bit of chaos for a few days, but it's smart management."

"I hope you're not thinking of replacing Honey? She's been there forever."

"Exactly. And nothing is forever." Margo put down her mug and he grabbed her arm. "I'm assuming you'd be very grateful to have your old job back with its pay raise. As I'm sure you're grateful for me helping you out tonight." He rubbed his thumb over her skin.

Margo wanted to jerk her arm away, but instead she withdrew it carefully from his touch.

"Grateful? For your help?" What was she going to do? She was terrified of pissing him off. She needed her job. "Yes, I am grateful." She looked at her watch. "Oh dear. I didn't realize it was so late. My family will wonder where I am."

"I thought you lived alone. You should invite me over to see your place."

"No, I live with my big burly son and his honey badger. And their cat is ferocious."

He held up his hand. "Wait. Why don't we go somewhere nice next time? We could get a drink, now that we're friends."

"You're my boss, and a very considerate one. Thank you again for tonight."

She left as quickly as she could and tried not to slip and slide on the icy sidewalks. Her phone buzzed. A text from Mike, *Where are u?* and one from Monty, *Did you get it sorted?*

She hopped in her car, turned it on, and locked the doors. It was cold, so she pushed the seat warmer button immediately. Ronnie was just hurrying around the corner of the store when she stepped on the gas and had no choice but to pass him. He waved, trying to flag her down. She waved back with a big, oblivious smile, and kept going.

She looked at him in the rear-view mirror and scowled.

"Thanks a lot."

Chapter Nineteen

It was time to look for an apartment. Margo didn't want to be living with Mike and Olenka when the baby came; she'd hate to leave the precious doll to go to work. And she wouldn't get a wink of sleep worrying about every little cry at night. It was one thing to come over and relieve the parents for a few hours, and quite another to be right on top of them. New moms and dads were often sleep-deprived and fraught with uncertainty, and that often led to bickering. Margo didn't want to be involved in that.

At least they had the baby's room sorted, to a point. The new crib and dressing table were up, thanks to Gerda, and Margo had bought a little bassinette for the first month or so. She couldn't afford to splurge. Michael went over to Gerda's and took a comfy glider Olenka liked for the baby's room, but Gerda and Margo agreed more could be done.

"They haven't even painted the walls a nice colour." Gerda shook her head. "And she's got an old blanket covering the window. She keeps saying she'd going to get blackout curtains, but has she? I have no idea where she comes from. She's completely uninterested in anything that doesn't have fur or scales or claws. I think she'd be thrilled if she gave birth to a puppy or a chipmunk."

The need to move became urgent in Margo's mind the day Olenka yelled down the stairs, "M! Can I borrow a pair of boots? I have a big hole in mine."

Margo yelled back, "Sure honey," and continued to pour herself a bowl of Rice Krispies. And then she remembered. She tore up the stairs and got to the bedroom just in time to see Olenka removing the vibrator from the laced-up boot.

"Oh god," Margo groaned.

Olenka grinned and handed it over. "No need to be embarrassed. Did you know that female masturbation has been observed in some non-human primate species? Orangutans fashion leaves or twigs for use in genital stimulation. Female chimps sometimes use mangos."

"I think I'd rather be a chimp. But I'm not sure I'll look at mangos the same way ever again."

There was no use in finding another hiding spot. Olenka already knew about it, so Margo just shoved the vibrator in another boot. Mike wasn't interested in her footwear, hopefully. Back downstairs Margo sliced a banana into her bowl of cereal. That got her thinking about mangos. She grabbed a pen and scribbled *batteries* on her grocery list under *broccoli* and *sharp cheddar*.

⸎

On April Fool's Day, besides dodging the still relentless admiration of Ronnie, Margo got a text from Julia while she was at work. *Come for supper...I have a list of apartments for u to look at*

She was in the back room, so she texted back. *Thanks. I have a list too.*

U do?

You said I should start looking, so I've been looking.

Huh

Typical. It sounded like Julia didn't believe her.

Andre wasn't home, which was unusual, but Margo should have known when she looked at her plate. Fish sticks and fries.

"Where's Andre?"

"He's playing squash with a friend. What I wouldn't give to be smashing something against a wall." Julia placed a plate in front of Posy, who licked her lips in anticipation.

"Mommy! I want more ketchup!" Hazel shouted from her seat.

"Say please, please," Margo reminded her.

"Please please can I have more ketchup?"

Once the girls trotted off to use their new markers on a random Amazon box, Julia poured some tea and took out her list. She also had her tablet so her mother could see pictures of the places. Sometimes the internet was handy. Margo had her list of three.

Julia frowned. "You're picky."

"I have to be close to you guys and not spend much money. These were the only choices. Did you know—I sound like Olenka—did you know the average two-bedroom apartment is $1,550 a month? How is that even possible? I think our first apartment was about $120 a month."

"First of all, do you need two bedrooms?"

"I think so. I'd like Eunie to be able to stay over when she's in town."

Julia took a drink and it was too hot, so she waved her hand in front of her mouth before lowering the cup. "Frig. Be careful drinking that. Realistically, how often does she come to town? And she's getting older."

"She's not dead yet, unlike poor Wilf. Besides, I want the girls to sleep over. I think you and Andre might enjoy that. You know, if this is going to be my life, I don't want to be in a tiny cubby hole like a university student."

Julia nodded. "Fair enough."

They went through the options. Too much, too far, not big enough, too fancy, too grungy. Then they got silly. "Okay, this is obviously cat-lady central."

"I'm going to kidnap Stan. Magoo is Mike's cat. The other day I came downstairs and he was draped over Mike's shoulders while he worked."

Julia tapped the next post. "Don't bother with apartments near UNB. University students invade like termites and you'll never get any sleep." She kept scrolling. "And this place is obviously where the mafia hang out. You just got rid of one Tony Soprano; you don't need another."

"Stop it. Dick never killed anyone."

"How on earth would you know? He kept some pretty big secrets." She touched her mom's arm. "No. I take that back. If he was capable of murder, he'd have killed Carole a long time ago."

The next weekend the two of them went to look at three places. Margo didn't point out that every one of them was from her own list, not Julia's.

The first one was the cheapest, and they found out why in a hurry. The building itself was no great shakes, there was no elevator, and the apartment was on the top floor. Never mind getting all the furniture in, Margo was worried about practical matters. "I'd have to lug groceries up the stairs, and in every murder mystery on Netflix, people are killed or raped in stairwells."

Julia looked at her. "You're an odd woman. Every apartment building has a stairwell."

"You tend not to use one if you have access to an elevator."

"Hello? You can be killed or sexually assaulted in an elevator as well."

Margo frowned. "Thanks for reminding me how vulnerable I'll be in an apartment complex."

Julia started down the stairs. "Sorry, but people are killed and assaulted in their own houses, too."

"Can we change the subject?"

The second place was okay, but as soon as they walked into the building it had a funny odour.

"You know how sensitive I am to smell," Margo said. "This would bother me. What is it?"

"Industrial cleaner, cabbage, and burnt rubber?"

"Let's go."

The last apartment didn't look that promising. It was an older building and the wooden balconies were weathered. Margo worried they might be rotten. So much for sitting out on a sunny day—but since they were next to a highway, she doubted she would anyway.

The apartment was on the first floor, which bothered Julia.

"Why?"

"Because some yahoo stumbling home drunk could jump on your balcony and break in no problem."

Margo was getting annoyed. "What do you want me to do, Julia? Burrow underground like a prairie dog?"

"You know what? Olenka is rubbing off on all of us. Posy told me this morning that baby langurs are born orange."

"What has that got to do with anything? Let's find the super."

They were shown into the apartment and it was a typical boring, completely ordinary white space...but it was clean. Really clean. And that made all the difference. It was at the very top of Margo's budget, but it was also smack dab in the middle of where she wanted to be: work was ten minutes away in one direction, and both kids were ten minutes in the other.

She clasped her hands together. "Not too hot, not too cold, just right. I'll take it."

Margo couldn't believe she said those words. Couldn't believe she'd be living on her own. She'd never lived on her own. It was scary, but she didn't want Julia to know that and worry about her. Of everyone she loved, Julia's opinion mattered the most. Her daughter was often exasperated with her, as though Margo were a naughty child, but deep down Margo knew that Julia loved her fiercely and was always ready to do battle for her. Who else would've gone into that lion's den to take back those silver bells? Mike was a sweetheart, but he was a follower, not a leader. Olenka had that sewn up.

Julia changed her tune on the first-floor business when she discovered what a breeze it was to move her mother in. No having to book an elevator to take furniture up. They went in the front door, turned left, and halfway down the hall on the left was her mom's new home. Apartment twelve.

Margo tried not to be insulted about how enthusiastic Mike was about getting her settled in her own space. She mentioned it to Monty as he passed her with a box of dishes.

"He is a little Energizer Bunny, isn't he?" He grinned.

The girls were with them for the move. They were very excited to be helping and they wanted to know where their beds would be.

"Don't you worry, my little blueberries. When Gogo gets the money to buy two twin beds, this will be your room! Won't what be fun?"

"I'm not a blueberry," Posy reminded her. "I'm a strawberry."

When everything was brought in, Mike hurried off to be with Olenka. Margo gave him a huge hug before he left. "I can never thank you enough, sweetheart. You two put up with me and I couldn't have managed without you."

"No problem. But ahh...I was thinking. You know, with you working all day, Magoo might get lonely. I'm home, obviously, and

Olenka will be on maternity leave, so there will be a lot going on... maybe it would be better if Magoo stayed with us?"

"I think you're right. He'd be much happier with you."

When Mike left, they looked around. No one said anything, but they were all thinking the same thing. Finally, it was Byron who voiced it. "This place looks like Mike's. What were you thinking, Margo? You should have taken more furniture with you."

"I realize that now, but at the time I wasn't interested, so there's no point fretting about it."

Byron kept nodding. "You know what, Monty? That couch downstairs, the one we never use? We should bring that over. And we also have that coffee table stuck in the corner and two bookshelves we can spare. That would fill this room up nicely."

"True."

"Oh, thank you, guys. That's brilliant, as Monty always says."

"Wait!" Julia jumped in. "I have two lamps downstairs I don't need."

Margo frowned. "Oh, no. I hate those."

"My mother hated them too. That's why she gave them to us," Andre said.

"Don't say hate," Hazel reminded them.

While they still had the U-Haul, the fellas went back to Monty's and picked up the couch, coffee table, and bookshelves. Byron also grabbed a canvas that was stacked amongst others against the wall in the corner. "This one always reminded me of Margo."

"Is that why it's in a dark corner, hidden away?" Andre grinned.

He turned it around. It was a watercolour of a sheep leaning against a barn door, its face partially hidden, unsure if it should go outside or not. The whole thing was awash with golden light and almost the exact shade of Margo's hair.

"Believe it or not, it's called *Indecision*."

They went back with the items and the space looked much better. Margo loved the painting. "I think I'll put this in my bedroom."

She hugged them goodbye and thanked them for being so kind. "Hopefully this is the last move I make for the foreseeable future."

"It better be." Byron waved.

Just before Margo closed the door, Monty appeared again and shoved some rolled-up bills in her hand. "This is from me. Consider it a housewarming gift. Go and buy the girls their beds."

She kissed his cheek. "Thank you, Granddad. You're the best."

The first night was unsettling. Margo wasn't used to the building's noises, and hearing footsteps above her head took some getting used to, along with the muted sounds of someone's television. Which reminded her. She'd have to get one. And then she thought maybe not. Who needed the aggravation? She detested remotes. Why bother when she could watch Netflix and CBC Gem on her tablet in bed? And she could get books and audiobooks at the library.

It was only when it got dark that Margo realized she had no curtains. There she was, exposed to the neighbourhood thanks to her living room's sliding doors. And it turned out there was a bus stop right in front of her. Hell's bells. She had to get a stick for this door so an axe murderer couldn't open it if he jumped up on her balcony, which was only about three feet off the ground. Great if there happened to be a fire, but she'd be dead with an axe in her skull.

She kept the kitchen light off, and since there was no overhead light in the living room, which was ridiculous, the place looked dark. She'd live in the bedroom and bathroom until she could run to the store tomorrow on her lunch hour and buy a broom handle for the door and heavy curtains and fixtures for the window. She could pick up Julia's ugly lamps, too, which she'd need in a hurry once the curtains were up.

Margo really didn't sleep that night. The box with the bedsheets was somewhere, but darned if she could find it. She wrapped herself up in her duvet. She made lists in her head and finally got up and took a pen from her purse but couldn't find any paper, so she wrote things down on a paper towel.

She had to remember to take the keys to the apartment and figure out if the key went up or down in the lock. Then there was the lock for the outer doors and she got them confused. Management assigned her a parking space and she hoped it would be close to the back door, but it wasn't. She was in the farthest row away by the huge green recycling and garbage bins, near the highway. Hmm. A perfect place for an axe murderer to lurk.

Julia had her spooked. Margo wanted to call her, but she didn't want to linger at the back of this parking lot, and she was going to be late for work if she didn't get going. Since figuring out how to use the phone in the car was never her strong suit, the call would have to wait.

Somewhere some young thing was chatting away on their car phone and using their GPS with no problem and clicking remotes willy nilly. She was not that person.

The morning was slow. Margo would much rather a busy lineup than a clock to watch. That's when she noticed her sore legs and stiff neck. She was rubbing her neck when Ronnie said in her ear, "Would you like me to do that?"

She jumped. He'd snuck up on her from behind. The man was relentless. "No! No. Thanks anyway. I'm fine."

"Must be all that looking down at the cash register. Too bad you didn't take me up on my offer to go back to cosmetics, but that door has shut, I'm afraid. Tit for tat and all that."

And he sidled away. Margo stuck her tongue out at him and a kid nearby started to laugh.

On her lunch hour, Margo waited outside the store for Julia to pick her up. She sniffed the April air. She'd been so busy she hadn't been outside in ages just to go for a walk. It was that in-between stage where you never knew what jacket to throw on and it was always the wrong one. Today it was chilly out, but she knew the minute she got in the car her coat would be too hot. It was probably too warm for the store, too, but she was on a curtain mission.

Julia pulled up in her SUV and Margo hopped in. Julia suggested HomeSense, but Margo wanted to be frugal so she thought Walmart instead.

"Mother, I am not going to rummage through packages with folded-up curtains. I barely know how long an inch is, let alone a centimetre. I need to see it, and they have them hanging at HomeSense."

"But they'll cost—"

"I'll buy the bloody curtains."

Margo had forgotten to measure the length and width of the sliding doors, so Julia had to take a wild guess. She bought four panels instead of two to keep them full and covered. They had to buy a rod and hardware and needed help but there wasn't anyone around.

Julia was steamed. "Most people run into a store on their lunch hour. It would make sense to have extra staff around between the hours of eleven and one. Don't you think?"

Margo nodded. "You should rule the world, Julia."

"I know."

Julia finally ran down an employee and practically took them hostage, but she got the necessary equipment and bundled the parcels and her mother in the car and drove rather quickly back to Shoppers. Margo smiled and turned to her. "Thank—"

"Get out. I have a meeting."

The afternoon went by at a crawl. Margo wanted to get back to her new home. That had a nice ring to it. What an amazing feeling to know she had a place to hide from the world, or invite it in, without worrying if that was okay with other people.

Five minutes before her shift was over, who walked in but Velma. She didn't see Margo and quickly disappeared down one of the aisles. *Please let her go to the back cash, or use the self-checkouts.* Margo kept her eye on the clock. She just didn't want to deal with Dick's daughter right now. And one of the reasons was that she looked like her dad.

Velma emerged, inevitably, from another aisle and came straight to Margo's cash register with contact lens solution, Tylenol, and two bags of Doritos. She looked up and saw Margo, and her face immediately turned stony as she put her items on the counter.

Margo rang them through. "Hello. How are you, Velma?"

"Not great, now that I've seen you."

Margo gave her the total and asked for her PC Optimum Card. Velma held it up and Margo scanned it. Then Velma held her debit card over the card reader and paid. Margo gave Velma the receipt. "I'm glad you're wearing your dad's jacket. That would make him happy."

Velma pointed at her. "You and that bitch daughter of yours are real pieces of work, you know that? Threatening my mother with the police. Who stoops that low? You better watch your back."

Velma stalked off.

What?

Margo's replacement showed up and Margo hurried into the lunch room to get her stuff. She tried not to be worried, but Velma was intimidating. Ronnie waved to get her attention, but Margo ignored him. She wanted to get home.

She rushed to her car and headed out. Ten minutes and she'd be home. Very convenient. She waited for a break in traffic before leaving the parking lot and glanced in the rear-view mirror. Velma was behind her. She recognized the car. It was hard to miss a large woman with a buzz cut.

No need to panic. She'd just left the store at the same time. Margo turned left onto the street and so did Velma. She drove straight for two kilometres and then turned right. So did Velma.

Five minutes later, a left. She was still there.

Oh my god. Velma was following her home! She was going to beat her up by those recycling bins. Margo didn't know what to do. Should she drive home or go the other way? She didn't know how to use the damn phone in the car. Margo fumbled in her purse for her cellphone but had to wait until she came to a traffic light to call Mike.

"What's up?"

"Mike! Velma is following me home! What should I do?"

"Why is she following you home?"

"She wants to kill me."

"What?"

"Mike! Believe me. She's right behind me and has been ever since I left work. She told me to watch my back before she left. I'm afraid of her."

"I hope you're not using your cellphone to call me. It's illegal."

"I'm not," she lied.

"How far from home are you?"

"Two minutes, but she'll beat me up by the recycling bins. My parking space is at the far end by the highway."

"Pull up to the back door of the apartment and go straight in. Worry about the car later. I'll stay on the phone with you. I'm sure it's nothing, but it's okay, I'm here."

"Actually, you're not here, but I appreciate it."

"Is she still tailing you?"

"YES. I'm pulling into the parking lot now and she's still on me! Oh no. There's a moving truck at the back door. What should I do?"

"Mom, stop panicking. Park behind it."

"Oh my god! She's pulling up to my passenger side window, she's...driving right by. She didn't even look at me...she's pulling into a parking space...she's getting out and she's opening the back door with a key...What's going on? How did she get a key to my apartment?"

"She lives there, Mom."

Chapter Twenty

When Julia came over that evening with the ugly lamps, she found Mike up on a kitchen chair screwing in hardware above the sliding doors for the curtain rod.

Her mother looked flustered. Lordy, now what?

"You're not going to believe it," her mom said.

"Let me guess, the curtains are too short. Why didn't you measure them?"

Mike turned around with a screw in his mouth. "No, you'll really never guess."

"So tell me. I haven't got all night. I have to go home and help Posy with a science experiment. Can you believe it? Grade One. At least we're just shaking whipping cream in a mason jar with a marble added in the hopes of making butter."

Mike turned back and screwed the screw in. "Guess who lives in this building?"

"Who?"

"Velma!" her mother shouted.

Julia closed her eyes, flopped her neck back, and sighed. "It's like we've been cursed with this infuriating and absurd family. Who else has an April, May, and June in their inner circle? And just think, we never would have run into these people if it hadn't been for you, Mother, hooking up with Icky Dicky Sterling."

"I'm changing my last name," Margo vowed.

"It'll cost you a fortune," Julia told her.

"Then I'm keeping my last name, but I'm never saying it."

"I wonder where she is in this building. Wait, I'll go look."

Julia ran out of the apartment and down the hall to the front where a list of surnames was featured above the intercom. She came back with good news.

"She's on the top floor. Hopefully she won't see your name anytime soon."

"I'm changing my last name," Margo vowed.

Mike was finished with the rod and they put the curtains on it. They were ten inches too short.

Julia sighed again. "That looks ridiculous."

Mike shook his head. "It's not a big deal. When the curtains are open you don't even notice it."

"Nothing is a big deal to you. Seeing as how she bought them to keep them closed so people can't peek in, they are ridiculous."

Michael got on his knees, bum in the air, and held his head a few inches off the floor. "Unless some bozo gets in this position on the cold wet slab of concrete out there, they aren't going to see much, are they?"

"Look guys, don't worry about it. I'll take them to Eunie's one weekend and get her to sew a border on them. She's got a whole closet of fabric remnants."

Julia said, "And expose your place for the weekend?"

"I'll put up a sheet, like Mike."

"Hey! I took that down a couple of months after I moved in."

With great dramatic effect, Julia plunked down on the chaise and held her arm over her forehead. "Please, Mother dear, do not leave this place. I don't care if Carole moves into the apartment next door."

Now Margo sat on Byron's sofa. "Did you say something about the police to Carole when you went back to get my stuff? Velma gave me an earful at the store today and told me to watch my back. I thought she was following me home to beat me up by the recycling bins."

Mike shook his head. "You're fixated on those bins."

"Watch your back?" Julia looked at Mike. "That's a threat. You need to be writing this down. All I said was that we could charge her with stealing, since that's what she did."

"Well, you shouldn't provoke a snake with a stick," Margo said. "I'm sure Olenka told me that once. Or maybe it was shake a stick."

Julia raised her head off the chaise. "Are you glad you got your stuff back? How else was it going to happen? Were *you* going to do something about it?"

"God, no. That's why I gave birth to you."

Now Margo was on high alert whenever she left her apartment, and the first thing she did before going out the back door was look for Velma's car. If it wasn't there, she walked to her parking spot. If it was, she kept her head down and hurried. Annoying, but necessary.

And then a week later the fire alarm went off. Wonderful. She'd just moved in and now the place was going to burn to the ground. She'd never been in a building where the fire alarm had gone off. And she wasn't exactly sure what she should do. She peeked out her door with the chain on but didn't see any immediate movement from anyone. But after a few minutes she did hear some doors slam shut, so she put on her coat. Maybe she could step out on her own balcony, but a fire truck arrived in front of the building, and she might be in their way.

She joined a few other people and went out the back door, mingling with the people already out there. There were dogs on leashes, cats in carriers. She saw one that looked like Stan and she missed him. Margo asked the lady next to her, "Does this happen often?"

"Not too often, but it's better safe than sorry. Some people complain, but some people complain about everything, don't they?"

And then she heard Velma giving the super an earful at the inconvenience of having to stand outside in the cold when there was obviously no fire. The lady next to her leaned over. "See what I mean?"

Margo nodded and held up her collar to walk quickly to her car, mindful of marauders. She stayed out of the light to avoid being seen and then realized she was a sitting duck by the bins, so she went back to the building but stayed at least twenty feet away from Velma, and every time Velma looked around impatiently, Margo turned away from her.

They got the all-clear and Velma was the first one to go back inside. That was another great thing about the first floor. Margo didn't have to wait for the elevator to get home, and she didn't have to join the more limber of the crowd on the stairwell.

⁓

Margo would go over to Mike and Olenka's now and then to cook a meal. Olenka was about two weeks from her due date, May 3. She was still working, and drove herself. Mike told his mom Olenka didn't seem to enjoy takeout anymore. Hallelujah. One night Margo and Gerda arrived at the same time. Gerda had her meal already made, so the four of them sat down to cepelinai, big potato dumplings with minced meat inside. Mike was in heaven.

Olenka had that nine-months-pregnant look about her. Weary, resigned, fed up. She was small-boned and carried this baby all out in front. If she walked away from you, you wouldn't know she was pregnant, other than her lumbering gait.

She had her elbow on the table to prop her head up as she picked at her food.

Her mother reached over and tucked Olenka's hair behind her ear. "You're near the finish line. Won't be long now."

"All I want to do is sleep on my stomach. And tie my own shoes. I never realized all I own are Keds. Who knew this baby was going to be so big? Thanks a lot, Mike."

He answered with a mouth full of dumpling. "Hey! I'm not a sasquatch. I can't help it if I'm tall like my dad."

"The doctor said the baby could be up to nine pounds."

"Nine?" Gerda looked concerned. "You were only six."

Margo put up her hand. "I'm to blame, I guess. My kids were eight and nine."

Now Gerda looked shocked. "You?! How is that even possible?"

"I had C-sections."

"Did you know that when a three-hundred-pound panda gives birth, their baby only weighs three and a half ounces? How come I couldn't sign up for that?"

"Don't worry, honey. The doctors will know what to do."

"I don't think I'm going to go to the hospital..."

Gerda looked like she might faint. "What are you talking about? Don't tell me you're planning a home birth?! Olenka, I really can't take much more. You're not married, you tell me don't want this baby baptized—"

Margo looked at Mike. "You don't?"

He shrugged.

"What am I supposed to tell Father Andrius? And now you want to give birth here?" Gerda continued.

"In a pool, if possible."

Margo looked at Mike. He shrugged again.

"Have you lost your mind?!" Gerda shrieked. "A tub of water? The child will drown!"

Olenka shifted her bulk in the chair. "Mom, lots of creatures are born in water. Baby sea otters are so fluffy they can't drown."

Gerda threw her fork and knife on the plate. "That's great if you're having a sea otter, but as far as I know this baby is human."

"Baby orcas—"

Gerda turned to Mike, shrieking, "And you are okay with this? You really want your baby to be born in water?"

"It's whatever Olenka wants."

"I have to agree with Gerda on this," Margo ventured. "It's wonderful that you want to support your wife, but this is your baby too, Michael. You do have some say." She turned to Olenka. "No offence."

"None taken."

Michael stopped eating. "I do know one thing. I don't want you giving the mother of my child any stress. And she is the mother, in case you've forgotten. She's the one dealing with this pregnancy, not you two."

The grandmothers looked at each other. Gerda was still too distraught to speak, so Margo asked, "Have you made plans for this, honey? Do you have a doula or does the doctor know your wishes? Have you made arrangements with a midwife or a nurse? There's usually quite a waitlist. I'm sure there are a lot of things to be taken care of before you make this a reality."

Olenka's face became uncertain. "Not really. I only thought about it a couple of days ago. I mean, mammals give birth hundreds of different ways all by themselves, without checking in with a higher authority. Giraffes don't go to the hospital. Their calves fall six feet to the ground when they're born. That breaks the umbilical cord and gives them the incentive to take a breath."

Gerda clasped her hands together in prayer. "If you go to the hospital to have this baby, I will personally lift you six feet off the bed and the baby can fall into the doctor's arms. I promise."

Olenka threw her arms up. "Fine! I'm sorry I even mentioned it. It was just an idea. You don't have to have a cow! But if you did, the calf's front feet would come first." She sat back and gave a great sigh before patting her belly. "You hear that, kit? Your grandmothers are as tenacious as border collies." She struggled out of her chair. "I need a banana. Did you know that newborn pigs recognize their mother's voice?" Olenka disappeared into the kitchen.

Gerda reached out and grabbed Margo's hand. "I think we dodged a bullet." She got up from the table and hurried after her daughter.

Mike resumed eating his dumpling before he glanced at his mother. "Olenka tells me that long ago the closer women lived to their mothers, the greater the chances their own kids survived. I'm starting to understand why."

❧

The girls' beds were delivered and Margo did spend some money on pretty new sheets, pillows, and two animal print comforters. She put the beds together in the middle of the room thinking they'd get a kick out of that. She would pick away at the room and add a few things as she could afford it.

Margo wasn't sure who was more excited, the kids or their parents. Julia said they would go out to a nice restaurant, bring home some wine, and practice on their g-force mattress. They kissed the girls and waved as they left. They held each other's hands walking down the hallway. Margo always loved that about Julia and Andre. Monty had never held her hand, but he did tuck her arm through his as he walked beside her. Dick always walked ahead of her and told her to hurry up.

She had gone to the library and taken out a whole stack of books to read to them. She'd also gone over to their house when Julia had the girls at gym class. Andre helped her go through their old toys that were packed away. Out of sight, out of mind. They would become brand new again at Gogo's place. She had strawberry ice cream in the freezer, but that was it. No store-bought cookies, and they were having salmon and rice and veggies for dinner.

They ate on the floor, another thrill, and after dinner they made a fort with blankets over the kitchen chairs. Margo bought bubble bath and they had a fine time splashing each other and were so surprised when their grandmother handed them a few of their old bath toys. Hazel held up a battered yellow duck. "When I was a baby, I had this."

Warm and soft in their pyjamas, they snuggled into their beds, giggling because they were so close to each other. Margo sat on the edge and read them many books. Hazel fell asleep, and Posy looked tired, but she kept her eyes open.

Margo kissed her. "I'm going to say goodnight, sweetheart. I'll leave the door open and I've plugged in a nightlight. I'm just in the next room, okay? If you need me, you call me."

"Okay."

Margo was busy cleaning up the living room and kitchen when she heard thunder outside. She opened the curtains and sure enough, a flash of lightning filled the sky. Did she have a flashlight in case the power went out? Luckily, she found one in the junk drawer she'd created as soon as she moved in. That was always the first thing that needed doing. She turned around and there was Posy standing in her pyjamas.

"Oh dear, can't sleep?"

Posy shook her head. "What's that noise?

"It's raining out, and I think there's a little thunder and lightning."

"I'm scared. I want Daddy."

"You come with me, sweetheart." Margo sat on the couch and slapped her knees to let Posy know she could sit on her. Posy crawled up and Margo wrapped them both in a throw. "There now. We'll sit together and listen. When I was a little girl, I woke up one night during a thunderstorm and my parents were out too, and I was afraid, so my grandfather let me sit in his lap in a rocking chair and we watched television until the signal went off and 'O Canada' came on. Back in those days, the television shut down and said goodnight in a civilized manner."

"The television said goodnight?"

"Let's just say it bid us adieu whether we liked it or not."

Posy scratched her nose. "That wasn't very nice."

"I didn't think so either, but now I wish it did. People need to rest, just like animals."

Posy yawned. "Lenka says koala bears sleep for twenty-two hours a day."

"Amazing."

"Lenka's having a baby."

"I know! Isn't that exciting?"

"Mommy says she'll probably have it in the woods, like a damn moose."

Chapter
Twenty-One

Margo was dealing with Oscar the Grouch disguised as a sweet little old lady. She banged her finger on the counter, her wedding rings wrapped up with dirty white adhesive tape so they wouldn't spin like a roulette wheel around her shrunken flesh. They certainly weren't going to come off. Her knuckles were the size of cherries. No wonder she was grouchy.

"I gave you a twenty-dollar bill."

"I'm sorry, you actually gave me a ten. See, it's right here on top of the drawer." Margo picked it up and showed it to her.

"That's not mine. I gave you a twenty! Are you calling me a liar?" The old lady looked around and spoke to the lineup of people behind her. "She's calling me a liar!"

Everyone in the lineup just wanted to get out of the store. Including Harman. She waved at Margo and Margo gave her a big smile. She hadn't noticed her. "Why don't I call the manager and you can speak with him?"

Oscar kept banging on the counter with that witch's finger of hers. "I'm speaking to you, young woman."

Margo picked up the intercom. "Manager to the front cash, please. Manager to the front cash."

Ronnie took his time coming. The woman continued with her tirade and some people went to the self-checkout machines. One man just dropped his stuff in the nearest bin and gave Margo a filthy look as he left, as if she were the one holding up the works.

Eventually Ronnie showed up and asked the lady to move aside so he could speak with her. The next customer came through and rolled her eyes at Margo, and then it was Harman's turn. Harman put her purchases on the counter and patted Margo's hand. "How are you, my dear? It's been so long."

"I've missed you!"

"I've got an idea. Are you doing anything for supper? Why don't you pop by our house around six? Are you off then?"

"Yes! That would be wonderful. Thank you, can I bring anything?' She nodded at the display case. "Gum, breath mints? Or what about Lotto tickets?"

"Just yourself."

Harman left and the drama continued. The old woman was going to have a coronary, and by the looks of it, Ronnie was too. The people in the lineup should have been eating popcorn, they were so mesmerized by the show. Finally, Ronnie turned around and approached Margo. "You were mistaken. This lady gave you a twenty. Give her the proper change."

No please or thank you? She handed the old grouch an extra ten. Surely that would shut her up.

"I want an apology!" She looked straight at Margo, and Ronnie had the nerve to bolt up the aisle and disappear into the back, which annoyed Margo to no end. What a coward. The four people in the lineup were still on high alert.

Margo was convinced this was a stunt the old dear pulled everywhere. She made eye contact with her. "I'm sorry you've had a bad experience. I hope this doesn't prevent you from coming back to our store."

"I'm never setting foot in this place again." And out she went with the ten-dollar bill in her hand.

The next customer approached her. "Clever. Good for you."

Finally, the day was over. She waved to Honey as she hurried out the back door. The first place she wanted to go was home so she could freshen up. Working with the public and money all day made her feel grimy, but she did stop at the liquor store to buy a bottle of wine. Something cheap and cheerful. She was in such a rush to be on time for supper, she zoomed into the back parking lot of her building and didn't notice Velma and Carole getting out of Velma's car. They almost physically crashed into each other at the curb by the back door.

Carole couldn't believe her eyes. "As I live and breathe, the man-eater. Are you stalking us?"

"Of course not."

Velma took a step towards Margo. "Why are you here, then? What else do you people want from us?"

Margo instinctively shrank back, her hands gripped around her purse strap. "Nothing."

"Ah, sweet Jesus, Velma! She lives here!" Carole closed her eyes, flopped her neck back, and sighed. "It's like we've been cursed. What are the chances?" Then she opened her eyes again and glared at Margo. "Don't you go near my daughter. You hear me?"

Margo looked up at Velma's imposing athletic bulk. "I wouldn't dare. She could squash me like a bug."

"Don't tempt me!" Velma practically spit. "Let's go, Mom."

"Man-eater!"

The two of them walked towards the door. This was almost over—and then Margo found her feet moving towards them. "Just a minute."

They turned around.

Margo didn't know what she was going to say until she said it. It came rushing out of its own accord. "I did not go to bed with your husband while you were married, Carole. We had three dates. When I found out he had a wife, that was the end of it. He lied to me. He lied all the time. That's why I have to live here."

Velma took offense to that. "What's wrong with this place? Not good enough for you? You and that chic, snotty daughter of yours think you're so special. It makes me sick."

"That's all I wanted to say."

Carole dismissed her with a wave of her hand. "Like I'm going to believe you. You ruined my life, lady, and someday you'll get yours. I hope I'm around to see it."

They went through the glass doors and disappeared. Margo took a deep breath and exhaled. She felt shaky, but the fact that they knew she was here would put an end to her skulking through the parking lot every morning.

She was ten minutes late driving up her old street. It was a very odd feeling. As she parked in Harman's driveway and looked over at the house, all she could think of was that terrible night. The good times they had had were so far away she couldn't reach them. That night wiped away everything.

But she was happy to be at this door. Harman opened it and the memories of their friendship spilled out. "I'm sorry I'm late."

Harman gave her a quick hug. "Hardly. But I do have an unexpected guest. I swear this wasn't planned." She rushed her into the dining room where her husband, Amir, was sitting at the table with another man. They both stood up, and Amir gave her a quick kiss on the cheek. "So nice to see you again, Margo. We've missed you."

"Thank you. Me too."

Harman nodded to the other guest. "Margo, this is my cousin Hari. He surprised us by showing up out of the blue, as usual."

"Hey. That's what annoying cousins do. Nice to meet you, Margo."

He seemed perfectly fine, but this suddenly felt like a dinner party, and as Hari asked her questions about everything under the sun over delicious butter chicken, she started to close down.

"I do know what it's like to live alone," he said. "I'm divorced now and it's quite an adjustment. Especially dating. It's hard to meet someone nice. Do you find that?"

"No."

Hari held out his hand towards her and gave his head a little toss. "Of course not. A beautiful woman like you. They must be falling all over you."

"They can fall all day, but I'm not picking them up."

Harman leaned over her plate. "Margo is not interested in dating you, Hari."

Margo gave him a little smile and saw Harman throw Amir a look, whereupon he quickly stood up. "Let's take our coffee and dessert in the den, Hari, and let these ladies get caught up. They haven't seen each other in a while."

Problem solved. Harman brought out their coffee and a plate of chocolate digestives. "I was going to make gulab jamun, but Hari arrived and that ended that."

"This is perfect." Margo took a sip of coffee and picked up a cookie. "I need this. What a day." And she told Harman about her run-in with the Sterlings.

"I can't believe Velma lives in your building. What are the odds? But you stood up to them, Margo. You do realize that?"

"I did?"

Harman took a cookie and dunked it. "That's more than you would have done a year ago."

"I've never been hated like that. I needed her to know I wasn't his mistress."

Harman finished her mouthful then said, "I'm glad you did tell her, but now leave it alone. You will never change her mind. And what she thinks of you is none of your business."

"I hate it when they say rude things about Julia."

"Understandable, but do not engage. They will eventually hit a brick wall if you don't respond."

Margo laughed. "Like an olm."

"What are you talking about? What's an olm?"

"A cave salamander. Olenka told me they can stay still for seven years, boring their enemy to death, I imagine."

"Sounds like my boss."

Margo looked out the window at her old house. There were lights on. "Obviously someone bought the house?"

"Yes. An older couple. I've waved to them a few times but get no response. Who knows what's going on in their lives? I try not to judge."

"You must be the only person in the world who doesn't. It's become a worldwide sport. I worry about Posy and Hazel growing up in this atmosphere."

"They are protected by their extended family's love and kindness. That will counterbalance the unpleasant things in life, hopefully. Don't think too far ahead. You'll miss today."

"I think I better start paying you for these therapy sessions."

"Great. Leave your two hundred dollars by the door."

They agreed to be in touch more often. Harman stood on the back porch as Margo walked to her car.

"Promise me you'll let me know when the baby arrives, whether it's a squirrel or skunk."

"They're all skunks until they're potty trained." Margo blew her old neighbour a kiss and got in her car. She looked over at the house again. And felt nothing. She didn't belong there.

So she drove home.

⌒∾⌒

A few days later Margo was playing the girls' favourite game. Tonight, they were ordering ice cream, what Hazel called hangerbers, chocolate bars, and pizza. Margo was the store owner this time, as Mr. Toucan. All the stuffies took turns.

"How much do you want?" Mr. Toucan asked.

Both girls shouted back. "Five hundred dollars and a week!"

Margo shook Mr. Toucan in the air. "WHAT?! How am I going to cook all that? Oh well, I better get started." She hummed and bounced Mr. Toucan along the toy box at the end of Posy's bed, suggesting he was a very busy cook.

Julia came in the bedroom. Margo was surprised. "Bedtime already?"

"No." She frowned. "Mike just texted me. He wants you to call him. Wouldn't tell me why."

"Oh gosh...maybe it's about the baby. But she's not due yet."

"Well, she's pretty close. Not every baby is nine days late, like Miss Posy."

Mr. Toucan quickly served the girls' feast and then lay down to take a nap after all that cooking. "I'll be right back, girls," said Margo. "I have to phone Booboo."

She went downstairs and called her son. "Hi, honey."

"Mom, could you come over?"

"Come over? Of course. Is it the baby? Please say it's not the baby."

"No. But Olenka and her mother had a big fight and I got mad at Gerda and she just stormed out of the house. Now Olenka thinks I'm the big bad wolf and I'm not sure what to do."

"I'll be right there." Margo put the cell in her purse and yelled up the stairs. "I have to go, Julia."

Julia came running down. "Is it the baby?"

Andre showed up from downstairs. "Not staying to give the girls a bath? I love it when you do that."

Margo put her coat on. "Sorry, Mike just called. I have to go. No, it's not the baby, but its baby related. Olenka and her mom had a big fight, and Mike's not sure what to do."

"Hormones are nasty little buggers," Julia said.

In no time Margo was stepping from one household into another. Magoo came to the door looking concerned. Margo reached down and stroked his head. "Don't worry. It will all blow over."

And then she heard Mike and Olenka arguing upstairs, so she took her coat off and joined the mix, knocking on the bedroom door. "Only me."

Olenka was on the bed with a beet-red face from crying. She had about six pillows around her as protection from something. "You called your mother?" she yelled.

"Yes!" Michael yelled back. "To try and get you to calm down. If you don't stop this, Olenka, the baby will fly out of the womb just to get away from you." He turned to his mom. "I can't deal with this. You take over." And his footsteps rushed down the stairs.

Margo looked at the soon-to-be mom. She was worn out and defeated. "I'll be right back." She ran down the stairs too.

Mike had just sat down in front of his computer. He turned around. "What are you doing?"

"I'm making some tea." Margo went into the kitchen and plugged the kettle in. Then she went back to his chair and said quietly, "Give me the Coles Notes version."

Mike crossed his arms. "They've been having the same damn discussion for the last three months and finally Olenka had enough. Gerda has it in her head that since we aren't married, which is bad enough in the eyes of God, that if we don't baptize the baby, we're all going to hell or something. She doesn't understand why Olenka won't do this for her, and tonight she said that Olenka's father would be very disappointed in her. Olenka blew up. I told Gerda to get out of our house. So she stormed off and now Olenka thinks her mother hates her and she hates me for ruining everything."

"All pregnant women hate everybody at this stage of the game. You can't win. But you did the right thing by taking Olenka's side. She just can't see it yet. Can I fix her something to eat?"

"Bring her a banana."

Margo went back to the kitchen, put a banana in her pocket, and poured a cup of chamomile tea. She took it upstairs and put them on the bedside table. "Just one more thing." She went to the bathroom, grabbed a face cloth, held it under cold water, then wrung it out and brought it over to the bed. "Now lean back and put this over your eyes, then press it against your neck. You'll feel better."

Olenka was now a dejected pussycat. She had no energy to be anything else. She sipped the tea and ate the banana at least. "I suppose Michael told you what happened. He had no right throwing my mother out of the house."

"You of all people should know that what Michael did was protect his den. That's his job. You were in trouble, and he removed the threat, that's all. He doesn't hate your mom, you don't hate your mom, and your mom doesn't hate you two. Everyone's nerves are frayed."

"Why is she insisting on this? She knows Mike and I don't go to church, and it doesn't have any meaning for us."

Margo looked out at the street light just outside the window. A robin was perched on it. She took her time. She was nervous and wasn't sure what to say. What if she got it wrong? She finally turned back to Olenka.

"This is your mother's first grandchild. In a grandmother's mind, it's her baby too. We want to protect it. For a woman of faith like your mom, the baby being baptized is the ultimate protection. And she believes your father is with God, and she wants her family to be together when the time comes. Does it really matter if she has this small ceremony? The baby doesn't know what's going on. And the only thing that *is* going on is your mother loving your baby the way she loves you."

Olenka nodded slightly but didn't say anything. She put her head back on the many pillows and closed her eyes.

"You get some rest, sweetheart. I'll be downstairs with papa bear."

"Grizzly bears are absentee dads and will sometimes kill and eat cubs, even their own."

"Forget I said anything."

"Mike will be a penguin or a water bug. They're the best dads." Olenka pulled up her quilt and settled in.

Margo went downstairs and sat in Mike's lounger. "You're forgiven."

He looked at her in amazement. "How did you manage that?"

"Using an animal analogy. They're very handy. I'm going to make some tea for myself. Want some?"

"No, I've got a beer."

Once Margo had another cup of chamomile tea in her hand, she went back in and settled into Mike's new couch. When she'd taken her furniture away, he'd realized how empty the room was and bitten the bullet. He and Olenka went out and picked a couch and a love seat. When Julia saw it, she'd shaken her head and whispered to her mother, "How is it possible to buy new furniture that looks old, drab, and slouchy, like big roundish lumps of olive-green marshmallows?"

"Take a seat," Margo had told her at the time.

Julia sat. "Whoa. You'll never get out of this but...damn, it's way more comfortable than mine."

Now Mike sat in his old lounger with Magoo in his lap and mother and son talked for a long time, something they never got to do enough.

"You're going to be a great dad, Michael."

He gave her a grin. "Ya think?"

"An amazing water bug."

And because Margo was used to living there, and Mike was comfortable having her there, they both fell asleep where they sat.

Chapter
Twenty-Two

It was the middle of the night when they heard "Mike!" from the top of the stairs. Poor Magoo was unceremoniously dumped on the floor as Mike took off and Margo had no idea where she was. When she clued in, she had a devil of a time getting up.

When they got to her, Olenka was standing but hunched over. Mike tried to hold her but she put her hand out. "Don't touch me. Oooooh."

"Is it happening? Where's the hospital bag? I'll get the car."

Margo knew he was panicking. "Just a minute Michael! Calm down. First babies take a long time. It's not like in the movies. Her water hasn't even broken yet."

If it was possible for a woman in labour to look sheepish, Olenka did. "That happened a couple of hours ago. Water can break and you still have about twenty-four hours before the baby is born. I didn't want to wake you."

Margo tempered her words. "There's no rush if you aren't having contractions, but it seems you are. You should have let us know."

"I'm sorry. They just started with a vengeance."

"Did your water break on the new mattress?" Mike asked.

Both women looked at him.

"Sorry! Just wondered. It's new."

"No, as it happens, on the bathroom floor. I tried to clean it up with a towel." She leaned over again and held her lower back. "Oooooooh. I thought you were supposed to feel contractions in your belly. This is like I have the world's worst backache."

"Okay." Margo wanted to throw up. Instead, she said, "Let's be on the safe side and get you to the hospital. You might be walking the halls for hours, but you need to be there. Mike, call the doctor or whatever you're supposed to do and find that bag. You should have left it by the front door. I'm sure they told you that at your Lamaze classes."

"We didn't take Lamaze classes."

Margo looked at Olenka. "If you tell me that zebras don't take Lamaze classes, so help me—"

"Well, they don't."

"Mike, stop standing there and start the car. Olenka, I'll help you get dressed."

That didn't happen. The poor girl was in a bad way. She should've been having periods of relief, but it didn't sound like she was, so Margo gingerly put on her bathrobe and slippers and wrapped a blanket around Olenka, and lead her to the stairs. "Michael!"

He came running in from outside. "The car's on. I can't find the bag."

"Forget the damn bag. Let's get her in the car."

It took them fifteen minutes to do that with all the stairs and Olenka stopping to groan. It didn't help that it was drizzly out and she had to stop again before she got to the car. April at four in the morning was cold. Margo yanked open the front door of the car and screeched, "Do you ever clean this thing?!" She started firing empty A&W litter off the passenger's seat into the back. When they tried to fold Olenka into the car, it wasn't happening.

Olenka started to cry. "I can't, I won't fit! It's too painful. I want my mom!!"

Mike looked at his mother with helplessness. She still wanted to throw up. "Let's get her back inside." That was the same nightmare in reverse. There was no way they could get her back to bed. "Mike! Go get your comforter and blankets and pillows. We'll put her on the floor."

He took to the stairs three at a time, Magoo racing after him.

"It's all right, sweetheart. Everything is fine. You're doing a great job."

"This is bullshit!" Olenka cried. "Why did I wait? I'm a lousy mother already."

"That's nonsense. You're a great mom."

"I'm going to be a spotted hyena! Eighteen percent of first-time mothers die when their penis-like genitalia rips open. And that's what it feels like! I want Mom here."

Mike arrived with the bedding and they placed her on the floor, but she wanted to get up on her knees. Mike knelt beside her and Olenka grabbed his shirt collar and nearly strangled him. "Why isn't this letting up? Aren't there supposed to be minutes between contractions?"

"I don't know!" Mike said desperately.

"Well, you would know if we went to Lamaze class, but nooooOOOOOO!" Mike tried to move one of his knees but she pulled him down. "You stay right here."

Margo called 911 and tried to be calm for the kids' sake, but when she said her daughter-in-law was having a bunny instead of a baby, she knew she was rattled.

Then she called Olenka's mom. Gerda answered the phone with, "Is it the baby?"

"Yes! Come to the house," Margo said more frantically than she intended. She went back into the living room. Magoo was up on Mike's desk, his eyes as round as saucers. She understood how he felt.

Margo leaned down towards Olenka face. "Your mom is coming and so is an ambulance. Everything is going to be fine. You're safe. Mike and I are here. Nothing is going to happen to you."

"Why isn't this pain going away? What am I doing wrong? I don't understand," Olenka cried.

Michael said, "Maybe you're too tense."

Olenka gave his shirt another yank. "Shut your face, daddio."

Margo kept herself busy boiling water and collecting towels. They only owned two sets of sheets, and one pair she wouldn't wrap a fish in. She once read somewhere that you could tie an umbilical cord with dental floss if you had to, which was useful to know, because the only scissors she could find were small. She threw them in the pot of boiling water anyway.

She kept looking at her watch. It seemed like hours since she'd called 911. Surely the ambulance would be here soon. At that very moment, there was a pounding on the door and Margo rushed to answer it. She tried not to be disappointed that it was Gerda. She'd forgotten she called her. "Where's my baby? I'm coming, Olenka!" She pushed Margo out of the way.

"Mama!!"

Olenka let go of Mike and her mother got on her knees. "I'm here, baby. I'm here."

"Mom, I think I want to push!"

"OH!" Gerda looked at Margo. "How long has she been in labour? Should she be pushing yet? What do I do?"

Margo looked around but Mike had run into the kitchen. Now Margo got down on the floor. "Olenka, listen to me. You need to slow your breathing down. Big easy breaths in and blow out. Pretend you're a jellyfish floating in the ocean."

"Jellyfish don't breathe," she croaked.

Gerda blew up. "Why are we talking about jellyfish?! This is a real live girl and she's in agony! What do I do? A hot compress? I know...she loves jellybeans. Do you want a jellybean, Olenka?"

"Mom! Stop panicking!"

Gerda started crying. "I'm so sorry I yelled at you. Forgive me."

Margo spoke up in a loud voice, trying to get Olenka focused. "Pretend you're an otter—"

"Again with the animals?!" Gerda yelled.

Margo ignored her. "Olenka. Pretend you're an otter sleeping in the water. Keep that image in your head and try and relax your legs. I'm going to get you a warm towel and your mom will massage your lower back. Remember, you're an otter, just drifting whichever way the water moves you." Margo put her hand on Gerda's shoulder. "Rub her back and sing her childhood songs."

"Oh no...I can't think of anything...Row, row, row your boat..."

"I think I still need to push! I'm an otter. I'm an otter. I'm an OTTER."

"My daughter, the otter, got hotter one day, so my daughter the otter went outside to play..."

Margo missed Gerda's rendition of the second verse as she ran into the kitchen to call 911 again. Mike was by the fridge, his eyes red with unshed tears and his hands on the top of his head. "Why aren't they here yet? Help me, Mom."

"I'm calling right now." She called again and was told they were on their way. "Well, tell them to hurry up! We have a pup ready to pop!"

She turned to Mike. "They're coming."

He was wringing his hands now. "I'm such a shithead. Why didn't I insist we go to those Lamaze classes? Just because hippos don't need them doesn't mean we don't! And I can't find that bag! And nothing's ready! And if anything happens—"

Margo slapped her son across the face.

He looked stunned but at least he stopped babbling.

"Sorry, dear!" She ran back out to the living room to join Gerda who was still singing about her hotter otter daughter.

"Mom, please shut up," Olenka whimpered. "I've got to get down on my side." Her legs were shaking. Both grandmothers helped her move into another position.

"I've got to push!! I can't help it. OOOOOOOOOOOH. MIKE!"

He hurried over and knelt by Olenka's head. He held her hand and stroked her hair. "I'm right here. I won't let anything happen to you."

Thank God in heaven there was another knock at the door and two paramedics showed up. Is there anything more wonderful than having the cavalry arrive? Two huge strangers dressed in all kinds of gear, ready for any emergency you can throw at them. Their whole demeanour screamed *We're here and we'll handle it.*

Both grandmothers got off the floor and moved to the side. Gerda turned away. She couldn't look. Then she hissed, "Why are you here, Margo? Mike kicked me out of the house, but you're allowed to come over? Does that seem fair to you?"

"Because he asked me to," Margo hissed back. "He said you made Olenka upset and he was upset. So, I came over to calm things down."

Gerda pointed at her daughter. "Does she look calm to you?"

"I have to push!" Olenka kept saying.

And the wonderful paramedic said, "You go ahead. Push."

He helped Olenka through a lot of pushes. Soon Margo realized what a gift this was. She never saw Julia's babies being born—not that Margo wanted to; she would have just fainted. Julia wanted only Andre present. She was lucky Hazel came when she did, in January 2020, because four months later during Covid, even dads weren't allowed in delivery rooms. She watched Michael as much as Olenka, how he lifted her shoulders and let her push against him. It was a team effort.

And then there he was. No suctioning needed. He opened his mouth and screamed as if to tell them all off for making him show up earlier than he needed to with all their nonsense. He was put on Mommy's chest and Daddy cut the cord. Margo and Gerda cried and hugged each other. Eventually, Mike lifted his head and gave them the biggest smile, his eyes bright with excitement.

Gerda was kissing Olenka, but the paramedics wanted to get mother and baby on the gurney and take them to the hospital. The two were bundled up in warm flannel blankets, with Mike right behind them. Gerda said she'd follow them to the hospital, and she disappeared in a puff of smoke.

He turned. "Mom..."

"Julia and I will bring your car to the hospital." He nodded and they went out the door. Margo thanked their heroes. One of them turned around. "They better name the kid after me."

"What's your name?" Margo smiled.

"Bubba."

Then the other paramedic turned around. "He tells that joke every time."

After they left, Margo collapsed into Mike's lounger. Magoo immediately jumped in her lap and started to purr. She stroked his head as she looked at the mess on the floor, then tucked him behind her to lean forward and retch. Thankfully, that's all it was.

She wasn't sure how long she sat there before her cell rang. It was on the chaise longue. "Hello, Gogo!" Monty almost shouted. "Mike just called me. A son! Isn't that marvellous?!"

"He's precious."

"Did you get to hold him?"

"No. They were in a hurry to get them to the hospital."

"Mike says you were brilliant."

"I think I was in shock and he assumed I was calm."

"It must have been scary."

Margo started to tear up. "It was so scary, Monty. I didn't know what to do."

"Apparently you did. Now go take a bath and we'll talk soon. Thank you for being there to bring our grandson into the world."

The minute she hung up, Julia called. "MOM! Michael says you're a rockstar! I can't believe I have a nephew! Way to go! Was it terrifying? You should've called me."

"I didn't even think to. He has a head full of dark hair, and a loud scream."

"Just like Mike."

Margo spent the rest of the morning cleaning up, throwing away some towels that had taken the brunt of baby's arrival, washing and drying the good set of sheets and remaking the bed, finding the hospital bag, making sure things were organized in the baby's room, and cleaning out their fridge before she wondered what the heck she was doing.

Since babies were kicked out of the hospital in an unseemly hurry these days, everyone was going to wait until he came home to see him. Everyone except Margo. Julia came by and tailed her while Margo drove Mike's car to her apartment. She needed a quick shower.

"Do your best to clean up the junk in this car while you wait, will you?"

"How did he get to be such a slob?"

Once Margo got to the hospital, she grabbed the baby bag and Mike's car keys. Julia leaned out her window. "Kiss that little sweetheart for me! Although I think I read somewhere you shouldn't kiss newborns. Hug him instead. Call me when you want a ride home."

When she got to their room, the whole little family was asleep. Mama in the bed, Daddy in a chair, and baby tucked in a cot. She tiptoed over and peeked at him. His skin was flaky in spots. He looked like he'd been squished through a wringer and had a few red marks his face. The fingers that peeked out over the swaddling blanket were wrinkled, like he'd been in a tub for hours.

Margo smiled and rubbed her thumb against the beanie cap on his head. "You're perfect," she whispered. It was lovely to be here, everyone quiet and peaceful after the mayhem of his birth. Poor Olenka. If she ever had another baby she'd have to live in the hospital for the last trimester to avoid this happening again. You read about unfortunate mothers who had their babies too fast. It was a sin. Over before they even had time to register it was happening. What if it had happened on one of Olenka's field trips? She really would have given birth in the woods.

Baby started to fuss a little and both his parents' eyes popped open.

"Hi, Mom," Mike yawned.

Margo waved, reluctant to stop looking at her little man.

Olenka held out her hand. Margo stepped to the side of the

bed and sat down with her, giving her hand a squeeze. "Hello, dearest. You were so brave."

"Thank God you were there."

Mike said, "Well, she was nice to you. She slapped me."

Olenka turned to him. "What? I don't remember that."

"It was in the kitchen and you were busy."

Baby started to squirm and make mewing noises, so Mike went over and picked him up. To see her son with his son was... well, it just was.

Michael put the baby in Margo's arms and she held him close, pressing her cheek against his ear. "Hello, precious. You and Gogo are going to have a wonderful time. Yes, we are."

Olenka pulled back his cap and cradled his scalp. "Look at him. He's like a conehead from *SNL*."

"You shoot out of a narrow cannon at a hundred miles an hour and see what you look like. Don't worry, that will go." She looked down at that little face. "Did you pick a name yet?"

Mike looked at Olenka and let her spill the beans. "Jonas Montgomery Donovan. Jonas after my dad, but we're calling him Kit. All kinds of babies in the animal world are called kits. Badgers, muskrats, woodchucks, so he's in good company. Even otters. It was so strange. I kept thinking about otters for some reason."

Margo touched the baby's nose with the tip of her finger. "Hello, my little Kit and caboodle."

"MOM. Don't."

Chapter Twenty-Three

It was now June. A year since Dick died. Where does a year go? Kids get bigger, trees get taller, the world and weather get crazier. And Margo's hair had started to go silver.

Julia commented on it as her mother cut Hazel's nails over a tissue on the coffee table. "Naturally, when you stop dying your hair it's an amazing shade of silver. No Brillo pad grey for you. I better be the same way."

"Your dad has salt-and-pepper hair. That's nice."

Hazel looked confused. "Dad-dad has salt and pepper in his hair?"

Julia was eating a peach but it was a little too hard, so she put it aside. "You're only sixty-three. Joan Collins is ninety, and she's still a brunette."

"I'm not a movie actress, and it costs too much to keep dyeing it. I have to be frugal."

Julia pursed her lips. "Are you lonely, Mom? Do you ever think about dating?"

Margo kissed Hazel's fingers. "All done, sweetie." She scrunched up the tissue. "Put this in the garbage for me, please."

Hazel went off on her mission and Margo leaned back on Julia's beautiful but not quite comfortable couch. "The last thing I want is a man. And I'm surprised you of all people would want me too. You never liked Dick. Do you really want me to make another mistake?"

Julia shrugged. "You're allowed to have companionship."

Margo shook her head. "I'm not interested. I like living by myself. I loved your dad, still love him, but he hurt me. Not intentionally, but he uprooted my life and I had to start over. And then Dick came along and hurt me very badly with his complete disregard for my welfare and his own, and I had to start over. I don't want to be in that position ever again."

Julia looked impressed. "Where did old Mom go?"

"Old Mom? She's still here, crawling her way into the light. Maybe I don't feel the need to have someone because I'm surrounded by family, as Holly reminded me. By the way, I'm going to Eunie's on the weekend. She's going to fix my curtains."

"You haven't done that yet?!"

"We're not all as perfect as you are, dear."

Margo ran over to Mike's on the way home, to see if they needed her to pick up anything. It was really just an excuse to see Kit. He was two months old now, his head perfectly round. Most of his hair had rubbed off, so he looked like Charlie Brown. Gerda's car was in the driveway, as usual. The woman never left them alone, but they were happy to have her. It gave Mike a chance to work uninterrupted and Olenka time to get some sleep.

Mike was on a call, so he just waved and kept talking, Magoo asleep in the cubby hole on his desk. Olenka was folding clothes on her bed, watching some sort of nature program; Margo recognized David Attenborough's voice. Olenka waved and kept folding.

Margo peeked in baby's room and there was Gerda like a mother hen, rocking Kit in her arms, completely content. She tiptoed over. "How is he?"

They both looked down at him. His round cheeks were red and his mouth moved as if he was nursing. "I should put him in the crib, but how can I resist?" Gerda whispered.

Margo whispered back, "Isn't it something? Hold him while you can. Posy is now six and doesn't want me to kiss her at the bus stop anymore." She bent down and kissed his downy head. "See you later."

Gerda said, "Oh! The kids picked a date for his christening. The Sunday after next. We'll have a lunch at my place afterwards."

Margo gave her a thumbs up. That meant six hundred people were coming. She poked her head back into Olenka's bedroom. "Need anything at the store?"

"More bananas."

"I'm surprised Kit isn't a little monkey."

❧

Margo left for Eunie's right after work on Friday. She had her things in the car so she didn't have to go home. She thought back to how Monty and Byron had ferried her to the old homestead a year ago, remembering how lost she felt.

It was still a great drive, and she stopped at the usual Tim Horton's, only this time she took her wallet to get coffee, not her purse with her makeup bag. Makeup was expensive. And she had enough to last her a lifetime.

A sense of peace came over her as she pulled into the yard at dusk. Fred and Ginger were grazing as usual, and Hazen was puttering by the barn. It didn't look as though Holly was there, but Eunie opened the back door and waved. Margo popped the trunk and got out.

"I'm home!" she shouted.

Hazen wandered over, wiping his hands on an old towel. "How are ya? Are you eating enough?"

"Why do you say that?" Margo started to collect her overnight bag and the bag with the curtains.

"Your face looks, what's the word...bleached."

"Thanks, Hazen. I'm fine. I just lost my crayons." She went over to the fence. "Hi, guys." The donkey's nodded their heads at her.

Hazen walked up too. "Unless you have something, don't talk to them."

"They expect a reward every time you go near them?"

"Pretty much." He put his hand in his pocket and gave them a humbug each.

"You spoil those critters."

"Nothin' better to do."

Eunie held the door open for Margo, who put her things on the floor by the kitchen table before she hugged her sister. "So good to see you, Eunie."

"You feeling okay?" Eunie asked.

"Not you too. I'm not wearing as much makeup. Tinted sunscreen is about it."

"Put a little colour on your cheeks. Remember Grammy? She used that gold lipstick tube with the little lever on the side to make the lipstick go up and down? She put that red on her lips and her cheeks."

"And she looked like Raggedy Ann."

"True."

Stan heard Margo's voice and ran down the stairs. He jumped up on the table and started purring. "Hi, Stan." Margo reached over to pat him and he rubbed his face against her fingers, but he still wasn't speaking to her.

"What a traitor," Eunie tsked.

"Stop being jealous. He loves you too."

"He doesn't sleep with me. Hey, wait a minute." Eunie reached over and touched Margo's hair. "You're going au naturel?"

"It costs money to look young. Ask anyone who lives in L.A. What's for supper?"

"We had our supper, but we did save you a plate. Grammy's chop suey."

"The furthest thing from Asian food possible. Ground beef fried with chopped onion, three cans of spaghetti, all mixed up with an undiluted can of tomato soup. Put crushed crackers on top and throw it in the oven. How is it possible that it tastes so good?"

"Memories."

"I wonder if I'm brave enough to make that for the girls some night when they sleep over. I bet they'd love it, but Hazel would probably tell on me."

Margo picked up one of her bags and pulled out a curtain. "I need ten inches of something sewn on the bottom of these."

Eunie pushed them back in. "We'll deal with that tomorrow. Have your supper. I need to speak to you before Holly comes home."

"Okay, and I need to show you Kit's latest pictures. He's such a little pudding."

Eunie and Stan watched Margo eat. She felt she better hurry for some reason. Eunie brought over tea and Oreos and sat across from her. "Now, Holly's birthday is in August. She'll be twenty. Hazen wants to do something special for her."

"Okay, that's nice. What do you want me to do? Organize a surprise party?"

"NO. She'd hate that. But she loves the Blue Jays."

Margo made a face. "Baseball? She's into baseball?" She took apart her Oreo and scraped the white icing off the cookie with her teeth.

"Yes, and she's never been to a game, and I was wondering if you'd come with me and we could fly to Toronto for a long weekend and take her one."

"Me? A baseball game? Why doesn't Hazen go? I can look after the donkeys."

"You? As if Hazen would trust you with Ginger and Fred after the last fiasco. He doesn't trust anyone. I'd take her myself, but I've never been to Toronto and I'd be nervous. Holly's never flown either, and you've been to the city a couple of times. At least you'd know your way around the airport."

Margo put down her cookie. "Oh, I don't know, Eunie. I'm not sure I'm up to travelling just yet. I seem to be sticking very close to home. And I work too, don't forget."

Eunie looked dejected. "I suppose so. It was just an idea."

"Is there anyone else who might do it?"

"My neighbour up the road, but his wife is a jealous type. Not sure why. The poor man is as homely as a hedge fence. And my good friend Luanne might have come with me, but she's recovering from hip surgery."

"The other reason is I can't spend money like that. Monty's offered to lend me some and even Julia, but I want to look after myself."

Eunie brightened a bit. "Oh, I forgot to say that it's my treat. I've got money stashed away. I've never had anyone to spend it on, and now that I do, I'd like to use some of it. And truthfully, I wanted you because Holly said she likes you. She's never said that about anyone but us. I think it would make her happy if you came along."

Oh, brother. Now she was stuck. "Look, Eunie, let me think about it, okay?"

"Hey, if I'm fixing your curtains, I think you owe me."

Stan and Margo went to bed early.

Holly was at the breakfast table when Margo showed up the next morning. "Hey," she said. "I like your face."

"I like yours too," Margo answered back.

Holly continued to eat her All-Bran cereal. Margo looked at the box. "You enjoy that stuff?"

"Nah, but my roommates are boring-cereal people, and I forgot to buy some. And I didn't mean to imply that I didn't like your face before, it's just you've always looked like you were going out to dinner, even first thing in the morning."

"You're right. What a waste of time." Margo sat down and looked around. "How are your roommates, anyway? Their health okay?"

Holly nodded. "As far as I know, but I think the two of them are plotting something. They shut up when I come in the room. It's fucking annoying. But I can't stay mad at them, even though they keep buying this gross cereal. It tastes like stuff Fred and Ginger should eat."

"I have an idea. Why don't you and Eunie come up and visit me next weekend? I have twin beds in my apartment, and you can see the baby. Maybe we can go to dinner and whatnot."

Holly nodded her head, looking pleased to be asked. "Just to let you know, babies aren't my thing, but I'll do anything for food."

Margo broached the idea while Eunie set up her sewing machine on the dining room table. She gathered her bags of remnants to see if she could match the right texture with the curtains. Margo said the colour didn't matter, that her place wasn't exactly fashionable.

"What do you think? Holly said she's willing to come."

"That sounds nice. I'm dying to see Kit. I wish they'd call him Jonas. Such a nice name."

"Gerda thinks so too, but she's keeping her mouth shut for once. She got the christening she wanted, so she's quit while she's ahead."

Eunie licked her two fingers and threaded the needle on the machine. "Life is about picking your battles."

It seemed like a simple thing to sew a bit of fabric onto the end of a curtain, but it wasn't. By the time Eunie ripped hems, measured and remeasured, cut straight, pinned straight, sewed straight, fixed the bobbin, made more hems, cut thread, and then repeated it four times, it took up most of the afternoon.

"This is why I hate sewing," Margo realized.

"Nonsense," Eunie said, using her teeth to cut a thread she'd overlooked. "Most of the time I enjoy it, unless I have someone sighing in my ear through the whole process. You really are a very impatient woman. Oh, before I forget, Hazen wants to talk to you."

"Where is he?"

"Where do you think?"

Margo went outside and looked around. Clouds were gathering in the sky to the west, big and dark. She loved looking at the sky. There was always drama, always something brewing, good or bad. She remembered lying in the hayfield when she was a kid to watch the clouds turn into amazing shapes. Just when she'd spot a dog's face, it became a witch, and then a fish. But her favourite clouds were the ones that quickly passed by a full moon, with the light outlining them from behind. Romantic and scary all at the same time.

She couldn't find Hazen or the donkeys anywhere. Not in the barn, not in the paddock. And then she heard Fred hee-hawing down by the orchard. She moseyed over, keeping her eye on the skies. Hazen was clearing away brush, the donkeys wandering with him like cats. She reached up to touch the branches of an apple tree.

"Do you think this will be a good year?"

Hazen leaned on his rake. "I doubt it. We had a late freeze, so that's going to affect them."

"All it takes is one brutal day to mess up everything. I should know."

"Everyone knows. That's life in a nutshell. Now, listen, are you willing to go on this little trip with Eunie? She doesn't ask much from you, girlie—"

Margo raised her hands in surrender. "I'll go, I'll go. Just don't say anything to Holly, because we have to decide when, and I have to see if I can get a Monday off, and it will take me forever to figure out booking tickets online. I could ask Julia, but I don't want to. Give me some time to prepare. And by the way, I hate baseball."

"It's not about you, is it?"

She stuck her tongue out at him before she went over to pat Ginger, who was looking adorable with her big brown eyes.

Hazen took something out of his overalls. "I can give you this, then." He held out a bit of paper.

Margo took it. "What's this?" This was a cheque for fifty thousand dollars. "Holy mackerel!"

"That's your share of the money we made when we sold the two hundred acres."

"And if I'd said no to the trip to Toronto?"

"It would've stayed in my pocket." He grinned.

"Are you sure, Hazen? You don't need it?"

Hazen looked annoyed. "You're the one scraping the bottom of the barrel, losing your home, living in a dinky apartment, having to work on your feet all day because of that bastard you were married to. You should be retiring. We're fine, and we're not spending our share except to send Holly to the police academy at Holland College. Not that she knows that yet. The money will be sitting here if you need more. This was Mom and Dad's property, and Eunie and I are leaving everything to our next of kin. Which is you, God help us."

Margo hugged him until he wiggled away from her. "Get off me, woman."

Fred trotted over and pushed Margo's backside with his snout. "Hey, mister!"

Hazen approved. "Ya see that? He takes care of his old man."

The first few raindrops fell, so they walked through the orchard and back to the barn. Once the donkeys were settled, they opened the barn door and the heavens opened. They scurried back to the house, getting drenched in the process. Eunie ran around putting newspapers over the floors. She passed them some towels to dry off.

"So, ya comin' to Toronto?" Eunie asked.

Margo wiped her hair. "I said yes before I knew about the cheque, I'll have you know."

"And I sewed your curtains before I knew your answer, so we're even."

Chapter
Twenty-Four

Ronnie was becoming even more of a pest. Margo wasn't sure what to do about it. Every chance he got he was in her space for one reason or another. He never put his hands on her, but she felt like he was touching her all the time. With his eyes, and his smirks. It was depressing.

And then Honey motioned her over to the makeup counter and said, "I'm thinking of packing it in. Hubby just retired and we want to visit our grandkids. Would you be interested in taking my place? I can put in a good word with Ronnie."

"Once upon a time I would have loved that, but I don't want Ronnie to do me any favours. I'll never hear the end of it. I'm better off where I am, with the sometimes-nasty public, if you can believe that. So, thanks anyway."

Holly and Eunie were driving up that day to spend time in Fredericton, going around to the shops before meeting Margo at work so they could have dinner out before heading back to her apartment. Margo wasn't sure when they'd arrive, and she was so busy she didn't notice them when they came in.

There was finally a lull in customers just as Ronnie came trotting up the aisle to show Margo yet another bogus problem with the orders. Margo was a cashier. She had nothing to do with any of that. It was just an excuse for him to stand next to her while pretending to show her a particular line on an order sheet. She stepped away from him and noticed Holly standing off to the side for the first time. Eunie came up behind Holly and waved. Ronnie didn't notice either of them, and manoeuvred his body to block Margo from moving about the space.

Margo managed to slide through by pretending she needed to reach for something. She smiled at the women and was about to wave when Ronnie pretended to trip forward, almost knocking them both to the floor. He grabbed Margo around the chest to keep her from going down. Margo righted herself in a hurry and pushed his hands away, but before she could say anything, Holly stepped forward. "Hey, asshole. Get the fuck away from her."

Ronnie turned around to see who was talking and who they were talking to. When he realized the only two women around were glaring at him, he got red in the face. "Excuse me?"

"You heard me. Fuck off and take your slimy thoughts with you. And don't you dare bother my aunt again or I swear to God I'll come in here and cut your balls off."

Ronnie looked aghast, but he moved away. "Who do you think you are?"

"Oh, you don't want know." She leapt forward as if to go after him and he scurried away. Holly leaned on the counter and shook her head. "Jesus Christ, Margo. Get your act together. Don't ever put up with shit like that. What is it with 'nice' people? It's not your job to be polite to perverts."

Lesson learned.

It was amazing how good Margo felt. She still had fifteen minutes until her shift was over, so while Eunie stayed by Margo as she finished up, Holly wandered down near the back and kept her eye on Ronnie behind the pharmacy counter. Every time he moved one way, so did she. Olenka would have been proud of her stalking ability, the way she prowled, her eyeballs like lasers. Everyone behind the counter was suddenly aware of her. Ronnie stayed behind the safety of the glass. Another man came to the counter window and said, "Is there something you want?"

Holly pointed at Ronnie and said loud enough for his coworkers to hear, "I want this perv to stay away from Margo. Or I'm coming back. Ya got that, asshole?!"

And then the three ladies went out for supper.

Back at the apartment, Eunie admired the job she'd done on the drapes. "They look almost custom made."

Holly sized up the chaise. "What's this? How is this comfortable? Who buys a fancy psychiatrist's couch?"

"Try it," Margo laughed.

"No, thanks. I need arms on furniture for my Coke and nachos."

It was like having a sleepover. Although Holly couldn't understand why Margo didn't have a television.

"I can't get the hang of remotes," Margo confessed.

Holly sighed. "Have you always been this pathetic?"

Margo tapped her index finger against her lips. "Pretty much."

"Stick with me. I'll show you how the real world works."

They said goodnight to each other and Margo lay in her bed listening to her guests laugh together on the other side of the wall. It was nice hearing other voices in the dark. Maybe one day she would get lonely and go looking for someone. But not now. She was just very happy for Eunie. This unexpected gift of a daughter so late in her life was changing everything for her. And Hazen.

Saturday was all about the kids. Eunie couldn't get enough of Kit, and he snuggled into her folds quite nicely, while Olenka and Holly shared donkey information. Everyone suddenly realized that

Kit's christening was the next day and Mike asked them to come to the ceremony. Holly spoke up. "We'll go to the church, but we have to leave after that, right, Eunie?"

"Right," Eunie agreed. One party with all of Gerda's multitude of friends crammed into her apartment had been enough for a lifetime.

The three of them were then invited over to Julia and Andre's for dinner. Pasta alfredo, fresh rolls, and baked apples.

Holly couldn't get over the house, and kept looking around as she ate. "This looks like a magazine. I'd be afraid to wear shoes in here."

Julia was annoyed. "It's not that precious."

"It's close."

The girls wanted to show her their rooms. Holly went up the stairs and looked around at the pink-and-purple décor. "You do know that princesses are boring, right? Don't be a princess. Be a pirate."

Right after the three of them left, Posy came downstairs and told her mother she wanted to be a badass.

The christening was heavenly to Gerda, special to Margo and Monty and Eunie, sweet but nerve-racking for Julia and Andre keeping the girls in their seats, a trial for Olenka and Mike, and an absolute bore for Holly and Byron. Gerda's gang of supporters were gleeful and Kit was super grumpy and not cooperating at all.

Eunie and Holly said goodbye outside the church to the relatives, who were now on their way to eat cake and mingle, if mingling was even possible with the number of Gerda's guests invited. Julia turned up beside Holly before she got in the car and said quietly, "Do not use vulgar language around my girls."

Holly nodded. "Sure thing. But if they were pirates, it wouldn't be a problem."

Off they went, Eunie waving out the back window, Margo waving back. Julia stood by her mom. "That Holly gets on my nerves."

"Really? I love her. She's such a badass."

ᘒᔷᘐ

It was like walking into a different store. Margo saw neither hide nor hair of Ronnie when she arrived for her next shift, which was unusual, since he always stationed himself near the back door when she came in. When she finally did see him as she put her things in the back, he turned around and went the other way.

What heaven was this? All from a few well-chosen words. Margo wasn't going to make this mistake again. And then she had a thought and hurried over to the makeup counter. Honey was getting ready for the day.

"Good morning. I've decided I'd like to take you up on that offer after all, but I think I'll speak to Ronnie myself."

"Go for it. You're wasted on the front cash."

"Thanks, Honey. I hope you and your husband have a wonderful retirement."

"We're going to be busy. We have grandchildren in Alberta, Florida, and Spain. Can you believe that? Our kids obviously couldn't wait to get away from us!"

Before Margo lost her nerve, she went into the back and knocked on Ronnie's open office door. He was at his deck and when he looked up, his eyes widened, only this time it wasn't with pleasure.

"What do you want?"

"Honey is retiring. I'll take her place. As she says, I'm wasted on the front cash, seeing as how I can sell cosmetics to a nun. It makes good business sense and I'd hate to have a conversation with human resources and bring up your name, but I will."

And that's how Margo got her old job back. She was so excited, she called Julia, even though she was at work.

"Mom! I'm proud of you. That's all it took? Was your boss bothering you?"

"Yes! Didn't I tell you?"

"No!"

"Sorry, with everything else going on I forgot. It wasn't until Holly came in the store and told him she'd cut off his balls that things changed."

"I suppose her potty-mouth comes in handy. I just wish you'd told me."

Margo recognized Julia's whiny, jealous tone. "Sweetheart, you've been my protector all your life. I never would have made it this year without you. Holly is a character and I'm very fond of her, but she's not my daughter. That's you. And I thank my lucky stars every day that you are in my corner."

"Well, thanks. I feel the same."

"Oh, by the way, Eunie and I are taking Holly to a baseball game in Toronto."

"Gotta go, Mom." And Julia hung up.

Monty and Byron took her out for a meal to celebrate the good news. They shared a glass of champagne with their mushroom risotto. Then she told Monty about the large cheque.

"Do you need financial advice?" he asked her.

Byron rolled his eyes. "She's capable of asking someone at the bank. She just threatened her boss. I think she's good."

Margo smiled at him. "Thanks, Byron."

She was delighted to be back behind the cosmetics counter, not realizing how much she'd missed it until she began to talk to customers about skin care. She counselled women her age on the best tinted sunscreens, glycolic acid, retinol, hyaluronic acid, and vitamin C treatment for older skin. And the gratifying part for her was when customers commented on her own nice skin. They were finally seeing it. She did have her own regime, but her skin ultimately came from her grandmother and mom. Eunie had the same soft complexion. It ran in the family.

One day she got in a rather intimate conversation with one woman who shared she was a widow and was finding it hard to get the glow back in her cheeks. "I feel old. Like I'm drying up from the inside out. I want to feel youthful. Do you have anything for that?"

"We have lots of great products that luminate the skin, but remember we need to drink lots of water at our age, and walk or do yoga to lubricate our joints. So many things can make you feel better. If you want an all-over glow, you might want to look at the end of aisle four. And don't forget batteries."

Margo hummed a lot. Olenka noticed it when she'd come over to visit Kit and kiss his chubby cheeks.

"You're a hummingbird," she said. "Did you know that when a hummingbird flies close to a person's face or hovers nearby momentarily, it's a sign that positive energy is present or that transformation is imminent?"

"Is that true?"

"It's one way of looking at it." Olenka felt her breasts to see which one had the most milk. "But more scientifically, they are fiercely territorial and when they fly close, it may be because it perceives the individual as a potential threat and is attempting to assert its dominance or protect its resources."

"I like the other interpretation."

Olenka laughed. "You would. At least you're not a scrubbird anymore."

Margo kept jiggling Kit on her knee. "A scrubbird? That sounds dreary."

"They are shy and secretive and occupy dense undergrowth."

Margo stopped jiggling. "That's how you saw me?"

Olenka never minced words. "Yes. But now you're a hummingbird."

Margo stopped humming the day she was ticking off items on her order sheet away from the cash register and heard someone clear their throat behind her. She turned around with a smile and was about to say "May I help you?" when she realized it was Carole.

Carole looked just as shocked. "I thought Velma said you worked in the Shoppers across town. I wouldn't have darkened this door otherwise."

Margo heard Holly's voice in her head about "nice" people being too polite. She leaned across the counter. "Then why don't you turn around and leave? I have no time for bullies like you."

Carole narrowed her eyes. "What did you call me, you self-righteous bitch?"

Margo didn't back down, even though a few customers glanced their way. "A bully. The biggest bully I've ever met. You have the manners of a warthog. And I am through being intimidated by you. We are nothing to each other, so stay the hell away from me. Don't ever speak to me again. Don't ever look at me again. And I'll do my very best to forget I ever met you, your husband, and your daughter."

Carole stood there with her mouth open. Margo picked up her sheets and walked to the back room, locking herself in the employee bathroom. Her hands were trembling. This sticking-up-for-yourself business was terrifying. Why was she still dealing with these people? Margo should've just kept her mouth shut. Now she was afraid to go home, in case she saw Velma, because no doubt Carole would be on the rampage and set her bulldog after her.

After work, Margo went straight to Julia's without telling them she was coming. Julia wasn't home yet but Andre didn't care. She watched him cut up zucchinis like French fries, coat them in egg wash with garlic, and roll them in Parmesan cheese to bake in the oven.

"Have I ever told you how much I love how you take care of my grandchildren, Andre? You really are the best."

He smiled at her. "You tell me all the time. The only upsetting part is that I can never partake in horrible-mother-in-law jokes."

Posy ran in looking for a sieve. "We're panning for gold." She grabbed it from the lower cupboard and ran out again.

Ande shook his head. "I don't ask anymore. It's amazing what they teach kids these days." He reached for a dishtowel and wiped crumbs off his hands. "Julia tells me you're going to Toronto with Aunt Eunie and Holly?"

Just the way he said it put Margo on alert. "Is Julia upset about it?"

"Not upset. Just surprised."

Margo groaned and covered her face before straightening up. "It's something I got roped into. It's for Eunie's sake. As Hazen so delicately put it, she doesn't ask much from me, and I'm aware she's getting older. The two of them want to surprise Holly for her birthday. She loves the Blue Jays apparently, and they want her to go to a game in Toronto. Only for a long weekend. Eunie's nervous to go by herself and Hazen won't leave Fred and Ginger, so I'm the logical choice. They are even paying my way, so it seems churlish not to do it."

"Maybe, but are you sure you want to go? You sound reluctant to me."

"Do I?" She picked up a cherry tomato and popped it in her mouth. "To tell you the truth, Andre, I'm afraid. I haven't travelled since Covid and I don't really want to. I haven't seen a lot of the world, but I've seen enough to know I'm quite happy where I am. And I'm a nervous flyer. I've been feeling jittery for a year now. What if I have a panic attack on the plane? What if Holly does? She's never flown before. How will I cope?"

"Ask her to bring a few edibles." He smirked.

Margo hit him with a tea towel. "Julia told you?!"

"Julia tells me everything."

She smiled at him. "I know she does."

Andre started to unwrap the sole fillets. "Hazen and Eunie love that girl, don't they?"

"She's made all the difference. They never had families of their own and now they do. Holly is a young girl, rough around the edges and tough, but she's got a good heart. How that's even possible when her parents dragged her up by the hair is beyond me."

The front door opened and Julia shouted, "Mom? I didn't know you were coming."

Margo went out to greet her daughter. She waited for her to put down her portfolio and grocery bag and then gave her a massive hug. "Wanna come to Toronto with me? My treat."

"Seriously? Why would I want to go to a ball game? I hate baseball."

Andre yelled from the stove: "It's not about you, Julia."

They ate their delicious supper and Gogo had fun giving the girls their bath. The best thing in life was watching the two of them in their pyjamas on their step stool in front of the mirror as they brushed their teeth. Hazel spent the whole time doing exactly what Posy did, spitting at the same time, putting the brush under the tap at the same time. She loved her big sister.

And Margo loved hers.

She'd better give Eunie the okay to tell Holly they were going and get started on those airline tickets, as much as she was daunted by the thought. She truly hoped Julia would come with her so she could deal with that—but then she checked herself. That was old Margo. People booked plane tickets all the time.

But then, they used remotes all the time too.

Margo had, miraculously, forgotten all about Carole until she got closer to the apartment. The first thing she looked for was Velma's car. It was parked in its usual spot. She pulled into her space and looked around by the recycling bins for unfamiliar shadows before getting out of the car. She headed for the back door, listening to the zoom of the traffic on the highway behind her. Where was everyone going in such a hurry?

Too late, she saw Velma standing just inside the glass doors. For a split second Margo wanted to be brave and took another step. She knew she should stay in the light, but when Velma charged out the doors, Margo turned around and ran for her car. She'd almost made it when Velma grabbed her by the arm and spun her around, almost knocking her off her feet.

"Let me go!"

Velma shook her like a Polaroid picture. "You skinny little toothpick! How dare you speak to my mother like that? Mouthing off in public, causing her embarrassment and humiliation."

"She's not capable of being embarrassed or humiliated! Remember your father's funeral? The woman is a drama queen, and you're just like her."

Velma's hand tightened on her arm. "You better shut your mouth."

"Or what, Velma? Are you going to beat me up? For God's sake, you're a high school teacher and you're behaving like a goon on your mother's behalf. Let her fight her own battles. You don't have to hate me anymore. It's over. Your dad is gone."

"NO! He's not. He's in my bathroom because you didn't want him and mom didn't want him, so I'm stuck with him. Why didn't you two just bury him like normal people? The entire family was gathered over his grave and suddenly you guys are passing him around like a hockey puck!"

Margo pulled against her, which didn't accomplish anything. The woman was three times her size. "Let go of me or I'm going to get mad."

"Ooooh...I'm so scared, you yappy little mutt. You're not worth my time." And she shoved Margo backwards and walked away, not seeing Margo hit the car first and then land awkwardly on the pavement.

Chapter Twenty-Five

Margo knew she was on ground but wondered why she was there. It was raining. She went to pull herself up, to go before she got wet, and felt a stab of pain in her left wrist. Had she fallen? She couldn't remember.

And then she did.

She wanted to cry, but she'd do that later. She had to get off the ground. She couldn't move very well, and she was shivering so much her teeth were chattering. Thankfully her purse was on the ground next to her. It took a minute to open the zipper properly, and she reached for her cellphone. She knew it would be charged, because Mike had taught her to pretend that fifty percent power was zero, the same way he told her to get gas when the tank was half full.

And because she was thinking of Mike, she called him. He sounded very sleepy. "Mom? What's up? It's almost midnight."

"I'm on the ground in my parking lot and I can't get up. I'm so cold."

"What?! Okay. Okay. I'm calling 911. I'll be right there. Hang on."

Margo laid her head on her purse. How nice. Mike was coming.

In rapid succession, Mike arrived, then Julia, then Monty and Byron, and then the ambulance. Margo wasn't sure who she should be talking to, because they were all yammering over her head at the same time. The paramedics told the family to move over and let them do their job. Margo decided if she was ever going to date again, it would be one of these guys. No, they were too young. Maybe a retired paramedic.

She moaned as they put her on a gurney. She couldn't seem to move her hand at all. It was flopped over like a dorsal fin on a killer whale. Olenka once told her that flopping was caused by age, stress, injury, or altercations. Margo was four for four.

Julia got close enough that she came into focus through Margo's fog of pain and bewilderment. "What happened, Mama? Did you trip over something?"

"Velma pushed me."

Julia went off like a firecracker. Margo could see her distress. She was sorry she'd said anything. She reached out her good hand and Julia grabbed it for a moment. "Julia...she didn't mean it." And then she was too tired to talk. The lovely paramedics shut the door in Julia's face and she was at peace, while her family stood in the parking lot and watched her go.

"Do you know what she just told me?" Julia shrieked. "Velma pushed her!"

Mike looked at the back door. "I'm going to kill her. Where are Mom's keys?"

Monty held up his hands. "Guys! Stop it. We don't know that for sure. Your mom was delirious. The paramedic said it looked like she was outside for a while. She could have slipped and knocked herself out. We can't believe anything she says at the moment, and running in and threatening someone, or indeed killing them, is not what your mother needs right now. Okay? If we have to, we can deal with Velma in court. It might be July but it's still bloody freezing out here with all this rain. Let's get out of here before we all come down with pneumonia. You two go the hospital. God knows how long she'll have to wait to be seen by a doctor in emergency."

Mike nodded. "We'll call you in the morning. Thanks for coming."

"Okay, talk soon. Don't worry, she'll be all right." Monty and Byron went back to their car and pulled out of the parking lot.

"Let's go," Julia said, putting her mother's purse strap over her head and out of her way.

They unlocked the back door and Julia went to check the number of Velma's apartment again before they headed for the elevator and pressed the button for the top floor. They didn't speak. The minute the doors opened they looked around and realized they had to go left. It was at the end of the corridor. They stood in front of it.

"What do we do?" Julia whispered. "It's the middle of the night. We'll wake up the neighbours if we pound on the door."

"So knock." And she did. They waited but there was no answer. Then he knocked. Still no answer.

"The bloody coward," Mike said. He pounded on the door. "Velma! Open up."

Not a peep.

"She's got to be in there." He pounded again.

And a door opened, all right. The one across the hall. A big guy in his underwear filled the space. "Keep that up, and see what happens."

They took off and jumped back on the elevator. "Damn," Julia said. "Where was she? We have to go be with Mom."

The doors opened to the ground floor, and who was standing there but Velma with a large laundry basket in her arms. She took one look at Mike and dropped the basket. "Wait! I only yelled at her!"

Mike faced her dead on and kept advancing until Velma was backed up against the wall on the other side of the hallway. "You pushed her to the ground and she was lying out there unconscious with a broken hand for God knows how long! How does it feel to pick on someone who weighs about a hundred pounds? So help me God, if you ever so much as breathe in her direction ever again, I won't be responsible for what happens. And that goes for your charming mother too." Then, looking Velma directly in the eye, Mike picked up her laundry basket and scattered its contents all over the grubby hallway floor.

One of Velma's sports bras landed at Julia's feet. Julia picked it up and threw it at Velma, but bras aren't heavy enough to throw, and it flopped to the ground directly in front of Julia. She deliberately stepped on it instead.

Outside, the siblings gave each other a high-five and sped off in their cars towards outpatients.

☙

Mike ended up having to leave the hospital, because Olenka called and said Kit had a bit of a fever. Julia assured him she'd manage. She watched him tear off. First-time parents were hypervigilant. Human meerkats. She remembered those days; they'd learn. By the time younger siblings come along, they can have blood dripping off them and no one bats an eye.

It was a long night and a long morning, with the wait, the X-rays, and getting the cast put on Margo's broken wrist. The doctor said she didn't seem to be suffering any ill effects from her blackout or time outside.

Margo was very tired and wanted to get home. Julia bundled her into the car. "You're coming home with me."

"No. I'm not."

Julia started the car and then looked at her mother. "Mom. You have to be with someone."

"Did the doctor say that?"

"Well, no...but you cannot go back to that apartment. Velma lives there, and I am not going to let you be assaulted by that nutcase ever again. You're going to have to move. I don't care how inconvenient that is, your health is more important."

Margo turned her head. "Listen to me very carefully, Julia. I am not going to your house. I am not moving, and I'm going to be fine. I broke my wrist. It's not a big deal. I will not be treated like a fragile flower, someone everybody else has to rescue and take care of. I'm a grown woman and I'll make my own decisions, thank you very much."

Julia was stunned speechless. She drove her mother back to her apartment, and helped her mom out of the car. As they walked into the building through the lobby, Velma came from around the corner and instantly froze. Julia was about to open her mouth but her mother grabbed her arm, so she kept quiet, and so did Margo.

Velma looked at the cast on Margo's arm and her face fell. "I'm sorry. I never meant to hurt you like that. I have anger issues, obviously..."

"Obviously," Julia snorted.

"Julia, keep your mouth shut," her mother said.

Julia couldn't believe it, but she did.

"I feel really bad," Velma said.

"And I feel bad that my actions at the graveside caused you distress. Handing your father's urn over to your mother like that. It wasn't right and I shouldn't have done it. You were there to see him buried that day. If you'd like to have that happen, the grave is there and paid for. You can use it. I can't afford a marker. That would be up to you, but I want you to have that option."

Velma's eyes filled with tears. "Thank you. I might just do that. I'll let you know. And thank you for giving me Dad's things. I'm sorry he hurt you, but I can see you're moving on anyway. I wish my mother would learn how to do that. I'm going to take a lesson from you because I'm ashamed of myself. Sorry, Julia. Tell Mike too."

"If you need me, you know where I live," Margo said, and then she walked down the hall, Julia behind her not believing what just happened.

Julia helped her mom into her pyjamas and washed her face and hands. Then she heated up a bowl of soup and buttered crackers because that's all Margo wanted to eat. Julia got her settled in bed and insisted on feeding her; her mother had no strength left.

"I want to sleep," Margo said.

"Okay. You sleep all day, and call me when you wake up. The phone is right here. I'm going to call the store and tell them you won't be in today and that you'll be in touch."

"Thank you, sweetheart. You get some sleep too."

Julia kissed Margo's forehead and locked the door behind her. Then she sat in her car and blubbered.

She was so damn proud of her mom.

ᕮᔕᕳ

Margo called Ronnie and told him what happened and said she'd be wearing a cast for six weeks. He said no problem, he'd put her on short-term disability. Just get better and he'd see her then. Margo looked at her phone when she hung up. Holly was on to something. Margo should've started telling people to fuck off years ago.

Then she called Eunie. Hazen answered. "Hey, girlie. What's new?"

"I broke my wrist."

"Honest to God, you'll say just about anything to get out of this trip! I'm taking my money back!"

"First of all, Hazen, it's not your money. It's my share, and if I was going to try and get out of this trip, I'd tell you I was in traction, not just a cast on my arm. People can fly with their arm in a sling."

"So how did you do that? Head in the clouds, I suppose."

"Exactly. So why don't you tell Holly, and we'll plan it for a month from now. The first of August. I'll be feeling stronger then. Whenever the Blue Jays have a home game. We don't have to worry about it being a weekend, because I'll still be off work."

"Hot diggity-dog!"

"Are you sure you don't want to go, Hazen? It's only a long weekend. You must have a friend who would look after the donkeys."

"Have you ever known me to take a trip? There's a reason for that. Some people were meant to keep their feet on the ground."

"You're afraid of flying? I never knew that."

"I'm not afraid of nuthin'. If other people wanna be traipsin' up there in the sky, that's their business. I'll wait until the good Lord calls me and not before."

A half an hour later, Holly rang her. "So, this is what they've been planning! You can't go with a broken wrist. I won't have it. I'll go next year."

"Next year you'll be at Holland College for police training."

"I will??"

Margo would have hit her own forehead if she had a hand that worked. "OH...sorry...that's another Holly I know."

"I'm going to brain those two."

"Please don't say anything. Hazen will kill me."

The rest of that week, Margo lay on her chaise longue like Marie Antoinette. One night Andre, Julia, and the girls came over with a pizza that Andre made, so it was whole wheat, vegetarian, and delicious. Posy and Hazel were very careful touching her cast because they'd never seen one before.

"I wanna cass," Hazel informed her parents.

The next night Mike, Olenka, and Kit showed up with Gerda's potato dumplings. Kit was growing bigger every day, with rolls on his rolls. Olenka sat on the couch and nursed him. They wanted to know how Margo was feeling and she said better, because all she did was rest.

Olenka looked down at Kit as his little fist opened and closed like a kitten. "That's exactly what you should be doing. Did you know Margaret Mead said that the first evidence of civilization was a fifteen-thousand-year-old fractured femur found in an archaeological site? In societies without the benefits of modern medicine, it takes about six weeks of rest for a fractured femur to heal. This particular bone had been broken and had healed."

Margo lifted her arm a little. "They told me six weeks, so not much has changed in fifteen thousand years."

Kit stopped nursing and Olenka put him over her shoulder to burp him. "In the animal kingdom, if you break your leg, you die. You can't run from danger; you can't drink or hunt for food. Wounded like that, you are meat for your predators. No creature survives a broken leg long enough for the bone to heal. You're eaten first."

Mike nodded. "See, Mom? You're lucky we picked you up off the pavement."

Olenka continued to pat Kit's back. "The broken femur that healed is evidence that another person took the time to stay with the fallen, they bound up the wound, carried that person to safety, and tended to them through their recovery. A healed femur indicates that someone helped a fellow human, rather than abandoning them to save their own life."

Margo was impressed. "You amaze me, Olenka. You know everything. You should go on *Jeopardy!*"

"Just don't ask her where the laundry detergent is, or toilet paper. The important things in life," Mike muttered.

Another evening Monty and Byron arrived at Margo's apartment with a pot of beef stew. The three of them sat at the table and Byron poured them all a glass of ale.

"This is really nice. Thanks, guys. Cheers."

They clinked glasses.

"Cheers to you, Margo," Monty said. "Julia told me how you handled Velma, and I've got to say, I was very impressed."

"That girl just needs to take a vacation from her mother. And she took me up on the offer. I let the cemetery know and she buried him. I have no idea if she told her mother or not. I have a feeling she didn't."

"So now you're going to have to buy another plot," Monty tsked. "That was a waste of money."

"I didn't want to be buried there anyway. I want my ashes scattered under my father's apple trees. Remember to tell the kids."

"You tell them. I'll be dead first according to every chart in the world. Men don't last."

Byron lifted his glass. "You'll be all right, dear. You're not married to a woman."

Margo only remembered to call Harman a week later, and nothing would do but for her to come bearing a huge plate of samosas to the invalid.

"These are divine! The meals I've had this week, I might have to break more bones."

"I've got to say, despite your injury, you're looking well, Margo. You seem content."

"That's the word. I am. Even in this hobbled-together apartment."

"I'm delighted. It's been a journey."

"I'm about to go on another one."

They had a nice visit and just as Harman was leaving, she said, "Do you play bridge, by any chance?"

"Once upon a time, but no one likes to play with me because I can never remember the rules. I guess I'm not 'suited' to it."

"Ha. You should brush up. Amir and I belong to a bridge club and they are constantly looking for new players. And to be truthful, there's an awfully nice chap there. A widower. Now I know you said you don't want to date, but this isn't a date. It's just a chance to meet other men our age, without having a drink in your hand. And since I doubt you're into pickleball, I thought this might be a nice idea. We could try it when you get back from Toronto and your cast is off. It's just one game. If you hate it, you don't have to come back."

"Maybe. We'll see."

Harman gave her a grin. "He's awfully sweet. His name is Hamish and he's a retired firefighter, I think, or maybe a paramedic. I'm not sure, but you can ask him."

❧

The three amigos flew to Toronto. As far as everyone knew they were having a marvellous time. And then Mike's cell went off, but he was bathing the baby and couldn't get to it. Olenka was out having lunch with her mother. Her last words were, "I'm starting to look like an aye-aye. I've got to get out of here for an hour."

"What's an aye-aye look like?" Mike shouted.

"Me!"

Once Kit was diapered, dressed, fed a bottle of breast milk, and cuddled, Mike put him down for his nap. He took the monitor and sat down on his lounger. Magoo appeared like magic and jumped in his lap demanding his head be rubbed. Eventually he settled down and they both drifted off until Olenka came home feeling a lot better.

She threw herself on the couch. "Everything okay here?"

"I'm a father penguin, remember?"

She smiled at him. "True. You know, I've been stuck in this house so long, I forgot what the world looked like."

"Please God, the whole world doesn't look like a suburb of Fredericton."

"Well, everyone I love is here, so I'm happy." Olenka laid on her stomach and snuggled into the pillow on the couch. "Hopefully the pup will sleep for a couple of hours."

Mike got off the lounger and Magoo switched allegiances and jumped on Olenka's back. "Ooof. Magoo, you need to go on a diet."

Mike sat at his desk and saw his phone. "Oh. I missed a call from Mom." He listened to the message. Olenka watched his face look confused, then pleased, then horrified, and then he started laughing. He pulled it away from his ear.

"What on earth was that all about?"

"Get this." He played it again on speaker so Olenka could hear it.

"Hi honey, it's Mom. I know we're supposed to be coming home tomorrow, but we're going to be delayed. Tell your dad and Julia and Hazen that we decided to spend a few more days here because we're having such a great time. I don't want them to worry. It's going to take me that long to get Eunie out of jail and for the police to drop the charges against Holly for disturbing the peace.

She caught a home-run ball and two people tried to take it from her. Eunie went nuts. It's all a big misunderstanding, but I'm dealing with it. Love you two. Kiss my little caboodle. Bye bye."

He looked at the phone. "Was that my mother? My mother who couldn't figure out her own recycling?"

"Older females are the world's most adaptable creatures."

"Oh yeah? How do you know that?"

"I've got eyes, Michael. I've got eyes like a brownsnout spookfish."

Lesley Crewe is the *Globe and Mail*–bestselling author of fourteen novels, including the *Globe and Mail*–bestselling *Recipe for a Good Life, Nosy Parker,* which was named one of Indigo's Top 100 Books of 2022, *The Spoon Stealer,* longlisted for Canada Reads 2022, *Beholden, Mary, Mary, Amazing Grace, Kin,* and *Relative Happiness,* which was adapted into an award-winning feature film. She has also published two collections of essays, the Leacock–longlisted *Are You Kidding Me?!* and *I Kid You Not!* Lesley lives in Homeville, Nova Scotia. Visit her at lesleycrewe.com.